CW00685611

To Jea
With

The
DAMSON TREE

Roger Whale (signature)

Roger Whale

Orca Publishing

First published in 2009 by Orca Publishing
Ponsworthy.

www.orcapublishing.co.uk
roger@orcapublishing.co.uk

Text copyright @ Roger Whale, 2009

The right of Roger Whale to be identified as the
Author of this work has been asserted by him.

ISBN
978-0-9562256-0-3

All rights reserved.
This book is sold subject to the condition that it shall not,
by way of trade or otherwise, be lent, hired out or otherwise
circulated in any form of binding or cover other than that in which
it is published. No part of this publication may be reproduced,
stored in a retrieval system, or transmitted in any form or by any
means(electronic, mechanical, photocopying, recording or otherwise)
without the prior written permission of Orca Publishing.

This is a work of fiction. Names, characters, places, incidents and
dialogues are products of the author's imagination or are used fictitiously.
Any resemblance to actual people, living or dead, events or locales is
entirely coincidental.

Printed by
Short Run Press Ltd.

ONE

"You can drop me at the cross-road if you will"

"Sure?"

"Yeah, I can walk from there, it's a nice afternoon and I've been sitting long enough as it is. What do I owe you?"

"Fifteen quid"

The taxi drew to a halt.

"Thanks a lot, keep the change, I'll give you a ring when I'm ready to go back, be a week or two I expect."

"O K mate"

Frank Naraway got out of the car, raised his hand in a gesture of farewell to the driver, stretched and looked around him. He stood six foot in his boots, jeans and brown suede leather jacket, broad of shoulder and slim waisted. His dark brown hair was cut short, though not excessively so, and would be curly if allowed to grow. His eyes, set in a well tanned and angular face were blue-grey. On a sunny day they looked more blue than grey; in fact his mother always said that they were blue, but then he was her only son. His hands were large with strong square ended fingers. He had the air of a man who had confidence in himself and his abilities; a man who was used to making decisions. This was hardly surprising; he was Staff Sergeant Naraway of the REME with nearly fifteen years of service behind him, service that had taken him all over the world maintaining vehicles for the fighting men of the Army.

He shouldered his rucksack and set off up beside the road with the fields on his right and heather and short gorse to his left. The grass was cropped short with a few gorse bushes and the flattened brown remains of last year's bracken. Where the fields gave way to moorland he turned right, away from the road and following an animal track made his way up towards the jumbled pile of granite rocks on the top of the tor. He climbed easily, shortening his stride and slackening his pace to accommodate the gradient. Walking on the moor was second nature to him; he had been born and raised here and had lived here for the first seventeen years of his life. He was above the bracken line now, heather and whortleberry bushes to either side, and reaching the rocks he scrambled up to the top of Brown Tor. The view was one that he never tired of, Dartmoor all around him. On his right against the horizon the long ridge of Hameldown with its two distinctive beech hedges running up to the top. Ahead of him he could see the saucer-shaped pan of Redacre head, and far beyond the trees of Fernworthy. To their left were the tors of the high moor with the pyramid-shaped rock formation of Longaford standing proud against the sky. To his left the more rolling hills of Holne Moor, Crane Hill.and the Hessary Tors near Princetown.

He couldn't see the farm yet; it was tucked away in the valley ahead, where the lower slopes of Brown Tor Down met the Redacre Brook.

The path that he was on ran through a patch of black sticks where somebody had recently been swaling. The smell of burning was still there but the green shoots of the new growth were already showing. Like all local kids he used to love swaling time, running in and out of the smoke, carrying fire to the next patch to be burned. The sight, the smells and the general excitement of it all, were especially good at night when you could see the line of red fire running up over the hill and the silhouettes of the people taking part. Years ago women would have gathered these black sticks, probably of the previous year's burning, and taken them home to burn in the copper that boiled the weekly wash on Mondays. Ahead the gorse and heather was taller and Frank wondered why it too hadn't been burned. A lot of the heather was dead and grey, probably killed by heather beetles. They didn't seem to affect the young growth but they killed the older bushes. Swaling on the other hand might burn off the top growth but the plant soon regenerated, stronger than before. New people moving into the area and an urban government were making changes to the moor that weren't for the good.

There was little stock on the moor, just a few ponies searching for the new green shoots. Soon the sheep would be there, getting their wool grey from the black sticks as they passed between the burned remains. On a piece of open grass a group of skylarks were strutting around, the cock-birds singing whilst on the ground instead of high in the sky. Frank remembered seeing this before, he felt sure that it was a part of their courtship display. He listened for the warbling song of the curlews, they always used to come up around the end of February, but of recent years there seemed to be few if any in the wet ground at the head of the valley. He remembered how the old folks used to say when they had heard the first curlews of spring 'one more rough spell to come'. It sounded very wise, but of course at that time of year it would not be surprising if there were more winter weather to come.

He made his way through the clitter on the valley floor, the path now joining a larger one which led to a clapper bridge. Two huge flat stones resting on stone piers at either bank and on a large square rock set in the middle of the stream. A bridge that was almost as old as time, built high enough to be above the reach of the water even when in flood. He crossed and joined the road coming up the valley, and as he turned he put his hand on the old damson tree that stood at the corner of the first field of the farm. It had often puzzled him as to how such a tree should have been planted there, so far from the farmstead. Maybe somebody had just thrown away a stone and it had germinated and taken root. There were various marks cut into the bark and a few initials, obviously a tree that could tell a tale or two.

Wistworthy had been farmed since Roman times. The downward course of the brook turned through a right angle at this point, first running east to west and then north to south. With the fields all on the north and west bank, the land enjoyed shelter from the worst winds and weather.

Downstream the sides of the valley were steeper and had never been cultivated. Hawthorn and rowan trees grew amongst the bracken, heather and gorse on the lower slopes but these gave way to more short grass as one reached the vast pile of rocks on the top that was Wistworthy Tor.

Upstream the valley sides were far less steep and there was a lot more of the tussocky Bent grass that seemed to cling to your feet and legs, making it feel as though you were walking through six inches of water. Now in early March it was a very pale straw colour, almost white, giving the landscape the appearance of a desert or an African plain.

Though only sixty-five acres it was a productive farm by Dartmoor standards. It stood like an L shaped oasis of green surrounded on all sides by moorland. Recently, however, income was down due to its small size, the economics of farming had changed and small farms every where were finding it difficult. Frank's mother, Blanche, had turned to taking in people on holiday, a move that had not gone down too well with Frank's dad, Stan. He had wanted to continue the old traditional way which was just not profitable enough on its own. It had made him feel almost as though he could no longer provide, was in a way inadequate. Also the lack of privacy, with strange people in the house, was something that he had found difficult to cope with.

It was Frank's grandfather, Edwin, who had taken tenancy of the farm in nineteen forty-six. He had come down from North Devon with a wife and a son of three years. He brought with him a few head of Devon cattle, Red Rubies, which were his pride and joy and were the original blood-line of the herd on the farm today. When the estate was sold in the early fifties, due to crippling death-duties, Edwin bought the farm. As a sitting tenant he got it at a reasonable price, though not so low that he could manage it without borrowing. He worked hard and by the time that he died, before Frank was born, the debt had been paid off.

Now Frank had reached the farmstead. He crossed the yard to the little gate at the bottom of the course that led up beside the front garden to the house door. No barking dogs ran out to greet him, they were always kept in their kennel when not working, but they could still be heard. Those making the most noise were the two geese and the gander that came hissing and honking threateningly across the yard. As he reached the door it opened and his mother stood there to greet him.

"You walked."

It was neither statement nor question, a bit of both.

"Yes, I felt the need to stretch my legs."

"You always did like it up there on the top; you used to say that it was your church."

He threw his arms around her, a slightly round woman with a tanned face, laughter lines at the eyes and an almost imperceptible smile that seemed to be forever twitching the corner of her mouth. It was a warm, friendly face that seemed to exude love. Her dark brown hair, naturally wavy and greying at the temples, was worn short. Her eyes were blue and seemed to dance as she spoke; enhancing and adding expression to every word. He could feel her heart beating against him, much as he must have felt it when in his first moments of life he had lain on her breast, and the tears welled up and burst out. It was not so much for his dead father that he was crying but for this wonderful hardworking woman that he held in his arms. She looked old beyond her years, work on the farm and looking after his dad had taken its toll. Yet she was always smiling, always ready to help anybody, especially children. They stood there for a few moments locked in their combined grief, then she pulled away saying "I'll make us a dish of tea; I dare say you could do with one."

What ever the situation, good or bad, a cup of tea was the universal cure or drink of celebration. Whenever any body came to call the first thing she always said was "Come on in, I'll make us a dish of tea."

They went inside and she put the kettle on the Aga. A drop of water caught between the hotplate and the kettle hissed and spat and made the kettle bounce. The room still had the same feel; the same smell, warm and homely. She had been baking and a couple of dozen buns were on a cooling rack. A pile of ironing, neatly stacked was on one of the hard backed chairs. Frank went and sat, with his back to the window at the old scrubbed top table that had always been there; a table that had witnessed so much of their family life. It was used for cooking preparation, eating off, playing games on and for his dad to do the inevitable paperwork of which there seemed to be so much today. He looked around the room, cream walls and light blue painted doors to match the Aga. To the right of the stove was an old well worn armchair, the one that his father used to flop down into when he came in from the fields. Next to it was a smaller chair with wooden arms in which lay the ginger cat that seemed to have lived there forever, and across on the other side of the stove was a new looking settee.

"I see the old settle has gone."

"Yes, it finally fell to pieces and Dad took it out and burned it."

There were a couple of pictures on the wall of cattle and a farm calendar with reminders written in the boxes by the dates. On the mantelshelf was an old wooden clock with a white face and roman numerals. It had three holes for winding; time, strike and Westminster chime. He could hear its familiar ticking from across the room and could remember how its chime every quarter of an hour used to keep him awake for a while when he came home on leave until he became used to it. Not much had changed since he was last at home.

"Was it bad at the end?"

"No, he was quite quiet those last few days; it was as though he had found peace at last. He knew what he was doing; he had always known that that was what he had to do. It was just a bit sooner than I had expected. I suppose if he had left it any later he would probably not have been able, or might have made a mess of it."

"It was an incredibly brave thing to do, I'm not sure that I could have done it, but he did it out of love for you. He did it so that you wouldn't have to watch him die slowly and, for the rest of his life, spend all your time nursing him."

There was silence in the kitchen for a while as they drank their tea. Then she said, "He was a proud man, proud of what he had done and of what he could do. I suppose what hurt him most was knowing that he could no longer do what he always had been able to do. These last six weeks he was struggling to cope and he hated having to ask for help."

"Why didn't you write and tell me he was so bad, I'd have come home, I'm sure I could have got leave."

"I know you would, but that was the last thing that he would have wanted, t'would have been like rubbing salt into the wound. And another thing, he had bad moods from time to time, outbursts of temper that were quite uncharacteristic. He didn't mean it, didn't mean anything by it, but you would have found it very difficult to cope with."

"It must have been more than difficult for you to cope with it Mum, he was always so easy going, especially with you."

"Yeah, but I can't help but feel that I should have done more for him. We both knew that this was coming, Doctor told us so long ago. Could we have been better prepared I wonder?"

"I can't see as how you could have, like you said you didn't know when it would get this bad. Two months ago he was right as rain wasn't he."

"Well, yes and no, looking back I can see now that really he had started going downhill twelve months or more ago. He was so stubborn, would never give in, and kept it from us as long as he could. Like I say, he was a proud man, naught wrong in that either, 'cept I wish I'd known, I might have been able to have helped him more."

"Don't beat yourself up Mum; nobody could have done more than you did. What we've got to think about now is what happens next. Do you stay here? You might have to sell the stock and just let the grass. Mrs Turner over to Roundhill did that when her husband died. Fact, she used to say that she made more money doing that than they made when they were farming."

He got up from his chair and walked around the table to stand beside her. Putting his arm around her shoulders he said "Would you want me to come home and live here? I don't know what I'd do mind, I'm not sure that I could carry on the farm, I don't know that I would be good enough at it, and I don't know that I would want to either. There's so much to think about. I'm sure that you've done little else but think about it all, and like me the more you think the less sense you make of it all." She looked up at him and he bent and kissed her gently on the forehead. Then he turned and went to stand with his back to the Aga, his backside resting on the rail, polished by years of people standing in the very same way. After a moment's thought he said, "As for right now, is there anything that needs to be done now, anything for tomorrow?"

"No, it all seems to be in order, the undertaker has done me proud up to now, and friends have rallied round as well. Oh yes, I expect you'd like to see the cards and messages from folks, they're in on the dining room table, a lovely lot. People have all been so good to me. By the way, I've put your suit out by the radiator to air off a bit, there's a new white shirt on the bed. You are still a sixteen and a half collar aren't you? You can use Dad's black tie; it's all up there ready for you. Do you want to take the car and go out for a while this evening?"

"Thanks Mum. If it's OK with you I'll have a bath and after supper stay in with you, watch a bit of telly or something and then get an early night. It's been a long old day what with the journey and all."

"That's alright, just shout if there's anything you need."

"What time is the funeral? I forgot to ask."

"Eleven o'clock and then in the pub afterwards, they said we can have their big room, you know, the one upstairs."

"Oh, that'll be nice; I expect there'll be plenty of folks there. Do you suppose many of them will know just how he died?"

"I don't see how they should, Doctor was very good about it all, just said that the pneumonia came on a bit sooner than he had expected, that's all."

"Good…. by the way what about the trade, is there any thing I need to do, feeding up or aught?" He didn't notice that he was slipping into the local accent, it always happened when he came home.

"No, that's all taken care of, Phil German or that nice chap that works for him have been looking in twice a day and so you don't have to bother about any of that for the time being."

"Good, that's fine. OK then, I'll go up and change" and with that he picked up his rucksack and went off upstairs. The bedroom was just as it had always been, except that like so many things it always seemed a lot smaller each time he came home. His books were in the bookcase, and the model of a tractor that he had made years ago was on the top shelf. Pictures that he had collected over the years of his favourite places on the moor were on the walls, and on the dressing table, in a glass dish, were three flint arrow-heads that he had found on the farm. He put away his clothes and sat on the bed thinking for a while. He still wasn't sure that it felt like home.

TWO

The church was packed; it was standing room only at the back. Not that Frank was able to see or take in what or who was there, he walked beside his mother like an automaton, eyes fixed ahead on the four men carrying the coffin. They were all local men, most of them farmers like his dad, most of them about the same age as his dad. He felt quite calm and controlled as he sat down in the front pew. The sun, low in the sky, sent coloured light from the stained glass window which fell on the coffin giving the white lilies a rainbow hue. At the back of the church someone coughed, breaking the solemn silence. The querulous voice of a child piped up, asking its mother in a stage whisper where Mr Stan was, only to be shushed into silence. Then the organ started to play the opening lines of the first hymn and that did it. "All things bright and beautiful". It was a favourite hymn and very fitting for the funeral of a countryman, but one that had always filled him with emotion. Frank felt the tears welling up again; he put his right arm around his mother's shoulders. There was no point trying to sing, he just stood there with the tears falling on his service sheet.

His dad's friend, Phil German, who was also one of the bearers, read a eulogy. They had grown up together, joined the young farmers, done a bit of contract sheep shearing together and taken over their father's farms at about the same time. There they had often helped each other at harvest time and the like. Their relationship was almost that of brothers, without the jealousy or fighting. He was a big man, six foot tall and broad of shoulder and with just a hint of a stoop, years of hard work were beginning to show. Frank thought how like his father he looked, the same colour hair and eyes, the same way of holding his head, looking forward as though into the far distance. A country man, a man of the land, big of hand and big of heart.

The lesson that followed was one of his mother's favourite passages that started "Though I speak with the tongue of men and of angels", then after a few words from the vicar the last hymn, "Dear Lord and Father of mankind".

The bearers took up their places, turned the coffin around, and preceded by the vicar led the congregation out of the church. Blanche and Frank followed and this time he was able to see some of those who had come to support his mother. He nodded to one or two who were on the ends of the pews, resisting the urge to smile or say thank you. There'd be time enough for that later. Then it was out into the early spring sunshine to the grave, a double one so that they could be together again when Blanche's turn came. All around there were daffodils and narcissi on and around the graves, bobbing and dancing in the slight breeze.

The internment was bad for Blanche. There's a dreadful finality about seeing the coffin disappearing into a hole in the ground. Up until then there seemed to be something to do, some sort of job to be done for the deceased, but now that was all over. The undertaker offered them each a small sprig of heather which they took and dropped on the coffin. Then they turned, shook hands with and thanked the bearers and then moved through the crowd.

"Don't stand out here in the cold, come across the road for a while" said Blanche. They followed her and Frank across the village green to the New Inn where, upstairs in the function room, there was a splendid array of sandwiches, quiches and all sorts of savoury and sweet nibbles to be had. The mood then changed, more to that of a party. There was a lot of reminiscing on happy days and events shared with Stan. Frank did the rounds renewing acquaintances; he had been away and out of touch for fifteen years and was embarrassed to find that he had actually forgotten some people. People he really should have known. His only excuse was that time had altered him and them too.

Then across the room he saw her. Linda Passmore, well she wasn't that now, she was married but he had never met her husband and couldn't remember his surname. She still looked the same; tall and slim, dark wavy hair with large hazel eyes. She was wearing glasses now; that was something new, but they suited her and certainly in no way detracted from her beauty. She caught his eye and raised a hand to him so he made his way over to her.

"Good to see you again Linda, you keeping alright? It's been a long time."

"Yes," she said "It has been a long time, I'm sorry that we are meeting under such sad circumstances. I'm finding this difficult; I never know what to say to someone who has just lost a relative or a close friend."

"That's alright; I know just what you mean. The worst thing you can do is to say nothing, or to cross the street, pretending that you haven't seen me because you don't know what to say and are afraid of saying the wrong thing."

"You're certainly looking well Frank, army life seems to be suiting you. Will you be coming home for good now?"

"I don't know; it's too early to say yet, there's a lot to think about, not least would I be able to settle down to life on the farm? I just don't know. The only thing is I shall have to make up my mind pretty soon; I can't rely on the kindness of neighbours to keep on looking after the place and the stock and all. Incidentally, you look pretty good yourself; married life certainly seems to be agreeing with you."

"Oh I don't know about that" she said, blushing like a teenager, "We'll have to have a bit more of a talk another day, you wont be going back that soon will you?"

"No, I expect to be here for a week, more likely two, and it would be nice to get together and have a laugh. Perhaps we could meet for a drink, give us a ring soon and we'll arrange it."

16

"Sure, I look forward to it, bye for now." and with that she moved off into the crowd.

Frank turned to find Phil German standing beside him.

"Catching up on old times Frank?"

"Yeah, something like that" said Frank with a bit of a smirk on his face. A lot of people in the village would have known that he and Linda had been very good friends before he went off in the army. But they were only seventeen then and nobody knew what had or hadn't happened between them, or what might have happened had he stayed.

"This is a sad day, but a happy release for your mother. The thing now is what are you going to do? You've got some tough decisions to make, son, and I don't envy you. Your mother can't stay there on her own, and the farm don't pay enough for her to employ a man. Yet 'tis her home, has been for years, and I doubt she wants to leave it. I know the paying guests bring in a nice bit, but 'tis only a bit. Course if you was to come home 'twould help in a way, but would there be enough of a living for you as well?"

"I know Phil, I know only too well. I was hoping I might come around and pick your brains a bit. After all, two heads are better than one, even if they'm only sheep's heads. Besides, you know a lot more about farming than I do. Modern farming I mean, with all its paperwork and that. Things have changed such a lot since I was a boy here helping Dad."

"Yeah, you'm right there boy, 'tis naught but paperwork these days, enough to drive a man maze 'tis. But I'll certainly do my best to help in any way I can, you know that. How about you come round tomorrow evening? I don't think I've got anything on, though I don't know that my brains will be that much help."

"Thanks a lot, tomorrow would be fine, about seven be alright?"

"Yes, seven's OK."

"See you then, bye for now."

Frank moved over to where his mother was standing talking to a couple of her friends from the local WI.

"You'll be coming home from the army now I 'spect," said one. It seemed that every body expected him to leave his army career and come back, back into a farming life that he had left before he had started working for a living. Was this how it was going to be from now on? Would he be under the spotlight, everybody watching his every move to see what sort of a job or a mess he would make of the farm? They would be bound to compare him with his father, and he knew that that would have been a hard act to follow, even if he had stayed and learned the business properly. But he had been away, chosen a different career as an army mechanic and that was where he felt comfortable, sorting out engines and gearboxes, from motorbikes to tanks. He just smiled at them and said that it was early days yet, too much else to think about just now and moved on to get a drink.

18

He was finding this more difficult than he had thought he would.

An old school friend, Jim, joined him and they talked and laughed about old times for a while and then Frank said, "Everybody seems to think that I'll be leaving the army now and coming home for a life on the farm. Can't any of them see that I don't necessarily want to be a farmer? I chose to be a mechanic, Dad didn't like it, he wanted me to stay at home and follow him. God knows we had enough rows about it. The army gave me the opportunity and the training and I've never looked back. I admit I like it here, love it in fact, I've always loved Dartmoor who wouldn't? I'm quite happy to live here, but I'm not sure that I would ever be good enough at farming to make a success of it. Does that make sense? Then there was Linda; I know it probably seemed as though I was running out on her and I admit I was, but I had good reason, or so it seemed to me then. "

"Only you can know what will be best for you, and I certainly aint going to try to advise you. As for Linda, you may find that she is still very fond of you, at least she often asks after you and talks about you and the times you spent together in the old days."

"Really Jim, but surely she's a married woman isn't she?"

"You hang around a bit; I think you'll see what I'm getting at soon enough."

"Talking in riddles as usual Jim, but I must say that it sounds interesting, very interesting." What was it that Jim was trying to tell him, he knew from past experience that it could be just a wind up? But Linda, whatever could he mean and was that really what he wanted?

"Enough of this gossip, that's old women's stuff, I'll see you here for a drink one night, meanwhile I think I'll be getting on home now, if Mother's ready to go"

She was, and they left the room, saying their thankyous and farewells as they left and leaving Phil to close down the proceedings when he thought fit.

Once they were home Frank changed into some old clothes and went out to look around the old place. Everywhere was in tip top order, which was only to be expected. Stan was a good farmer and like any good farmer was determined to leave the land in a better state than it had been when he had taken over. As Frank went from field to field, kicking through the short grass that was hardly showing any new green yet, memories of work done in each came back. Hoeing swedes here, back breaking work in the early June sunlight; saving hay in the next one, pitching the square bales up to his Dad who built the load on the trailer. He remembered how he had made a sort of sledge to go behind the baler to catch the bales and leave them in heaps around the field. It had saved a lot of time and effort and he thought with pride of the praise his Dad had given him. He came to a stretch of stone wall. It had been the first bit of walling that he had put up on his own. "Build your hedges horse high, pig tight and bull strong" Stan had told him. It was good advice, handed down through the generations no doubt. At any rate it was still standing without the need of protection from stakes and barbed wire. But it was no good looking back, he had to go forward, hopefully with some advice from Phil he would see the way. It was strange though, how sometimes things seemed to sort themselves out. His mother had often said 'Something'll turn up, you see if I'm not right' and she generally was. Another good night's sleep was probably what he needed most.

THREE

The next day he was up with the lark. He was out in the covered yard when Phil's workman, Jeff, came to see to the stock. They exchanged a few pleasantries but it was hard to have much of a conversation over the roar of the tractor. Frank went on up through the fields and out onto the open moor. He turned right, up towards the head of the Redacre, hoping to hear the curlews. For some reason that he couldn't explain, he felt that if he could only hear them again this morning, it would be a good omen and perhaps even help him to make up his mind. There was a large rock at the edge of the wettest part and he sat and looked over the pan. The sunlight, shaded by Brown Tor, hadn't reached all of the valley. There was still a white covering of frost, after the clear night, that wouldn't be gone for a while yet. He and Linda had often sat here, making plans for the future though their plans had never included marriage. His were always to train as a mechanic and she hoped to become a physiotherapist, she had always been keen on sports and realised that sport and injuries went together. It would be good to be able to help her fellow athletes. Frank had seemingly always had a natural affinity with engines and things mechanical, right from an early age. In fact he had often saved his father money by doing small repairs to the tractor and farm machinery. Linda was always surrounded by lots of children; loved them and was naturally good with them. She was the oldest in a big family and, as is often the case with the eldest daughter, helped her parents with her siblings. She always said that she didn't need dolls to play with, she had the real thing. Only trouble was they needed real nappy changes.

He stood and started walking back up the hill to the rocks at the top of the tor. Then he heard it, the first three notes each curling upwards followed by that wonderful warbling song. So they were here, or at least one pair; the curlews that he so loved to see and hear, they had come back to breed. Perhaps that was all the sign that he needed, perhaps that was what they were saying to him, come back like us. Well he could, his fifteen years were almost up. In two month's time he could leave or stay in for the rest of his service life. If he stayed he would come out in his fifties and with a handsome pension. A few more days at home would help him to make up his mind, then he heard the curlews again and he smiled to himself. His mind was almost made up already.

He sat on the rocks on Wistworthy Tor, watching the sunlight melt away the frost patches in the valley. In the distance he could hear a dog barking, the sound carrying crystal clear in the cold morning air, probably Phil moving some stock. There was a tractor working somewhere off to his right, and above him the "pork-pork "of a raven as it flew overhead.

From this vantage point he could see all around him the tors he knew and loved so well. Horizon after horizon fading off into the distance, with the early morning mist lying in the valleys looking for all the world as though the tide had come in.

To some people, he realized, the moor looked a dark and threatening place, but to him it was a place of peace, reliable and continuous, a place that almost wrapped around him like a huge duvet, giving him a wonderful feeling of warmth and belonging. Many a time he had walked for miles enjoying the freedom of the solitude, talking to himself, often out loud, working over problems and puzzles. More often than not an answer would come to him long before he returned home. He had always felt that Dartmoor was far more than just a piece of land with all its varied flora and fauna; it was a living sentient entity that could, just by him being there, take away his negative feelings and any stresses and strains from which he was suffering. A very special place.

To leave the Army would not just be a matter of returning to the home where he was born and raised, it would be more like a return to his spiritual home.

He stretched, animal like, and then got to his feet and almost skipped down through the rocks along a sheep track towards the road below. A car was making its way slowly towards the farm. It stopped, where so many did, by the clapper bridge. There was an old gravel pit beside the road where people parked. The gravel was no longer dug to repair and surface the roads, tarmac had taken over that job and the sides of the pit had now grown over with short green grass. The grassy banks by the stream made it an ideal spot for a picnic. Children would play in the water and many, both young and old, had had their photos taken as they stood on the bridge. As Frank got nearer a figure climbed laboriously out of the car. At first he wasn't sure who it was, then he turned and Frank recognised the tall slender figure of the vicar, the Reverend Quentin Russell.

"Morning Vicar, lovely morning. Thank you for a lovely service yesterday."

"Morning Frank, yes it is a lovely morning, and I'm glad that you liked the service. I hardly need ask how you are; you look disgustingly fit and well. I suppose you've been out for a brisk walk, or was it a run? I know you army chaps like to keep yourselves in shape."

"No running this morning, just a walk on the top. I find that it's a good place for a man to think. When I have a bit of a problem I like to go up on the rocks. I just sit and let my thoughts wander, ask the natural world all around me what I should do, and most often the answer comes to me."

"Good for you, of course I would say that it is God who is answering you, but I suppose the important thing is that you get the answer. Where or from whom that answer comes doesn't really matter. In fact, by the look on your face I would hazard a guess that you have already got your answer, am I right?"

"Could be, at any rate I feel a lot closer to knowing what to do."

"I'm so glad to hear that Frank. Now, I've come up to see your mother, in case there is anything I can do to be of help. I didn't get the time to talk to either of you properly yesterday I'm sorry to say. I'll leave the car here and if I may we could walk up to the farm together. Before we go though, there's something I have always wanted to know. This tree here, a blackthorn is it?"

"No, it's a damson tree; I've often wondered how it got to be here."

"Oh a damson tree is it? And these initials carved on the trunk have always intrigued me. RB=SW, have you any idea whose they might be?"

"No, I haven't a clue, I just assumed that some courting couple came here for a picnic and carved their loving promise while they were here. There's a lot of people come here for a quiet time, it's a no through road and I suppose they think that they won't get disturbed."

"Yes, and I've no doubt that as a small boy you did your best to spoil their fun, eh?" he said with a knowing chuckle.

"Probably, I don't reckon I was any different from any other small boy."

They walked up the road to the farm together making small talk as they went. On their right the brook tumbled splashing and gurgling down through the rocks, some smooth and shiny,

26

others moss covered. On their left were the small fields, each surrounded by stone faced hedges, some with thorn or beech on the top. In places the hawthorn had their first green chinks of new leaves whilst the beech held on to last years brown ones. The vicar, a master at getting people to open up to him, asked Frank about his life and work in the army. Strangely, he didn't seem to want to know if Frank would be leaving soon and coming home, unlike so many of those Frank had spoken to the day before. Perhaps he already knew.

Frank found himself comparing their lives. In a way they had similarities; being posted from one place to another, living in accommodation that went with the job. And what sort of a life was it for the wife of a vicar? Always on show, having to be somebody, living up to public expectations, never being oneself, no it certainly wasn't the sort of lifestyle that he would like. The more he thought about it the more he felt a little sorry for Grace, especially as she was not that well thought of by the parishioners; looked upon almost as a figure of fun.

As they reached the door of the farmhouse it opened and Blanche predictably said "Morning Vicar, come on in, I'll make us a dish of tea"

"I'll leave you two to it, if you don't mind Mother; I still haven't unpacked my rucksack yet. Or have you already done that? You always were good at ferreting out any dirty washing I brought home, when I know I really should be doing it."

"No I haven't had time to go ferreting, as you call it. If there is any washing to be done just bring it down, it's no trouble, I only have to put it in the machine."

"Right ho Mum." And he was off up the stairs.

"Now then, Mrs Naraway, how are you? The house must seem very empty. Have you got a friend or relative who could come and stay for a few days?"

"Not really, I've got a cousin over to Newton, but she'd be more trouble than she's worth. Naught but fuss fuss fuss she is. Then I've got a sister up to Shepton Mallet, she wouldn't be able to do much though. She's got a bad hip, that's why she didn't come to the funeral. But her daughter Cathy might come down later, she's just taken her exams for to be a vet, you know. I think she has it in mind to come down here and join the local practice, if she does 'twould be nice if she chose to stay here for a while. She used to come here for her holidays when she was small."

She moved over to the table, busying herself with the cups and saucers "I'll be alright, Frank'll be here for a week or two and Phil or his wife Elaine looks in most days to see me. No, you don't need to worry, honest."

"Well I'm very glad to hear it, but don't be afraid to ask, any time. Grief is a funny thing, it affects people in many different ways, and we all have different ways of dealing with it. What's right for one isn't necessarily right for all. Some people will be able to help you and others will just be an interfering nuisance, but most of them will mean well."

28

"Yes, I'm already finding out just who my real friends are and who's just come round for a good nose about. 'Nother cup of tea Vicar?"

"No thanks, I'll be getting along now, now I know just how you are. I expect you've got a lot to do, what with Frank at home and all."

"Yes, I think I'll get him to take me into town to do some shopping. Things have got a little bit left behind just lately"

"I quite understand, and I want you to understand that you can talk to me at any time about anything. Goodbye and God bless you." With that he was off down the road to his car.

FOUR

At ten to seven that evening Frank drove into the yard of Manor Farm. There was a light on in one of the big sheds and the sound of an engine running, though to Frank's ear it sounded more like it was limping along. He went over and saw Phil standing beside one of their tractors with a puzzled look on his face.

"Cor, am I glad you'm here, you could be just the chap I need. You know all about engines an' that, can you tell me what's wrong with this bloody thing? Jeff an' I haven't got a clue when it comes to machinery."

"I don't mind having a look, but I'm making no promises. We always say in the mob, 'we can do the impossible immediately, miracles take a little longer'. Have you got any spanners?"

"Yes over here but you'd better put on this boiler suit first, you'll be stinking of diesel all night else."

Frank dressed and went to the side of the tractor, listening to the uneven sound of the engine. Taking a spanner, and out of Phil's sight he made some adjustments. Then, "Switch her off for a minute will you Phil."
There was silence and the occasional clink of metal as Frank worked.

"O K, start her up again, see if that's made any difference."

The tractor roared into life sending a cloud of black smoke up towards the roof of the shed, and then settled to a steady purr.

"I knowed you could do it, but I don't know how."

"Tis a gift" said Frank with a grin "You can't learn it."

"It may be a gift, it's certainly a godsend to me, apart from saving me at least sixty quid to have a man from Newton out to fix it, I can use that tractor tomorrow. Come on in and wash off, then we'll have a drink and a chat."

Frank peeled off the boiler suit, wiped his hands on a piece of rag and followed Phil up to the house.

It was a big house, some two hundred years old, set on a slight rise above the farmyard. Formerly the home farm for the manor, it was built in Georgian style with an arched granite porch over the front door. It replaced the old farmhouse, which was to the side of the yard, and was now occupied by Jeff. They went in and after a good wash in the butler's sink in the ample kitchen, moved into a warm comfortable lounge where a log fire was burning in the grate. The fragrance of the burning ash logs filled the room causing memories of many an evening spent there to come flooding back. The soft lighting and the muted colours of the furnishings all added to the relaxed and inviting atmosphere. Frank had always loved this room; it always made him feel at ease.

31

"Mrs German not here tonight?" asked Frank.

"No, she's off doing some good works somewhere. You'll have a drink I hope, something a bit special after what you've just done," and with that Phil put a bottle of Highland Park and two glasses on the low table between their two armchairs saying "You take it with just a dash of water, if I remember rightly."

They settled down to their drinks, at first the conversation was mostly about the past and their early days, farming, village life and people. Then Frank said "I hope you don't mind me asking, but how was Dad at the end? I don't like to ask Mum too much, she's been through enough already. She would probably try to protect my feelings by not telling me how it really was. Not that I can do anything now, but for my own peace of mind I would like to know."

"Yes I understand, but I don't think you need to worry. I didn't go there that much towards the end; it was mostly Elaine who visited. She told me that your Dad was peaceful and calm."

"Good, thanks for telling me. It's the last twelve months that I need to know about, I didn't come home that much and I feel bad about it. I know that I should have done more to help them both. Was Dad short tempered and hard to live with? I know that he could be when things were very difficult, and what could have been more difficult than what he had to deal with, both physically and mentally? "

"Don't punish yourself, you kept in touch by phone and letter and Mum would have made little of their problems, so how could you have done any more?"

"Thanks Phil, I've always found it so easy to talk to you and I needed to know. It's very hard not to feel guilty but sharing it with you has helped enormously." Then the talk moved to present times and the inevitable changes that had occurred, both in the parish and in Frank's field, mechanics.

"That's what I wanted to talk to you about, and seeing you at work down in the yard just now made me feel all the more sure. I reckon that there's a good living to be made here for you, in your line of business. There's scores of folks around here would be only too glad to have you maintain their cars, tractors and the likes. Servicing and repairs, the odd breakdown, you could do all of that no bother."

"D'you reckon so?"

"Yes I'm certain sure so."

"Well I'm glad to hear you say so; I must admit I was thinking on much the same lines this morning when I was up on Wistworthy Tor. I just wasn't sure as to whether there would be enough trade here abouts."

"Yeah, there's plenty. You've got a couple of good buildings that you could use for workshops and that. The cattle don't come into the old yard these days so it would be relatively clean. I suppose you would need a ramp or lift or whatever so as you could work underneath the cars. I'd be happy to put a bit of money into it if that would be any help."

"Thanks Phil; thanks for the offer, I've saved a bit, I should be alright that way. I must say, it would be nice to come home after all these years. I think I'm about ready to settle down. I can come out of the mob in just under two months."

"I knew it, you can take the boy out of Dartmoor, but you can't take Dartmoor out of the boy. Have another whisky and we'll celebrate your homecoming in two months time."

"Right ho, but let's keep this to just ourselves and Mum for the time being, I'm a bit superstitious that way, if you know what I mean."

"Of course, and I understand just what you mean, it'll be our secret for the time being."

They sat making plans for the future and enjoying the scotch and the fire for a while longer. The warmth of the room and the whisky had mellowed them both and Frank sat gazing into the fire watching the patterns of burning soot running up the fire-back; what his mother had always described as the hounds chasing the fox. A log fell in the fire sending a small shower of sparks up into the chimney, and the pattern of light on the walls danced brightly. After several minutes of quiet companionship they heard the sound of a car in the yard. A few moments later Elaine entered the room.

"Hello Frank, has Phil been looking after you alright? I see you've had a drink, but I don't suppose he's offered you something to eat."

"Thank you very much," said Frank, jumping to his feet "I really don't need anything, I hadn't realised it was so late, I must be on my way and leave you good people to get to bed."

So after a few more pleasantries he said goodnight and went back to Wistworthy. He felt supremely happy and he realised after a while why that was. He was coming home, and for the first time in fifteen years it really felt like home.

FIVE

It was a week later and the weather had changed, as so often happens in March. Now it was cold and dull and there was a keen north-east wind, a lazy wind that wouldn't go around but seemed to go right through you.

On several of the hedges the blackthorn bushes were in flower, white as snow, often referred to as a blackthorn winter. Frank came out of the gate from the church onto the village green. He had been in to check the flowers on the grave and remove the dead ones.

"Nothing worse than lot of old brown flowers, looks like nobody cares" Blanche had said as he left the house.

To call it the village green was a bit of a misnomer. At one time it had been nearly all grass but now it was mostly tarmac. It was triangular in shape, each side being over fifty yards long with a road entering at each corner. In the centre was a large horse chestnut tree, surrounded by a granite-paved area on which there were three outward facing wrought iron benches put there to celebrate the millennium.

The church and churchyard took up one side with the Old Rectory set a little way back down a short drive. On the second side were The New Inn, the Post Office/Shop and the three

Manor Cottages. These latter formed a short terrace of granite houses, each with a window either side of a door that was sheltered by a small granite porch, and three windows above. The whole was roofed in slate but the flat stones jutting out from the chimneys showed that the original roof had been thatch. On the third side stood the Village Hall and the old Primary School, now like so many in the countryside closed. Beside the Village Hall was a pair of gates across the drive leading to Edworthy Hall, home of Sir Harold Edworthy, lord of the manor. His family had been there since the Restoration and had seen good times and bad. Sir Harold seemed to be a better business man than most of his predecessors and had recently improved the family fortunes more than somewhat.

As he crossed the road Frank met Giles Cameron-Hyde coming out of the shop.

"Good to see you, my boy, are you going to join me in a swift half or would you prefer a cup of coffee at mine?"

"Coffee would be nice, Sir, very nice thank you."

They went through the gates into the Old Rectory. Like many a country parish the area was covered by a team ministry with one vicar ministering to more than one parish. The Reverend Quentin Russell lived in the next village and so the Old Rectory had become redundant a while before Frank had left for the Army and Giles had bought it when he retired. He was a handsome man of medium build with a shock of wavy snow-white hair and piercing blue eyes. He had served in the Royal Air Force from nineteen fifty to seventy five as a pilot. An exceptionally good pilot in fact, he had led the Black Arrows, the then RAF display team that in the fifties had preceeded the present day Red Arrows. When he left the air force he had worked for British Aerospace selling planes to Middle Eastern countries and the likes. Frank had done a few odd jobs for him in the past and had always liked him for his forthright approach to life and people. Giles had taken a particular interest in Frank and despite the age difference the two had become firm friends. They had had several long talks about Frank's future plans and hopes of a career as a mechanic. It was Giles who had suggested that it might be a good plan to go into the forces and had in fact helped Frank to find out more information on the subject. His interest in the young man had continued and he had watched Frank's progress over the years as he rose through the ranks to staff-sergeant.

"I'm so sorry about your father, it must have been a shock for you, was he ill long? I didn't get a chance to talk to you at the funeral, anyway that probably wasn't the right place or time for us to have a chat."

"Thank you Sir, we had sort of expected it. He had Huntington's Disease; it was diagnosed just before I went into the army. He had had some problem or other that nobody could understand. Then a new test in nineteen ninety three discovered it. It was a helluva shock to him and Mum, but it took a lot longer to develop than the doctors at first thought, so he was able to live his life almost normally until quite recently. Then when it started to get bad he did what he always said he would and……."

"Oh my God, I never realised, I don't suppose anybody else did, did they? It isn't the sort of thing you would want to broadcast. Terrible, terrible…..and how awful it must have been for your poor mother." He paused, shaking his head and staring at the floor deep in thought. "But what exactly is Huntington's Disease? I've heard of it, but I think all I've heard is that it can be hereditary in some cases? How about you, dear boy, are you affected?"

"I don't know, but you are right in saying that it can be hereditary. Any person whose parent has the disease is born with a fifty–fifty chance of inheriting the faulty gene. There is a genetic test which will usually be able to show whether someone has inherited that faulty gene but not at what age they will develop the disease. Apart from a natural worry, the word usually caused me some concern as to the accuracy of the result. Also I have read that the psychological implications raised by a pre-symptomatic test can be devastating. Do I really want to know now, if there is only a fifty-fifty chance that I have inherited this horrible disease? I'm not sure that I can answer that."

"I really don't know what to say, what a horrible predicament to be in, and what a terrible thing for your mother." Giles didn't like to say what he was thinking, first her husband, then her son.

"She puts a very brave face on it, seems to be able to put it to the back of her mind as far as my getting it is concerned. But no matter what she might say or think I have to be realistic. That was one of the reasons I left in such a hurry. How could I stay and marry Linda, especially as I always thought that she wanted a large family? I just couldn't take the chance, I had to go".

"How did Linda take it?"

"I never told her."

"You mean you just up and left?"

"Yeah, bit of a swine and a coward too. But I really couldn't say anything about the disease, I didn't know if I would end up with it. So I said that I wanted to be absolutely sure of my feelings, needed to go away for a while to help me make up my mind. After all we were both only seventeen and although I felt very strongly towards her we had never mentioned marriage, it was just sort of assumed, I suppose. I wrote to her once but she didn't answer, I didn't come home that often on leave we just sort of drifted apart."

"Well, have you had the test yourself, or do you have to wait until the first symptoms show up?"

"No I haven't had a test yet, I don't know if and when I shall either, frightened I suppose. It's that one word **usually**. Even if the test was negative I would always be worried in case….. And now of course, Linda's married and I'm not exactly looking for anyone to settle down with."

"Oh I see. Mmm… you never did come home on leave that much, if I remember rightly, was that to do with Linda or the difficulty you had with your father?"

"Bit of both I think, I spent most of my leaves going around the world visiting and sight seeing. I've been to every continent; I've certainly done my fair share of travelling. But I always wrote home to let Mum and Dad know where I was and how I was getting on. Some might say that I was just escaping."

"So you'll be going back to your regiment soon now I expect. Staying in for a few more years or have you got other plans? Perhaps I shouldn't ask, it really isn't any of my business, but whatever you decide to do with your life, I wish you the best of luck."

"Thank you Sir, I'd rather not say anything about any plans I might have, it might be bad luck. In fact I would rather you didn't mention any of this conversation, particularly about the Huntingdon's Disease, to anybody."

"Of course dear boy, of course, I know what you mean. Anyway I'm so glad we had the chance to have this little chat and any time you are home, do look in and see me, I'm always here and always pleased to see you."

"That's very good of you Sir, I'll certainly remember what you said and I'll look in on you again when I'm next home."

With that he took his leave and went out into the cold spring air. Across the green he

41

thought he caught sight of Jim disappearing into the pub and decided to join him.

Jim Blundel had been his best friend at school, playing, swotting for exams in each other's houses and going for long walks over the moor together. On leaving school Jim had gone to Bicton Agricultural College for two years. Then he had worked for a large local merchant selling feed and agricultural supplies. He was a good salesman and liked by the farmers who were his customers. They trusted him because he was a local boy and understood them, their way of life and their needs. Eventually he bought a large empty warehouse on the edge of town and set up on his own. It was hard going at first because he really didn't have enough customers, although he had thought that he had. Slow but sure, word got around and more and more of the local farmers put their orders his way and so his business had grown.He had married Pippa, Phil German's eldest child who worked in the stables down in the valley below the Church, and they had two children who were both at primary school. He was a little taller than Frank; about six foot two, with mousey coloured hair that was beginning to recede. He always looked as though he would break into a smile at any minute, his grey eyes twinkling. He liked a joke, was a terrible tease, and was not in the least put out when the joke was turned on him.

"Glad I caught you" said Frank as they raised their glasses, "I was hoping that you and Pippa might join me here tonight for a meal, it would be my shout. I know it's a bit short notice but I'll soon be going back and there's a lot I want to fit in. Besides, we haven't had chance to have much of a chat yet."

"That would be great Frank, I'll just ring Pippa and check with her a minute, she'll have to fix a baby sitter, but I'm sure that her Mum or Aunt Sal will be only too pleased to do that."

A short call on his mobile and a time was fixed. They sat at a table in the window comparing notes as to how life had treated them and what, since their schooldays they had been able to achieve. Looking around Frank remarked on the changes he could see that had been made to the old pub.

Four years before, Bob and Julie Peters had taken over what had been a somewhat out of date and run down village pub. Trade had been nearly all local and mostly drinks, with just odd sandwiches and snacks. Showing a great deal of sense, the changes they had made had been small and not so sudden as to be noticed immediately. Over the four years, however, they had achieved quite a transformation. Now it was a thriving destination pub with people coming from a good distance away to sample the excellent beer and food. Simple home-cooking, beautifully done and presented, and wherever possible using locally sourced produce. The décor also had seen some subtle changes. Before it had been old dark beams and horse brasses, a sort of stereotypical townies idea of a country pub but now it was lighter and brighter. The old seating, mostly dark oak with worn red leather, had been replaced with lighter

43

beech wood Windsor chairs and tables to match. It was still a village pub where the locals could stand at the bar and have a drink but now more and more of them were having a meal there with friends, especially at weekends. They left the pub together, happy in the knowledge that their friendship was still as strong as ever despite Frank's long absence.

When he arrived home his mother told him that Linda had phoned and would he ring back. After several rings she answered. "You said to ring and arrange a meet for a drink or something, so I rang, and you were out."

"Yes" said Frank, "I've just been talking to Jim, he and Pippa are going to join me for a meal in the pub tonight, any chance that you and your man could join us? It would be lovely if you could. I'm sorry I don't think I've met him and I don't even know his name. I feel it's awful of me to be so ignorant."

"His name's Eric, Eric Jordon. He's a teacher at the comprehensive school. I don't know if he'll be able to come, he does a lot for the school after hours so to speak. I'll give him a ring and tell him, but you can be sure that I'll be there, I'm not going to turn down the chance of a nice meal out."

"Great, I'll see you down the pub then, about half seven I should think."

"Lovely, I'm looking forward to it already. Bye."

She hung up and Frank went into the kitchen for one of his mother's inevitable cups of tea. Blanche could feel that his mood had lifted; he was a lot more settled and relaxed. She knew, however, that it wouldn't do to ask just yet, he would tell her soon enough, he always did. Although he'd been away so much and had spent so many of his times on leave travelling the world, she still knew him well, and his moods. The letters that he'd sent were full of descriptions, not just of the places and people but of how he felt and his reactions to his surroundings. Often there were photographs too, which had helped her and Stan to get a real feel for the life that he was leading and the man he had become. As usual, she wasn't thinking of herself or her loss, but of her son and his problems. No doubt her approach was also helping her to cope with her grief and his too. Although he and Stan hadn't got on too well when he was younger, on his few visits home they seemed to be much more friendly toward one another, especially of late. Stan was fascinated by the tales Frank brought home, of foreign places, the people and their customs. He always wanted to know about the way that they farmed, different climates and soils made for different techniques. Often the breeds of domestic animals too were unknown to either of them, but the photos helped. The wild life was different too and was especially a problem when it preyed on the farm animals, and sometimes their owners as well.

"They've got more to worry about out there than a few foxes" said Frank showing a couple of pictures of Massai warriors with their cattle and then a picture of a pride of lions feeding on a wildebeest they had just killed.

"It's so vast out there; the plains seem to go on for ever. It's a bit like standing on top of Fur Tor and looking down towards the top of Tavy Cleave, only a hundred times bigger. I remember standing on the rim of a vast crater watching the dust devils spiralling hundreds of feet below. The scale of it all is amazing, the climate is wonderful, it seems you can grow anything, it's no wonder the Brits settled there."

"Dartmoor must seem pretty tame after all that."

"Oh I don't know about that, every place has its own special charm and none more special than Dartmoor"

She smiled to herself at the thought of the two of them enjoying time together and then felt the tears pricking her eyes. Just one of many things, she realised, that wouldn't be happening again. She also had decided that she would have to make several changes in the house, move some of the furniture around a bit. The way it was at present it was still **their** house and she could still see Stan everywhere. She felt that by moving a few things it would become what it now was; her house. It wasn't that she wanted to forget Stan, far from it, she never would. She just didn't want to be a professional widow all her life, like some she knew. She had her memories, wonderful memories, so she didn't need objects to remind her. She would get Frank to help her to move a few things tomorrow. Then there were all Stan's clothes and things to be disposed of, some charity shop perhaps, maybe the Air Ambulance. She didn't fancy the idea of putting any of them in the village jumble sale. There was one coming off soon but, no, that wouldn't be the right place.

"If you're going out tonight you won't want supper, just a bit of bread and cream for your tea perhaps?"

"That would be just handsome Mum, just like old times."

SIX

Jim and Pippa were already in the bar when Frank walked in .Pippa was tall with grey-green eyes and long blond hair. During the day she wore her hair tied back in a pony tail, it was easier for working in the stables, but now it was hanging free over her shoulders. She greeted him with a kiss on the cheek and then asked "How's your Mum today? It must have been hard for her at the funeral, being pleasant to all and sundry."

"She seems to be taking it very well, thank you. She doesn't say very much about it now, in fact neither of us do, we just try to get on with life."

"Good for you. If there's anything we can do you know you only have to ask."

"Thanks a lot Pippa, you are all very kind."

"We've got a table over there by the fire," said Jim, "what are you drinking?"

"I'm driving, so I'd better have a pint of their weakest Real Ale, thanks Jim. I've asked Linda to come as well so she should be here soon. She rang earlier but she said Eric may be held up at school, we'll find out when she comes. Before she gets here though, perhaps you could tell me a bit more about him. How long have they been married, have they got any children?"

"They've been married eight years" said Pippa "And no, they haven't got any children."

"Not likely too either, Eric's been firing blanks." said Jim.

"Jim, that's hardly fair, you make it sound as though it's his fault. Well I know it is really, but it's not his intention. They tried for a long time, then they went for tests and it turned out that Eric has a very low sperm count, virtually nothing. Linda told me that it shattered his confidence, made him feel that he wasn't a proper man. It was awful for a while; he took to drinking a lot, got very moody and sulky. Things have turned around a good bit lately though, I understand. He has thrown himself into a lot of extra- curricular activities at school and that seems to have helped. Only trouble is, it means that Linda doesn't see as much of him as she would like to, still when she does he's in a good mood and that can't be bad."

"Poor Linda, she was always so fond of children, it must have been just as much of a disappointment for her," said Frank.

"I'm sure it was, but she 'borrows' ours from time to time, in fact she often baby sits for us. Tonight though, Auntie Sal is looking after them. She'll be picking their brains, trying to find out all the school gossip, as if a nine year old and a seven year old could tell her any gossip."

"Oh, I expect she'll find out something that she didn't know before, and then she can tell her friend Edna all about it. Its village gossip that keeps that pair going, I'm often tempted to make up a nice bit of juicy scandal for them to spread around."

"What d'you mean Jim, tempted? You are always teasing them with little tales of fiction. You've probably already told her that Frank here is in the SAS, fighting for his country in darkest Uzbekistan or something. Or else you've said that he's Dartmoor's answer to James Bond."

"Well she falls for it every time, she makes it so easy."

"Who's this Edna you spoke about?" said Frank "I don't remember her, is she new to the village?"

"Yes, relatively new," said Pippa "she and her husband moved down here to retire about eight years ago. They bought Number 2 Manor Cottages. He died four years ago. She and Auntie Sal had become good friends, shared a common interest you could say, an interest in everybody else's business. They are members of almost every committee and group here. They do do a lot of good really; because a lot of folks aren't prepared to do all the work that they do for the village. It's just that she gossips so much."

"Your mother summed her up proper" said Jim, "said her problem was that 'she had too much of what the cat licks its arse with'."

It was at that moment that Linda entered the bar and on seeing them came over to their table. She stood tall and composed looking down at Frank, her dark wavy hair cascading around her face, her eyes shining behind her glasses and a broad smile on her lips. They greeted one another with a hug and a kiss, and Frank felt the old feelings coming over him. So it wasn't just Dartmoor that he missed, he would have to be very careful.

"Eric will be a little late, probably another half an hour, but he said to start without him."

"I think we could wait a bit if it's only going to be that long Linda. What's he on upon now, d'you know?"

"Yes, its training for the Ten Tors. I think that it's mostly theory tonight, map reading and so on, they don't go out until next weekend for a practice walk."

Eric joined them a little later, and Frank thought that he seemed alright. He was full of good humour, smiling and joking and regaling them with tales of the amusing things that children do at school. After an exceptionally fine meal the girls went off to the loo together and Frank went up to the bar to pay. Jim joined him and, making sure that Eric wasn't near, said"I don't think its school work that keeps him late of an evening."

"What d'you mean?"

"I think he's got a bit on the side, one of the female members of staff maybe. He always looks so happy when he comes home late, never full of the usual woes that most people have at the end of a hard day's work."

"Has Linda said anything to Pippa?"

"Not that I know of, anyway she's more likely to talk to Beatie, you remember her, Pippa's sister. She's a nurse at Plymouth, so they have a bit in common what with Linda's physiotherapy and

51

all. They are really close friends, have been for years."

"Well it's been a great evening, good to catch up with friends and meet Eric; we must do it again when I'm next home."

They said their goodbyes at the door before going out into the cold. Was Linda's embrace a little prolonged Frank wondered? Was it just his imagination or was it wishful thinking? His thoughts had been in turmoil ever since he came home, trying to decide just what to do next. Now he was feeling the old feelings that he used to have for her, feelings that he thought had died. After all the years away, he felt sure that he had reached a stage where he didn't think of her in that way at all. Tonight he had held her in his arms, and though it was only for a brief moment he had felt seventeen again.

As he lay in bed later that night he tried to make sense of his thoughts. His first consideration must be for his Mum. If he didn't come home to stay could she cope? Would the farm just become an unmanageable burden? Would he feel increasingly worried as to her ability to run the place while he was away? It wouldn't be much of a life for him if he was always thinking of the farm, nor much of a life for her if the work-load were too much. She might be too proud to complain or ask for help even, she could be like that he knew. Perhaps he ought to talk to his Mum in the morning, ask her; but that would never do, she would say that she could easily manage the place on her own. She would say that because that was what she would think he wanted to hear. No he couldn't ask her, he would just have to go back and see how it felt when he was away from the place; he might be able to make a rational decision then. After all, if he did decide to leave the Army it would only be two months and then he would be home for good.

Then there was Linda. What did he really think of her? Not that that really mattered, after all she was a married woman. But if she did still have feelings for him it would only add to her problems if he came home and was always around. Why did life have to be so complicated?

SEVEN

The village hall was really a large wooden hut. When it was first put up in 1948 the intention was for it to be a temporary structure until more funds became available. So a sectional building, or rather two sectional buildings, were obtained and erected. Successive generations of willing helpers, craftsmen and enthusiasts had improved, extended, modified and modernised it, to the extent that the people of the village had become really quite fond of it and talk of replacing it had ceased long ago. Several and various were the organizations that used it. The baby and toddler group met there every Monday, Wednesday and Friday mornings. There was a whist drive every other Monday night that usually had at least ten tables. For several years the youngsters had held a youth club on Wednesday evenings, playing table-tennis and listening to music. Unfortunately numbers had dwindled and it had folded, computer games and other more hi-tec forms of amusement had taken over. The ladies circle met on Thursdays for craft evenings, and other parties and groups hired it as and when necessary.

It was the Friday after Easter and Edna Marriot and Sal Blundel were busying themselves arranging tables for the Easter Jumble Sale. Edna was a large lady who died her permed hair a whitish blond. She liked to wear a lot of make-up and gold jewellery; rings, bracelets and chains which made her look cheaper than she had intended. Sal was a lot slimmer with straight, mousey coloured hair, no make-up and no nonsense inexpensive clothes. They looked rather like a female Laurel and Hardy but despite their apparent differences they were good friends who worked well together, helping the many and various groups in the village. They were inveterate gossips who, despite never seeming to go anywhere, knew every thing there was to know about village life, its people and their lives. A number of boxes and bags of unwanted goodies were piled in the corner waiting to be sorted and arranged on the tables ready for sale. Edna and Sal enjoyed this sort of work helping the community, as much as anything because it gave them a chance to look over and comment on what each person had given. Not all the boxes had the donor's name on but this only added to their enjoyment. Guessing from whom the goods had come by recognising one or more of the items made it a sort of detective game.

"That's Betty Landers frock, I mind seeing her wearing it to several whist drives. Never did suit her, I'm surprised she hadn't got rid of it years ago."

"So these horrible plastic egg cups must have been hers also. No taste at all, that woman."

They were trying to get it all set up before the vicar's wife Grace arrived. They naturally felt that their way of doing things, tried and tested over many years, was not only the best, but the only way. Goods for sale should be arranged in categories, not according to value or price. In any case, regardless of quality or origin, it was easiest if everything on any table was of a similar type. So they would have a table for books, one for adult's clothing, one for children's clothing, one for toys, one for jams and pickles and so on, with particularly good items of clothing hung on a rail. That was in their experienced opinion the only way that would work. Grace on the other hand preferred a mixture of goods on all tables, the goods on each table all being the same price. Thus a ten pence, a fifty pence and a pound table etcetera.

"If we look sharp, we'll have most of this done before 'Close Up' gets here, and then she wont be able to alter it," said Sal.

Grace Russell was a small bird-like woman in her late sixties with thin grey hair and glasses, that she had never been seen wearing, hung around her neck. Most of the time she wore tweeds and sensible shoes and several of the younger members of the community reckoned that she also wore tweed knickers. She had an uncomfortable habit of getting very close to people to whom she was talking, uncomfortable that is for the listener. With her head tilted back and looking up she would get right under that unfortunate's chin; hence her nickname. She came from a long line of vicars' wives; curiously her mother and both her grandmothers had been married to the cloth, so to speak. So she felt that with her upbringing she knew, better than most, all about things to do with village fund raising affairs, an opinion that was not shared by the rest of the population.

"What are you going to bring for refreshments?"

"I shall bring what I always do, a round of shortbread and some ham sandwiches. What about you Edna, are you going to bring a quiche again? They'm always very popular."

"Yes I dare say I will, and a sponge too if I've got the time. There's never enough time these days though, don't seem to get a minute to myself."

"Telling about your quiche reminded me of old Mrs Sadler that always made the pasties for the Christmas Whist Drive. I don't suppose you knew her, I think she was dead and buried before you came here. Any road, she once said to me that after she'd been out in the garden and had got her hands all dirty and green with that there ingrained dirt, the finest way to get them clean was to make some pastry. Well, I tell you, I never ate another of her pasties after that."

"That's nothing, where we came from there was a posh woman, least ways she thought she was posh, married to a judge or something. Well she told me how she had broken her mixing bowl one day, you know, the old earthenware sort. So what did she do? Went straight upstairs and got the gazunder from under the bed; she reckoned it was proper, had a handle to catch hold to and all."

"That's posh for you. By the way, what are we raising money for this time? I wasn't at the last meeting."

"It's to buy some new crockery, there's an awful lot of cracked cups in the cupboard, Sal, and the committee decided we needed to get some new ones. So that's what this jumble sale is all in aid of."

"Quite right too, it might be alright for the likes of us, but it's never right, gentry having to drink out of cracked cups."

They continued busying themselves putting items on the tables, with the best items in front to coy the customers to buy. Space was a little limited so some things were left in their bags or boxes under the tables.

"That should do it" said Edna, putting the finishing touches to the table that she was working on. "I'm off home, I'll see you tomorrow Sal, I reckon we've done a good job here; time to go."

With that they left and locking the door behind them went to their respective homes, happy in the knowledge that the layout was as they wanted it to be and that tomorrow's sale would go like clockwork.

EIGHT

At ten to eleven next morning Grace Russell welcomed her band of helpers to the hall saying, "Lovely to see you all here today, there's just one thing I must ask of you. Please don't help yourselves to all the best bargains before the doors open, it's hardly fair on others."

"May not be fair on the others but tis the only perk we get for doing all the work and standing here all day." said one of the helpers under her breath. It was hard to tell whether the helper's bags under the tables contained more goods for sale to be brought up later as space allowed, or items that they had purchased pre-sale as it were.

The doors opened at eleven o'clock and a goodly crowd of people came in milling around the hall, joking with each other as they picked up, inspected and then replaced or purchased the various bargains. School holidays were not yet over and so there were families from afar to swell the numbers. Nevertheless as the day wore on the tables began to empty. Now more and more were sitting at the line of card tables and chairs along one side of the hall partaking of the very reasonably priced refreshments that the various ladies of the village had provided.

Linda and her friend Beatie were sitting at one of the tables enjoying a cup of coffee and a chat. They had brought Pippa's two children with them as she was busy at the stables.

"You had a nice evening at the pub the other week, when Frank was home."

"Yes it was lovely. Oh look you kids, they've just brought up another load of toys on that table, here's a pound each, why don't you go over and see if there's anything you'd like?" When they had gone Linda said, "I couldn't say anything while they were here."

"Why, what is there to say?"

"Well I don't really know, it's just that I got this funny warm feeling every time I looked at Frank, and then when he kissed me goodnight I felt ….I don't know…"

"Turned on?"

"Yes….no …oh I don't know, it's just that I always fancied him as a kid, that's all we were really. Then he up and went off to be a soldier and I suppose I still wonder what it would have been like if he'd stayed. Now I'm with Eric and …."

"The other man's grass?"

"Or in this case, 'the other man's arse', Frank really has got a gorgeous bum." They both laughed,

"Careful Linda, the kids are coming, we'll have to continue this another time, it sounds like you have got yourself a bit of a dilemma though."

"I'm not sure whether it's a dilemma or a delight, but whatever, it's good to have you to talk to, I certainly need someone to listen to my thoughts. They're all of a jumble at the moment."

The children returned with a small boy and after showing Linda their purchases went off with their friend to his grandmother, Rose, who was sitting at a nearby table.

Rose Stapleton was a striking looking woman in her late fifties who lived in a caravan in a clearing in the woods. These woods, part of the Edworthy estate, were in a valley on either side of a little stream that joined the Redacre Brook below the village. It was some thirty years before that Rose had arrived, driving an old single-decker bus. She was dark haired with olive skin, high cheekbones and flashing dark brown eyes. She wore layers of long loose fitting clothes, strings of beads and had the general appearance of a Romany. She was often to be seen in an old fur coat which she wore inside out The term used by a number of village residents to describe her appearance was 'A bit Totnes'. With her were two small children and a dog. Somehow she had been able to get her bus into the woods and into a clearing near to the stream where she had remained ever since. More of a puzzle to the villagers was how she had managed to persuade Sir Harold to allow her to park there and to stay there all these years. Many and various were the rumours floating around concerning this hippy-like Amazon. Could she be a relative or an illegitimate daughter perhaps? Did her free love extend to Edworthy Hall? But she had stayed and despite there being no Mr Stapleton her family of children had grown. There were now four and two grandchildren, and the campsite had also grown to comprise the old bus and two caravans. Few people visited the site, few knew of its existence even, tucked away as it was in a very private part of the wood.

The children had all attended the local school, were extremely well behaved and were now working at various jobs in the area. They all favoured Rose in appearance with their striking dark good looks. Despite rumour and the sort of speculation that always surrounds those who are a bit different and keep themselves to themselves, none had ever been in any trouble with the law or anybody else for that matter. Rose was thought to help out at Edworthy Hall from time to time and she worked for Giles and Nancy at the Old Rectory, both indoors cleaning and cooking, and outdoors tending to the garden.

At that moment a man approached their table and asked Linda and Beatie if he could join them. They flashed each other a glance as if to say shall we, but before they had time to answer he was sitting down. Linda smiled at her friend and mouthed 'You've pulled' and Beatie giggled. Their new companion was dressed in jeans, jumper, a faded anorak and dirty white trainers. He looked to be about twenty five with long hair pulled back and tied in a pony tail and a silver ear ring in one of his ears. Generally he looked a bit scruffy, as though he had been sleeping rough, or at any rate in his clothes. He had brought over to the table with him a plate loaded down with sandwiches and pieces of quiche and a cup of tea "Good do this, lovely food too and very reasonably priced."

"Are you on holiday?" asked Beatie feeling that she ought to be polite.

"No, just passing through. I'm going back home to Plymouth. I had the chance of a lift that brought me this far, but I thought that I would be able to get a bus or something on from here. Turns out there aint any buses till tomorrow. Is there anywhere hereabouts where I could spend the night? It's such a lovely location; I've always been fond of Dartmoor."

"Well there are several places that do bed and breakfast, I don't know how many of them will have vacancies, school holidays and that."

"Thanks, I'll take a look in a while, better finish my lunch first."

The children rejoined them, laughing, giggling and skipping around the table. "Can we go now Auntie? We want to go and see Mummy at the stables before she leaves. She said that there's a new pony there, a palomino. We want to see it, can we…. please?"

"O K, I think I've got all I want, you ready Linda?"

"Yeah," and with that they stood up and left the hall with the two girls dancing excitedly beside them and hanging on their arms.

"Bye, nice meting you" said the man with the pony tail, and he too got up and went over to get another cup of tea and some more food. When he finally finished eating he went to find the toilets. They were located in an extension at the rear of the building. He spent a long time inspecting the place almost as though he was searching for something that he had lost. Then, shouldering his large rucksack, he left the building and walked past the old school into the lane that led out of the village towards the East.

On his right the old granite church stood proud. Like so many Devon churches it had a fine tower with four pinnacles gracing the top, a peel of six bells and a flock of noisy jackdaws forever trying to get into the belfry. There were two old yew trees either side of the slate-roofed lych-gate, reminders of the days when all the young men of the parish had to own and be proficient with a long bow. Beyond it and running down through the graveyard a granite-paved pathway that led to the west door. Across the road from the church was a small row of cottages. The first had originally been the home of the local blacksmith and farrier. The old forge that adjoined it had long since been converted, the heavy wooden doors replaced with glass ones and the old open windows were also now glazed. Inside were tables and chairs for twenty people. The reminder of it's past was the anvil standing in the centre of the room, various tools adorning the walls and horse shoes fastened onto the beams. Though there were a few customers sitting at the tables drinking tea and eating scones and cream, business had obviously been badly affected by the availability of good inexpensive refreshments at the hall.

The second, Rose Cottage, had a pretty garden, climbing roses up its wall and a 'Bed & Breakfast' sign outside it. A black and white cat was sitting on the window sill washing itself and taking no notice of the two chaffinches eating from the nearby bird table. Unfortunately for the stranger there was also a sign saying 'No Vacancies'. In the yard of the next, Strawberry Cottage, were a large new looking four wheel drive vehicle and a posh German car. Both of these had registration plates denoting that they were from Oxfordshire. Not too difficult to guess that it was a holiday home.

He walked along the road until, having passed several dwellings; he came to the end of the village and the fields began. So he retraced his steps and this time left the village green by the road that led south. He passed the entrance to the Old Rectory, several more houses and a little way down the hill the stables where Pippa worked. Just below this was a pretty little bridge and he stopped for quite a while watching the water flowing swiftly yet peacefully by, the odd bubble on top marking its progress. Though slightly brown in colour it was clear and he could see to the rocks and gravel on the bottom. A few small trout, heads facing upstream, were lying almost stationary, just the odd swish of their tail keeping them in the same position.

A hundred yards or so further on he came to the main road where he turned right. He was between fields and hedges now, neatly trimmed and with the first spring flowers blooming amongst the grass at the sides of the road. After a short while he passed Manor Farm, no barns full of hay for him to doss down in, what hay there was, left over from the previous summer, was in large plastic wrapped round bales. Opposite Manor Farm was another former farm, now a thriving guest house with its redundant farm buildings converted into holiday cottages. That was far too upmarket for his wallet, so he carried on until he came to the cross-road and there he turned right which led him back into the village again. Of the fifty or so dwellings that he had seen, three did bed and breakfast but all were full. Perhaps it had been a mistake, availing himself of the offer of a lift that had brought him to this quiet backwater. It was too late to leave now; the last bus had left long ago so he would have to spend the night here. Perhaps a pint and a bowl of chips in the pub first, more time had passed than he had realised, and he was beginning to feel hungry again. He would check the bus timetable so that he wouldn't miss the one going towards Princetown next day.

The pub was busy, several customers enjoying a Saturday night out with a meal and a bottle of wine. The stranger sat in a corner with his third pint, reading a paper that some one had left. He had treated himself to a meal of ham, egg and chips, he felt that he could afford that small luxury seeing as he wasn't going to have to pay for a night's bed and breakfast. When half past nine came and it was truly dark, he left the pub and keeping to the shadows made his way passed the row of Manor Cottages. He crossed the road, slipped into the village hall car park and around the back of the building. It wasn't very difficult to open the old window of the toilets. He had inspected it before and had realised that with his pocket knife he would be able to slip the blade between the frame and the window and lift the latch. At the third attempt he had it open and was in the building. It was dark, so using his small torch he went into the main part of the hall and found some old cardboard boxes left over from the jumble sale. These he took into the toilets and used to cover the windows. That done he felt that it would be safe to turn on the light because if any chinks of light did show he was at the rear of the building and hopefully out of sight. The lights in the toilets worked but the heating was off. He discovered that it was on a different circuit and required a coin in the slot to operate it. However the hot air hand drier worked, so gathering up some more empty boxes he made up a sort of a bed below it. He then turned and jammed the hot air outlet with a piece of paper thus making it work continuously. The humming noise seemed very loud to begin with but he soon got used to it and lying on his makeshift bed was soon asleep.

Whether it was the noise that woke him or the discomfort of his sleeping position he didn't know, but wake he did. The noise seemed to come from the main part of the building and was a sort of roaring with the odd cracking sound. Switching on the light he opened the door into the hall and was horrified to see that the whole building was ablaze. He quickly slammed the door, gathered his few possessions and got out of the window as fast as he could. By the light of the fire he could see that the time was just after three in the morning. Not bothering to raise the alarm, some body would surely have done that by now he thought, he ran into the lane and off in the direction of Princetown.

It was Charlie Blundel that raised the alarm. Like many a man of his age he regularly woke in the middle of the night needing to go to the toilet. This night was no exception and, switching on his small bedside light he crept silently from the room so as not to wake his wife Sal. His bathroom was at the rear of the house, so it was the sound of the fire rather than the sight of it that he was first aware of. Somewhat puzzled by the noise he looked out of the bedroom window and saw the inferno across the road. Not even waiting to put on the dressing-gown that was hanging on the back of the door he ran downstairs and dialled 999 for the fire service. Then as he walked back up the stairs he remembered how one day, many years before, he had been talking to one of the retained firemen in Newton. He had asked what would happen if there was a fire in his village out on the moor. The answer that he got was 'Just keep it going till us gets there boy!'

By this time Sal was awake, so he went back downstairs and made them both a cup of tea and they watched from the bedroom window as the fire burned their village hall to the ground long before the fire brigade arrived. What with the noise and the flashing blue lights to arouse them, it wasn't long before a large crowd had gathered on the green. It seemed as though at least half the population of the parish were there, in various states of dress. Though still early in the morning, it wasn't yet light; the onlookers didn't seem to mind loosing their sleep. This was an event of some magnitude and the lights and noise, the smoke and steam all added to the drama. Men and machines working against one of the fearful forces of nature, this was to be marvelled at, almost to be enjoyed. There would be time enough tomorrow to wonder how it had all happened and worry about what to do about it all.

In the cold light of day it all looked very different. The fire engines had gone, the drama was over, and their precious village hall was nothing more than a pile of sodden, blackened ashes and a few pieces of half-burnt timber. The heat had been so intense as to have melted the plastic chairs, even the metal legs. Odd-shaped heaps were all that was left of the contents. To those who knew the whereabouts of the items that were kept in the various cupboards it was possible to guess what treasured objects had become these blackened mounds.

NINE

The Brown Bull Inn was just far enough away from camp not to be considered or used as a servicemen's pub. Frank and a few of his friends used it on occasions for a quiet night out, and on this particular evening, quiet was exactly what Frank wanted. He was with his best pals Rick and Charlie, Rick's wife. Frank always found it odd to call a girl by a boy's name, though there was no doubting that Charlie was 'all woman'.

He and Rick had joined the mob together and had been in the same unit for nearly all their service career. Now that Frank was about to leave the forces he wanted to use his friend as a sort of Devil's Advocate. Rick was a service man through and through and would do his best to persuade Frank not to leave.

They had finished their meal, through all of which Frank had been doing his best to explain how he was thinking and why he was going. Now it seemed it was Rick's turn.

"I've listened to all that you've been saying and I can understand a lot of your reasoning Frank, but I still don't think that you have seriously looked at what you will be missing. What you will be throwing away to put it bluntly. You have risen up through the ranks and will go a lot further I'm

70

certain. You are well respected by your fellow men; in fact the younger ones worship you. And think of the pension that you will get if you stay in to the end of your term. Besides, you will still be a relatively young man then, you would still be able to do your own thing in civvy street, running your own garage no doubt. Why be just a mechanic getting your hands dirty when you could be the boss of your own firm and pay somebody else to do the dirty work?"

"But that's just it Rick, don't you see? If I stay in I may well get promoted, but that would mean sitting behind a desk doing the admin side of things and telling others what to do. I have always lead from the front, I like being hands on. I suppose that's the thing that bothers me most about the prospect of staying in. I don't really want to be a Chief, I like being an Indian."

"What about all your friends then, wont you miss them, miss us?"

"Of course I will, but I'm not emigrating to the other side of the world. There's no reason why we can't keep in touch, in fact you pair would be more than welcome if you wanted to visit."

Rick got up and went over to the bar to get some more drinks. Charlie took the opportunity to say

"There's more to this than you are letting on isn't there Frank? I reckon that there's a woman in it somewhere. You have always fought shy of any long-term relationship with a girl. I some times wondered why, but I think that you have

71

been carrying a torch for some lucky young lady back home, am I right?"

"There used to be a girl of whom I was very fond. We were just teenagers who grew up together and liked the same sort of things, that's all. In any case she's married now, has been for a number of years. I could never marry her even if she were free. No that's not what is drawing me back, it's hard to describe to any body else just what it is, because I hardly understand it myself. I just feel this incredible pull, an intense longing to be in those wild places with all of nature around me, the wind on my face and the song of the curlews in my ears. I just can't imagine life, a happy life that is, anywhere else but on Dartmoor."

"So all of Rick's arguments have been in vain then?"

"Yes and no. Oh I know he hasn't persuaded me to stay, and in that respect he had failed. But if he hadn't made the argument, I wouldn't have had to think of my counter argument and work out just what all the points in favour and against were."

Rick returned with the drinks and said, "Have you had any better luck with him than I did Charlie?"

"No, but I think that between us we have helped Frank to see what really matters to him in life. I think if all we have done is to do that, then we've done a good job this evening, don't you?"

"So long as he's happy that's really all that matters. In any case a man of his calibre, with his qualifications, would have no trouble coming back if he really wanted to."

"I don't think that that is very likely" said Charlie looking over at Frank with a knowing smile. "Frank has done the Army bit of his life and now he's moving on, and I wish him well."

"So do I, in fact we'll drink to that, to Frank's new life."

They lifted their glasses in a toast. Three friends, whose friendship was unlikely to be quite the same as it had been for the last fifteen years, but the change didn't mean that it would be any less strong.

TEN

Grace rarely purchased any thing at jumble sales. It wasn't, she told herself, that she was a snob, far from it, it was just that she felt that it would hardly be proper for the wife of the vicar to be seen wearing or using someone else's cast offs. Apart from anything else, the last thing that she would want to do would be to cause any jealousy by seeming to patronise or favour one member of the community over others. However at the recent sale she had picked up a shoe box containing a small collection of postcards. The first few were old black and white photographs of local churches. Thinking that these would be of interest to Quentin, she happily parted with the two pounds asked for their purchase, as being her contribution to the cause.

On returning home other duties had prevented her from inspecting her acquisition any further, so the box of cards had been put in her desk and forgotten. Then, what with the fire and all, it was nearly a week later that she finally had a chance to look thoroughly at the collection.

As it turned out she was a little disappointed because there were only seven postcards of local churches. There were several pictures of villages in South Devon and a few moorland scenes showing ponies and tors. On more than one of these, the same group of ponies seemed to have mysteriously appeared in several different places in the same pose. There were however two pictures that interested her. They were old black and white photographs of Wistworthy Farm. The name was written across the bottom of the card in white capital letters sloping slightly backwards as though the writer was left-handed.

Although Grace hadn't been to Wistworthy for some time, she felt sure that there was now a group of trees in front of the yard that were not shown in either of the pictures. She had been intending to visit Blanche and this would give her an added reason to go and see her. So that afternoon she took her little car and set off to see one of the few women in the parish with whom she felt comfortable and at ease.

She was well aware that a lot of people regarded her as a figure of fun, a sort of caricature of a vicar's wife. And really that was the problem, she was not, and probably never had been, a person in her own right. She was the vicar's wife, an appendage almost, with no personality of her own. Her role in life had always been to support her husband, do good deeds for the parishioners on his behalf, and keep as much as possible in the background.

Blanche came into the yard from the fields, with her collie dog trotting by her side, just as Grace arrived.

"Come on in Mrs Russell. I'll make us a dish of tea. Don't often see you up this way, what can I do for you?"

"I've been meaning to come and see you for some time now. It's very remiss of me to have neglected you so, though I know that my husband has been to see you more than once."

"Oh that's all right, you'm here now, that's what matters," said Blanche, always ready to put others at ease. "Come in and sit down, we can have a piece of cake and a natter with our tea." With that she put the dog in its shed and the two women went into the comfortable old farm kitchen.

"I've just been up looking over the cattle, I find it takes a good bit longer than it used to. My old bones don't work quite so well as they did, still I shan't have to do so much when Frank gets back home."

"So he's leaving the army then is he? Coming home for good then?"

"Yes, he's finally made up his mind. I know it hasn't been an easy decision, but I for one can't wait till he gets here."

"You're a lucky woman to have a son, something that we were never gifted to have. We had always hoped that we would have a family, but it wasn't to be, it obviously wasn't God's will for us. But I greatly missed the joy of motherhood, missed that bond between a mother and her child. So as a result I have never felt totally fulfilled. Also as a mother I feel that I would have had a place in life, a place of my own."

"But you have a place, Mrs Russell, an important place as the vicar's wife."

"That's just it, my only place seems to be as a part of some one else. I want to be a woman in my own right. And please Blanche, call me Grace."

"Right; but I never realised that you felt this way Grace, I now can see from what you are saying that you're not really happy with the situation. But Quentin's a good man isn't he? Surely there's nothing there that you would want to change."

"Oh no, it's not Quentin, he's a very good man and a good husband. It's just that we are both of a generation and upbringing that saw the traditional roll of husband and wife very much set in stone, with the husband making all the decisions and the wife meekly doing her duty in the background. With you and Stan it was obviously a partnership, each maybe with your own separate roll to play, yet each roll of equal importance. I'm not saying that I want to be important, it's just that there are times when I would like to be me, Grace, not just the vicar's wife."

Blanche leaned across the table and put her hand on Grace's. She was beginning to understand what this unhappy woman had been living through all her life. Whilst her life on the farm had been physically hard and not always easy, she had been part of a team with Stan. They had always worked together, made plans and decisions together, been a true partnership. It had left her worn and a little older than her years; that was the price of hard work. She may have lost her man to an early grave but she had wonderful memories to look back on. More to the point, she had a fine son who was coming home soon to help and support her. Relatively speaking, of the two of them she was undoubtedly by far the better off.

"I must apologise for unburdening myself on you in this way, I had no right to do so but I have always felt that you are one of the few people around here who would understand, and on whom I could trust with a confidence. You are so natural and down to earth, probably because in farming you are so close to life and death and the things that really matter."

"That's alright Grace, 'tis good to talk and get it off your chest. Talking helps one to see things more clearly. You come up here any time you want to have a bit of a chat, I'll be only too pleased to see you."

"Thank you, thank you so much. You're very kind. Changing the subject completely, one of the reasons that I came up here was to show you these two postcards that I got at the jumble sale the other day. You are most welcome to keep them if they are of any interest to you. I've no idea when they were taken; it must have been quite some time ago though, because of the absence of those trees."

She pointed to the group of trees across the stream from the farmyard.

"Oh yes, I see what you mean. I don't know when they was planted, 'twas before my time, but 'tis true they have grown a brave bit in the last ten years or so."

"It's rare to get the chance to see how things were a hundred years ago. Some of the other pictures of village scenes show the people wearing clothes that very clearly date when the photographs were taken."

"Thank you Grace, thank you very much, I'm sure that Frank will be equally pleased to see them."

The two women stayed chatting for several minutes more, mostly about recent village events with the fire that destroyed the village hall occupying most of the conversation. Finally Grace left, feeling better for her visit, and feeling also that she had started a good and true friendship, a friendship which she felt sure would enrich her life no end.

ELEVEN

As the days passed people in the parish became increasingly aware of the magnitude of their loss and just how great an impact that loss was going to make on their lives. So many events and functions took place there, both routinely and spasmodically. An enormous part of the social life of the village was bound up in the hall. Of course there was the pub for a lot of people's socialising, older members of the community that is, but it could hardly be used by the young mum's for the baby and toddler group meetings, meetings without which many a young mum would have barely any social life at all. Then there was the amateur dramatic group, the Redacres, they were due to put on their summer variety show at the end of June. Rehearsals were well under way and a lot of new young talent were having their first shot at treading the boards. It would be a great shame if they were to miss out because the show had to be cancelled. It was all looking very bleak.

Then notices appeared in the pub and the post office. A village meeting was due to be held in the function room of The New Inn to discuss the future of the village hall. By the time the day of the meeting came most people had made up their minds as to what they felt would be best or at any rate what they wanted.

The function room was packed, there were nowhere near enough chairs for every one so many men were standing at the back of the room. Sal and Edna were sitting in the front row. They would be waiting to see which way the argument would go and then agree with whatever seemed to be the most popular idea. They felt, quite naturally, that proposing motions was not in their remit, they were there purely to see that the winning side won convincingly. If there was an opportunity to criticise the loosing side of the argument, then it was only right that they should do so in the interest of democracy. They would leave the gathering at the end of the evening confident in the knowledge that they had done their bit for the community.

Phil German was to chair the meeting, he being the chairman of the village hall committee. Two days earlier he had had a surprise visit from Sir Harold at eight o'clock in the evening. Over a glass or two of malt whiskey they had talked at length and now the result of their conversation was going to be put to the villagers. Phil was looking forward to the meeting and the reaction to the speech that Sir Harold was about to make. He called the room to order and after a brief preamble introduced the main speaker. Sir Harold was a tall slightly stooping man in his early seventies with thin greying hair and bushy eyebrows. He was wearing grey flannel trousers a cream cotton shirt and a tweed sports jacket with leather patches on the elbows. Most of the village knew of him, knew who he was but few actually knew him. Though he was lord of the manor and landlord to a few, he was a private man who kept himself to himself, preferring to do what he did for the village and its people discreetly.

He looked over the assembled crowd, smiled and started talking in a clear if rather soft voice. "First of all I would like to welcome you all tonight, it is a sad occasion that has brought us together but I am hopeful that by the end of this evening we will have planned a way forward. You don't need me to tell you that you have lost a very valuable asset, an asset that you urgently need to replace. Too many valuable aspects of village life are fast disappearing; most of the craftsmen that used to work here are long gone. Farming has changed so much and there are very few people left working the land. Other villages have lost their post offices, hopefully ours here is safe. Not three years ago our village school was closed. There was understandable concern that it might well be bought by some developer and turned into something of no benefit to this community. It was with that concern in mind that I bought the school when it came up for sale eighteen months ago."

A sigh followed by a murmuring followed this piece of totally unexpected news. Although there had been rumours that the school had been sold, nobody could discover who had bought it and speculation as to the resulting possible development was rife. Conversions of such buildings, disused chapels and the like were notoriously difficult. The resulting edifices were rarely pleasing to the eye, and if used as private dwellings were unconventional and difficult to arrange, not to mention difficult to heat.

"I had no idea at the time to what purpose I would put the building, I just wanted to ensure that it stayed in the village for the use of the village. Phil and I have looked over it and though a little dirty I think it is sound enough. We took a tape measure with us and I can tell you that the main room, the one that could be divided by a folding screen into two classrooms, is at least as big if not bigger than the hall was, though a somewhat different shape.. There are also two other rooms, one larger than the other, a kitchen, that will need equipping, and two toilet blocks. Oh I know, you will probably be thinking what good is all this to us. There's no way we can afford to buy the place, even if we only have to pay the price that I paid. You would be right, the insurance company will pay out a sum for your loss but it will be nowhere near enough to buy the old school, let alone do the necessary work on it that you would need to do to make it into a village hall. This is a problem of which I am well aware, so it is my pleasure to say that I would like to make a gift of the school to this village."

This time the gasp of astonishment and the hubbub that followed was considerably louder than before. Neighbour turned to neighbour chattering excitedly at the prospect of the new hall and already discussing plans as to what should be done and how.

After a while Phil called the meeting to order again saying that Sir Harold hadn't quite finished.

"Thank you Phil, all I wanted to say was this. There is a small price involved, oh don't get alarmed, it's not too bad. I would like it if you in return would give me the site of the now burned down hall. I want to build two three bed roomed cottages there, possibly semi-detached, to be let to local youngsters who are having such difficulty these days getting somewhere to live. Far too many houses in the Westcountry lie empty for a large part of the year. Whilst I have no objections to new people moving into the area, too many houses have been lost and are now out of the reach of our local boys and girls. In too many villages there are no lights in the windows during the winter months so that is why I want these proposed cottages to be to let and not ever for sale. I am fully aware that I shall have to get planning permission but I am hopeful that that will not be a great problem. Now, I am going to go downstairs for a drink, I've got a bit dry with all this talking. While I am gone you will doubtless want to discuss this offer, when you are ready I will come up again and we will finalise things, at least as much as we can tonight."

The people started clapping as Sir Harold made to leave, then one man got to his feet, then another and another until finally the whole room was standing, clapping and cheering. Deeply embarrassed Sir Harold left the room and after several minutes quiet returned and Phil regained some sort of order.

"Well folks, that was some surprise wasn't it? Is there anyone here who does not want to take up Sir Harold's kind and generous offer?...Don't all speak at once now....Right ho, I take it that you are all in agreement, we accept the offer and pass over the land on which the old hall stood in return. Sir Harold has already told me that he will be pleased to meet the total cost of this transaction and will instruct his lawyers tomorrow. I can't get over the man's generosity. I wonder what he would have done with the school if the hall hadn't burned down. I did worry as to what had caused the fire, I'm told that it was probably an electrical fault, right now I couldn't care less."

The babble of excited voices grew again, Phil let them go for a few minutes and then he went downstairs to get their benefactor. After thanking him once more Phil said that there would have to be a meeting of the village hall committee in a day or two. He felt that a representative of all those groups that used the hall should also attend, that's if any of them were not already on the committee, and that they should meet in the old school. The meeting was then adjourned, several staying for a drink in the bar to celebrate, and all went home with a feeling of euphoria and hope for the future.

TWELVE

Nancy Cameron-Hyde had been shopping in Newton. It was by no means a favourite occupation of hers; she could never understand the modern young women who liked to go shopping purely for the sake of it. Retail therapy it was not, not by any stretch of the imagination. For therapy she would always prefer a good walk with her highland terrier, Haig. The last two days had unfortunately been wet, very wet, and walking had been out of the question. Now as she was driving home the sun was trying to come out, maybe she would be able to get out after tea for a while. The bluebells were out now and maybe those lovely pale lilac-coloured orchids; she would see if she could find them later. Nancy was a keen admirer of the natural world, wild birds and animals were almost a passion with her, and though she knew the names of most of the wild flowers around her home she would often carry a small book on wild flowers with her. She disliked the idea of taking a flower home in order to identify it. The garden at the Old Rectory was not really her cup of tea; Giles liked the more formal approach, lawns and herbaceous borders full of flowers and shrubs. It was very nice to sit in with friends and have a drink and a chat, but for her the woods by the stream, the country lanes and the open moor were the places that inspired her. This time of year, with the rebirth that came each spring, was probably for her most fulfilling and exciting. The myriad of colourful wild flowers that she saw beside the road as she drove home filled her heart with joy. Thank heavens that some eco-friendly member on the council had decided recently that the verges shouldn't be cut till much later in the year. It made such a difference and was so worthwhile. Now she must get home, put away the shopping and get some tea for herself and Giles and then maybe she and Haig could go out for a walk.

Giles wouldn't want a lot to eat as he was going out that night for a reunion dinner. It was an annual event, men only, which took place in a different location each year. This year it was Giles' year to choose the location, so he had chosen an hotel in the South Hams. There was another member who lived in South Devon who also would benefit from his choice. The previous year they had all had to go up to Lossiemouth which was a bit of a drag. Despite the fact that it was a lot nearer this year Giles would be staying overnight, as he said, it would be a boozy evening and he had no intention of drinking and driving. They all wanted to relax, eat, drink and be merry and then fall into bed. He also wondered for how many more years they would be able to hold these reunions, they were all getting older and numbers were dwindling.

She arrived at the Old Rectory and Giles helped her to unload and carry in the bags and boxes of shopping. Then a cup of tea for them both; a piece of cake for Giles and some scrambled eggs for herself before he set off.

"Now my dear, I've left the phone number of the hotel on the pad by the phone. If you should need me for any thing just ring."

"And what good would that do, darling, you will be stuck there in a drunken stupor unable to walk, let alone drive home."

"Yes, I suppose you're right, you generally are. I'll see you tomorrow about lunch time." And with that he kissed her tenderly, held her close for almost a full minute and got into his car and left. They were a very close couple, spent a great deal of time together with their various hobbies, and so he particularly disliked spending nights away from her. For some reason that he couldn't explain he feared that he might not return. It was ridiculous he knew, after all when he was flying he had never given it a thought, they neither of them had, and the risk then had been several hundred times greater. But he had been young then and, with the not uncommon confidence of youth, believed himself to be immortal. They had all been like that in the squadron, they had to be. They had assessed the risk, done the training over and over and had become the polished professionals that they were, a team whose concentration on the job was total. But now that he was seventy-five he was well aware that 'they were picking them out of his pen' as his farming neighbours would say. He felt pretty fit and healthy, had an MOT every year and was told by his doctor that he had a wonderful constitution. Never the less he would feel, as he always did on these occasions, a great sense of relief when he got home again.

Nancy went back indoors to put on her walking trousers, boots and waterproof jacket. She took a rucksack with a spare jumper in it in case it got a bit colder before she returned and, with Haig running excitedly ahead of her, walked through the church-yard and down the foot path to the stream. It was a lovely evening, almost warm enough not to have a coat, but she knew that it would be a lot colder in the woods beside the water. She felt that there was something special about walking beside running water. There was life in the movement, it was always changing and it seemed to be talking to her. After the recent rains the water was well up, dark and beer-coloured with a lot of white water; the head on the beer. The path ran through an old meadow, rough grazing with gorse bushes and the new shoots of bracken just poking through. She came to an old hawthorn, in full flower like a giant snowball, and just beyond it were the bluebells. In amongst them were the little orchids that she had hoped to see. They didn't seem to last for very long, the previous year she had missed them, so she took her time walking slowly and enjoying the scene. The path was then fenced off from the fields with a post and rail fence, on the other side of which the horses from the riding stables were there grazing contentedly. Nancy called Haig to heel and leant on the rail talking gently, and soon she had three of the horses standing close to her. They were beautiful, sleek and shining, nodding their heads up and down, their tails swishing and feet stamping at the flies that swarmed around. She nodded in turn and then carried on on her way past a couple more pasture fields and into the woods. It was decidedly cooler in there beneath the beech and oak trees. They were just showing their first leaves, delicate and tender like green butterflies, another of the beauties of the time of year. She had to watch her footing now because in places the flood waters had washed away the soil from around the roots of the trees. It made the going tricky and she couldn't watch the stream as much as she would have liked, she was hoping to spot the dipper. He was a little dark-brown, almost black bird with a white breast who would stand on a rock in the middle of the stream and bob and curtsey. It was not easy to spot him as he was perfectly camouflaged against the dark brown and white water of the stream. Then he would walk into the stream with his wings held partially out to keep him down and feed on insects and caddis fly larvae off the bottom. It was more usual to see him flying away, low and straight along the stream, probably because Haig's barking would frighten him.

They had passed the awkward part when ahead of them Nancy saw a mother duck with her brood of six... seven... no, eight ducklings following her. Little brown and black bundles of fluff, squeaking as they ran to keep up, with their little necks stretched out. Nancy called to Haig but she was too late, he had already spotted them and was off as fast as his short legs would carry him.

The mother duck called to her young and then, with one wing trailing awkwardly to one side and the other flapping madly, she made off down the path with Haig in full pursuit, barking all the way. Nancy's calling was to no avail; to the small dog this was far more fun than ordinary 'walkies'. The ducklings had disappeared into the vegetation somewhere, as if to a well rehearsed plan, and then the duck jumped into the water.

"No Haig no, you silly dog, come back here!"

It was no use, he was in the water trying to catch up with his prey, but at his age of thirteen he had no chance. The duck suddenly took off and flew over the small patch of open ground on the opposite side of the stream. Instead of turning for the near bank Haig carried on not seeing the danger ahead. From a fast flowing but smooth pool the water had become a white torrent rushing between rocks, swirling this way and that.

Nancy realising his plight ran down the path calling all the while, hoping that he would reach the bank. But he swept on, his fur by now sodden and weighing him down, with his head barely above water. A tree ahead had fallen across the path, probably during the previous night's rough weather. Its branches were in the stream and Nancy hoped that Haig might be able to make use of them to get ashore. No such luck, he was swept on in under the branches and out of her sight. The trunk across the path was a little over waist height and the gap underneath it was a tangle of branches. She heaved herself up and over and fell awkwardly on the other side. A pain like a knife stabbed into her hip and shot through her left side as she landed in a heap on the path. After a moment or two she tried to get to her feet, the pain was horrendous and her leg seemed no longer to work.

"Oh God," she said, "You silly old girl, you've really done it now."

Feeling gently around the painful area she came to the conclusion, quite correctly, that she had broken her hip. She tried to move and a wave of pain shot through her again bringing with it the warm flush of nausea. She looked down stream to see if she could see Haig, hoping that he might be able in some way to help. But he was nowhere to be seen, he had been swept on and she would never see him again. She lay listening to the sounds of the stream and the wood. A green woodpecker flew by with its *hyah hyah hyah* call. Up in the top of a tree a song thrush was singing its heart out, its evening song filling the sky. Each phrase was repeated three or four times, *'tiddly-dee..tiddly-dee...tiddly-dee , go back..go back..go back, I love you..I love you.. I love you, no you don't..no you don't..no you don't'* . At any other time Nancy would have loved to listen to it but now it seemed only to emphasise its wellbeing and her dilemma. She looked around her, she recognised where she was, the path was narrower at this point and rising cliff-like beside it was a rock face some thirty feet high and sixty or seventy feet long. Trees were growing on the top of it and there were one or two large cracks running vertically from the bottom. One of these looked like a small cave; maybe if she could only get there she might get a little warmth from its shelter. She was already beginning to feel the cold, partly because she was no longer walking but mainly because of her accident. She shuffled around a bit and took off her rucksack. Then after a rest she took out her spare jumper, wriggled out of her coat and put them both back on. The effort and the associated pain had brought her out in a sweat and she had another rest for a few minutes. Then she took out her mobile phone, but who to ring? Giles was away, Rose didn't have a phone, perhaps Phil German would be the best bet. She switched on; only to find that there in the woods she could not get a signal.

"Oh God, you really are in a mess girl" she said, "I'll just have to try and get to that sort of cave thing over there." With that she pushed herself up onto her hands and one knee and painfully dragging her broken leg behind her crawled towards the rock. She had to stop frequently because of the pain and the waves of nausea that kept sweeping over her. Twice she fainted briefly but after some twenty minutes she had reached the cleft in the rocks and managed to get most of her body inside. It was remarkably dry, with a carpet of dead leaves on the floor. If she had to stay there until she was found, at any rate it would be better than where she had fallen. She wriggled herself into the least painful position that she could find and settled down. It would be for the night, she realised that. Nobody would be passing this way until daylight at the earliest. With a sigh of frustration and exhaustion she lay back and was soon overtaken by sleep.

THIRTEEN

Jimmy Stapleton was Rose's youngest son. He was a handsome young man with a ready smile and a winning way, particularly with the ladies. His latest conquest was a thirty-five year old divorcee who lived in the neighbouring village. Not wishing to broadcast his affair, Jimmy would park his car in an old disused gravel pit off the main road and walk the rest of the way to his assignation. This morning he was returning along the path beside the Redacre Brook when a hundred yards below the junction with the little brook he saw something white in the water. Looking closer he saw that it was a white dog. He scrambled down the bank and hooking a stick under the collar was able to get the animal out onto the bank. It was as he feared dead, so he searched the collar for identification. 'Haig Cameron-Hyde'. His mum worked for them, he must get home as quickly as possible, they would probably be out looking everywhere for their dog by now. Maybe not, it was still early, only half past six. Holding onto the collar with the dog as far away from his leg as possible so as not to get too wet, he set off for his car. He got home and went straight to his mum's caravan and shouted in through the open doorway, "Mum, I've found this dead dog in the river just below water's meet. It belongs to Giles and Nancy, where you work. They may be out looking for it, I think we ought to go over there and let them know that I've found it. It's best if you tell them, you know them better than I do."

Rose dressed and they piled into her car and drove down to the Old Rectory.

"The old man's away at some reunion, I think. I don't know if Nancy will be up yet, she tends to lie in a bit longer these days. Still, I know where they keep a spare key, though I'm not looking forward to telling her the sad news."

They arrived at the house and Rose jumped out of the car telling Jimmy to search the garden in case Nancy was out there looking for Haig. She then went and got the key from an outhouse and let herself in through the back door. She walked through the house calling, but there was no answer. Going upstairs she found the bed empty and looking as though it had not been slept in that night. She ran downstairs and searched the utility room for the walking clothes that she knew Nancy would be wearing if she had gone out. Then she looked in on the kitchen table for any sign of a note, and then by the telephone in the hall. Everywhere she drew a blank. Jimmy put his head in the door, "She don't seem to be any where out here Mum, have you had any luck?"

"No son and I don't think she's been here all night, her bed hasn't been slept in, that's for sure. I just don't know quite what to do for the best. She may be out looking for her dog, but I can't think that she would have stayed out all night. More likely she would have called on someone to help her."

"Yes Mum, and we all know who that would have been.... you."

"I think I'd best ring Phil German, he'll know what to do and who to contact, I'm sure they have his number here in their little phone book."

So Rose made her phone call, trying not to appear too worried, and passed on to Phil the job of organizing the search. Based on where Jimmy had found the dog Phil reckoned that it could have fallen into either stream, so the search should start at water's meet. Nancy could be somewhere in either valley, maybe. Then he rang the local police and Eric Jordon. The police wanted to know where Giles was and Phil told them as best as he could. They seemed to think that they would be able to trace him; he just prayed that they wouldn't frighten Giles too much. He had called Eric because he did a lot with the school children, training for Ten Tors and the like, and could probably get help from the local rescue group. "We'll meet at water's meet, how soon can you get there Eric?"

"Twenty minutes, maybe less, and I'll try and get a couple of friends to join me."

"Right ho, Beatie will come with me until Jeff finishes the yard work, then he'll take over so she can get off to work. See you."

Twenty minutes later a small group was gathered by the stream. Phil, Beatie and Phil's sheep dog together with Rose and her eldest son,

Will, were to search the Redacre, while Eric, Jimmy and two of Eric's friends would search the smaller stream. They also had a couple of collie dogs, well known for their ability to find people. Eric had also brought in his rucksack a large flask of hot tea and an aluminium rescue blanket.

"Make sure to search the bank as well as the water, there's nothing to say that she's in either but we've got to look. Keep calling to her, but remember that she may not be able to hear you, she may be asleep or something, so be sure to look everywhere."

So with these words of exhortation from Phil ringing in their ears the two groups set off up the streams. The water had dropped a little during the night and was a little less discoloured. The sun was out warming the air, and a slight mist was rising off the water like the breath of the stream. Although the paths beside the streams ran along one bank only, they were searching both in case Nancy had fallen in and been forced to climb out on the other bank. Where the valley was open, the meadows were easy to search and they spread out to cover as large an area as possible. In the woods it was a lot more difficult looking amongst the undergrowth and trees, both standing and fallen. This was where the dogs proved to be so useful, pushing into thickets and sniffing everywhere. None the less it took a long time to cover a hundred yards and all the searchers were frustrated by their lack of progress. They were all thinking of Nancy, trying hard to be positive and cheerful. But it wasn't easy, though they wouldn't admit it out loud the thought of a seventy-two year old woman spending the night out in the open, possibly in water, filled them all with dread.

FOURTEEN

Nancy was freezing; she was stiff, cramped and uncomfortable in her little shelter. But she was alive. She was well aware of her predicament and the danger that she faced from hypothermia. She remembered having read somewhere that if she were to tense her muscles over and over in a sort of rhythm, she would generate heat, hopefully enough to keep her alive. So she kept tensing her arm and upper body muscles over and over and found that it did seem to work. She was tired after a few minutes but definitely a good bit warmer. Feeling a little better she started wondering when she might be found. Who would find that she was missing? Would she have to wait until Giles got home from his reunion party? That might not be until midday, then how would they know where to look? She hadn't left any note or message with any one; she didn't think any one had seen her leave the house because she had gone through the churchyard. And what about poor little Haig, where had he got to, was he still alive? Surely if he were he would have sought her out by now, he was incredibly loyal. No, she was realistic enough to accept that her dear little dog was most likely dead. It was beginning to get light, she looked at her watch, ten past five, was this night ever going to end? It could be another twelve hours before she was found; perhaps this was the time when her life would flash before her eyes. No not really, but she started to think about her past life, slowly and thoughtfully, not in flashes.

She thought of her courtship, the dashing young pilot who had swept her off her feet, and how delighted she had been to be swept, and then their wedding with the guard of honour formed by the other young pilots all in their best blues. The honeymoon in the Scilly Isles in that lovely little B&B. It was a quaint little cottage with no electricity and she could still remember the smells and the sounds. She could picture them coming home at night, after a meal in the only pub, to the smell of paraffin and the hissing of the Tilley lamp. Then there was the birth of their son, Julian, not an easy one in a foreign land with none of her relations to support her. Giles had been marvellous, probably what now would be called a 'new man' helping around the house whenever he could. He even would change Julian's nappies, if no one else was around. Then the friendships she had forged with the other young wives on the base, with several of whom she still kept close contact. Two years later their second son David had been born, in England this time. Her mother had been able to come over and stay with them and help. She looked after Julian and Giles, which meant that he wasn't quite as involved with the chores as he had been when Julian was born. The two boys had grown up well adjusted, despite being dragged all over the world as is so often the case with service families. They had played well together

101

and fought only rarely. They had watched Julian grow up into a sensitive artistic young man with a love of music and art and a talent with musical instruments. David was more the practical type, more hands on, always making things and building dens and tree houses. It had been a joy to see their sons grow and they were so proud of them both. It had all seemed so perfect and then tragedy had struck, double tragedy, first David's death and then the awful business with Julian.

Julian had followed his father into the services, whether out of desire or a sense of duty she had never known, and had been doing well until the scandal blew up. Giles may have seemed a new man when Julian was born but he was really an old dinosaur. The fact of a son of his being 'gay' was an anathema to him. The scandal, the shame, it was almost as if it was his fault that he had sired this freak, as he now considered his son to be. Julian had left the forces and moved away. Giles and Nancy hadn't exactly told him to go, but he had felt most uncomfortable at home and if only for their sakes had felt that it was best course of action. Nancy, though not quite as homophobic as her husband, had done nothing to stop him. She was greatly disappointed, mostly because she would never become a grandmother. Perhaps she should have stood up to Giles a bit more. She did get the odd letter from Julian but it was all wrong that they never saw him these days. She would have to have a word with Giles about it, she felt quite sure that he wanted to see their son just as much as she. It was probably just his silly male pride that kept him from making the first move.

A dark wave washed over her and for a while she slipped into unconsciousness. Then out into the light again to hear a cuckoo singing. How ironic, she thought, that she should hear her first cuckoo of the year when she was about to die. She drifted away again and then when she came back in her jumbled thoughts she saw Julian walking up the path towards her. She called to him, but he didn't hear her, maybe he didn't want to see her or help her. She cried out loud, the tears of anguish running down her cheeks leaving water marks in the grime. Then he was gone. Had he really been there? She was finding it very difficult to make out what was real and what was just imagination or hallucination.

Then she heard Haig barking, she called to him but he didn't come, perhaps he hadn't heard her, her voice was very weak. Then she heard the barking again and a figure was standing over her. "Julian, oh my dear boy, you've come home." she cried out softly.

The figure above her moved and a voice said "It's all right, Mrs Cameron-Hyde, you'll be alright now. We'll soon get you out of here and back home. What's the problem, are you hurt and if so where? You've had us all worried sick trying to find you."

"It's my leg, my hip, my left hip. I think it's broken, it hurts rather a lot. Who are you?"

"I'm Eric, Eric Jordon; we must see if we can get you out of there, it's a bit of a squeeze isn't it."

He told Jimmy to get in behind her. "You're smaller than me and there's not a lot of room in there. If you can lift her shoulders I will lift her legs and hips." At the first movement Nancy gave a sharp cry of pain and then blacked out again.

"Quick now, while she's out she wont feel any pain. I know we shouldn't do it this way, but we haven't got much choice. We need to get her out of there and warm her up somehow."

Once they had Nancy out on the path Eric's two friends sat on either side of her, arms around her thin shoulders, bodies pressed tight in an attempt to warm her. Eric wrapped her in the aluminium blanket that he had brought and then poured out a cup of tea from his flask. He then took out his map and after studying it for a while wrote down the grid reference on a piece of paper.

"Jimmy, take this phone, go down the path a ways and then climb up onto the rock here beside us. I reckon you'll get a signal there. Then ring 999 and tell them we've found her and that we need the Air Ambulance. Read out this number to them, it's the grid reference of this spot so they'll know where we are. Then ring Phil German, his number is also on that piece of paper. I hope you'll be able to get him, if not ring the Post Office, their number is in the phone, OK, think you can do that alright? Good lad."

Jimmy disappeared down the path and Eric turned his attention to Nancy trying to get her to drink a little of the hot tea that he'd brought. After she had had a few sips she began to perk up a little and a bit of colour returned to her cheeks.

"What ever happened to you, do you remember? Jimmy found your little dog in the river way downstream. I'm sorry to have to tell you that he's dead. Then when there was nobody at home we realized that something was wrong and started a search party."

"Haig took off after a duck, silly little dog, jumped into the water after it. The current was too strong for him and he got washed down-stream.. I ran after him, calling to him to try to get him to the bank. Then I came to this fallen tree. I suppose I was in too much of a hurry or something, any way I had to climb over it and I fell awkwardly and it seems like I've broken my hip. I managed to crawl into that sort of cave and I spent the night there. Thank God you found Haig; I might have been here for days."

"Well you're safe now and we'll soon have you out of here. The Air Ambulance won't be long; as soon as Jimmy gets back we'll have a better idea as to when. The main thing is to keep you as warm as possible until they get here."

But it was another half an hour before they heard the whirring of the helicopter and a further ten minutes before the paramedics arrived up the path carrying a stretcher. They took over from Eric, much to his relief, and soon were on their way to their craft and a swift flight to Derriford Hospital.

FIFTEEN

The old school was a hive of industry with nearly twenty people working away to get it cleaned up ready for repainting and general decorating. Jim Blundel and his uncle Charlie were dismantling the folding wooden screen that in times past had been pulled across to divide the large room and thus make two classrooms. They were painstakingly undoing all the screws and removing each panel because, as Charlie said, they could come in very handy for building the surrounds of the stage or something else. Charlie was a great believer in make do and mend, he was of that generation. His shed at the bottom of his garden was a veritable Aladdin's Cave filled with pieces of wood and metal. To most people it would look like a load of old junk, but not only did Charlie know exactly where any piece was, but also to what use it could be put. Many a neighbour had cause to thank him for saving them time and money by providing just the piece or part required to fix their problem. Also as a former farm worker he could, like so many of that ilk, turn his hand to almost anything, and since he retired had found that his services were in such demand that he had little time to himself.

Structurally the building was sound, though there was one slate missing off the roof. This had led to a small drip in the kitchen area, but there were two men on the roof fixing a fresh slate and having a good look to see if there were any more problems that they could fix while they were up there. Inside the toilets would need a total makeover, apart from anything else the scale of all the fittings was too small.

Sal and Edna were washing down the woodwork with sugar soap prior to re-painting. As usual their minds and conversation were more occupied with the latest gossip.

"Terrible thing about poor Nancy, I heard that she was lucky to be found alive, what with a broken hip and that there hypothermia."

"Yes, and what about poor Giles coming home to find that his wife had been rushed off to hospital, that must have been a helluva shock. Just imagine if you was to come home Sal, and find Charlie had been took off to hospital whilst you had been out playing whist or something, imagine how you would feel. You'd be for ever blaming yourself for not being home when he was took bad."

"Yes, I know what you mean, except that Charlie always comes to whist drives with me so tis hardly likely to happen," said Sal with a giggle.

"Oh you know what I mean, it could happen any time, like when you're out shopping or something. Then there's all the hospital visiting and that, I mean, it doesn't bear thinking about does it?"

They had moved on to a small cupboard door that was standing against the wall.

"What's this old door doing here Sal? It looks too small to be from this room."

"I reckon that that's the old store cupboard door, from out in the passage, there must be another of them somewhere, they was a pair."

"There's some writing here on the back, looks like some names or something. Somebody pressed quite hard with a ball point pen 'cos they are almost cut into the wood. Can you see what I mean Sal, 'tis names of some sort isn't it?"

"Yeah, that's right, it's a bit hard to read them but it looks like BUDDY, TWINKLE, DAN DARE, SNOW WHITE, LUCY LOCKET .....Oh I know, I remember now, least ways I think I do, they was nicknames. We all had 'em at one time and for some reason they was all written in this cupboard on the back of the doors. I reckon there was a lot more on the other door."

"Can you remember who any of them were?"

"Oh yes, I remember one alright, Twinkle, that was my nickname, I don't recollect why I was called that."

"Can you remember any of the others, or any that aren't here but were in use at the time, perhaps on the other door?"

"Yes, Snow White; that was Blanche Leaman that was, you know, Blanche Naraway from over to Wistworthy. Charlie might remember a few more, let's ask him. Charlie, over here a minute, these here nicknames, d'you remember any of the other ones? There's another door somewhere with them on but we can't seem to find it."

Charlie came over and had a look and after some deliberation said "The only names I can remember were Mae West and Red Barron. Mae West was that plump girl from down the valley, what was she called? You know the one, bit plump and starting to sprout a pair of breasts, Heather something. Typical kids, cruel like, we called her Mae West, 'twas hardly fair, but what nickname was? As to Red Barron, I don't rightly know, fact is I'm not even sure what my nickname was, maybe the craze hadn't started when I was here."

"They probably called you Charlie Brown or Peanuts" said Edna with a laugh. "I remember they used to call me Eddie at my first school, it used to make me cry, so they called me that all the more then. Like you say, kids are cruel aren't they?"

"Blanche had a thing with Phil at one time, if I remember rightly. In fact when they were at big school they were quite an 'item' as they say these days. Then all of a sudden it stopped. I know he went off to college but when he came home in the holidays you would think he had never even spoken to Blanche. Dumped her good an' proper he did."

"What you seem to forget Sal," said Charlie in a stern voice, "is that the Germans and the Leamans had been at each other's throats for three generations. I wouldn't be surprised if Phil hadn't been told that under no circumstances was

110

he to marry a Leaman. Or if he did he would have to leave home and lose any chance of taking over the farm."

"What's all this?" said Edna, "Sounds like something off Dallas, tell us more, Charlie, don't leave us in suspense."

"Well I'm not rightly sure of the details; it was all to do with common rights. In those days, and I'm talking about Phil's great grandfather, Blanche Leaman's great grandfather had a big farm. It was a Duchy farm, as was German's, but Old Man Leaman was well in with Captain Sinclair, the Duchy agent. German's place was only small, not much more than a smallholding I suppose. Anyway, somehow or other Leaman got the common rights that went with German's little place, seemed to steal them like. 'Course, without those grazing rights his place wasn't hardly worth a light, and it wasn't as though Leaman really needed them himself neither. It really did lead to a helluva ruckus, they said at the time it was a wonder somebody didn't get killed. I've no idea how it all ended up, but I know that the Leamans didn't gain aught from it in the end."

"Was it really that bad? I thought all that sort of thing died out long ago."

"Well thank heavens it has now," said Charlie, "There's enough trouble in the world without neighbours falling out with one another. I was always taught to help my neighbours; I might need their help myself one day. I'm glad to say that in this village people do help one another."

"That reminds me, has anybody heard anything about Nancy, I haven't seen Giles for a day or two is she going to be able to come home soon?"

"Last I heard, Edna, there was complications, something to do with the hypothermia, and they don't expect her home this week at least," said Charlie.

"Oh, well I hope it won't be too much longer, poor old Giles is missing her. Rose may be a very good cook and looking after the house and that very well, but he's lost a lot of weight poor chap. Tis the worry of it all I reckon. I mind when my husband was ill, fortunately for him it wasn't for very long, I lost nearly two stone."

"Looks like you managed to find them again Edna."

"I was always built for comfort, not for speed. I always say that it's better to be a bag full of curves than a bag full of nerves. Never mind that, I hear that young Frank is coming home today, Blanche will be pleased to have company again, she's lost without her Stan, and the farm needs a man."

"So is he coming home for good, going to stay and run the farm then?" asked Sal.

"I really don't know, perhaps your Charlie could tell us, he knows a lot more'n he lets on as a rule. Charlie, what have you heard about young Frank, is he going to run the farm or what?"

"'S far as I know he is, maybe on a slightly smaller scale. Blanche said something about him starting up a mechanicing business as well. Tis what he knows best after all." With that Charlie left the two women and moved off to another room to help Jim.

SIXTEEN

Sir Harold had been down to the shop and seeing the men on the roof had crossed over to see how the work was progressing. He was a little concerned lest the repairs needed were greater than he had at first thought. He talked to Phil who reassured him that all was well and then took a quick look inside. While he was standing in the passage he overheard Sal and Edna's conversation about the nicknames the school children had given each other and the childhood romances. This conversation made his mind go back to a time over forty years earlier when he was a young man, fresh out of university enjoying a summer break before starting work. So it was that as he walked up the drive memories of that day came flooding into his mind, as fresh as if it had been only yesterday.

He had gone fishing, up the East Dart above Dartmeet. It was late afternoon; a hot slightly humid day and he hadn't had a great deal of luck, just two reasonable sized brown trout. He was on the west bank in the shade beside the woods. On the other bank in an open area of flat ground, much like a meadow, three girls were picnicking around a small fire, a wisp of blue smoke curling upwards in the still air. The sound of their teenage laughter came across the valley and mingled with the splashing and babbling of the river noises. He went on further, beyond the large cliff-like rock that sheltered one of his favourite pools. Here he had cast several times but without success, so he packed up his rod and crossing over on the stepping stones had returned on the east bank.

The sound of a splash and the sight of a flash of bronzed skin seen through the willows made him stop. He was at pains to make out exactly what it was that he had seen, then through the bushes and up the path towards him came an elfin like creature. It was a girl, no more than fifteen or sixteen, in a faded blue T-shirt, several sizes too large for her, which she was wearing as a mini dress. She was still wet from her swim, and the dress clung provocatively to her lithe body. Her black hair, slightly curly was cut very short, almost like a boy's, and her eyebrows slanted upwards, above dark brown eyes accentuating the pixie like image.

"I hope I haven't disturbed the fish and spoiled your sport," she said.

"No, I had packed up a while ago and was making my way back home."

"Do you live around here then?"

"Yes, not that far away. What are you doing here, apart from swimming and frightening the fish?" He laughed as he spoke, not wishing to seem upset by her behaviour.

"We came out on the bus to spend the day by the river and have a picnic. Trouble is I think we've missed the last bus home so it looks as though we'll have to spend the night here. It's OK

115

we have a couple of blankets that we brought to sit on and we've got quite a bit of food."

"Would you like a couple of trout for your tea" he said, and wrapping the two fish in a few foxglove leaves he held them out to her.

"Oh yes, that would be lovely, thank you very much," she said, taking the fish and putting them down on the ground beside her. She looked at him; one eyebrow raised quizzically, a coquettish tilt to her head and a most engaging smile twitching the corners of her mouth. She moved closer and then, standing on tip-toe, she put her hands on his shoulders and kissed him on the lips. Then she stepped back, the same impish smile still playing around her mouth.

It was a childish kiss, but Harold was so moved by it, by the innocence and honesty of it that he put his hands on her waist and drew her towards him again. She was chuckling, the lights in her eyes dancing, her white teeth flashing as he kissed her again. Her lips were parted and his tongue found its way in and touched hers. This was a totally new experience for her, different and exciting. Her whole body was tingling as though charged with electricity. What had started as an innocent peck on the lips had become a passionate embrace. Both of them were kissing fiercely, hungrily. Then suddenly she pulled back, almost breathless, and picking up her fish, turned and trotted away down the path. Where it opened out into the meadow-like expanse that ran from the river up to the foot of the tor she paused briefly, looked over her shoulder at him, gave him one last wonderful smile and said "You're beautiful."

Then she was gone, skipping across the meadow to join her friends at their camp fire. He watched her flashing brown legs made golden by the evening sun, her T-shirt bouncing up and down showing the smooth curves of her buttocks as she ran. Would he ever see her again? He doubted it; it had been one of those heart-stopping moments, a brief encounter, a moment to savour and maybe to remember. For the girl, it was her first kiss, something that she would never ever forget.

Harold had returned the next day, but of course they were long gone leaving no sign of her or of who she was. At the base of the tor, by a big rock, where the flat ground ended and the bracken-covered slope rose to the rocky tor above; a small pile of whitish ash was all that remained surrounded by a ring of short black-ended sticks. He poked the ashes and, still warm they rose with a wisp of smoke making a pattern in the air; a pattern which in his fancy looked like her elfin face with her cheeky coquettish smile and laughing eyes..

Not many days afterwards he was off to the city to start his career. Visits to Edworthy Hall were few and far between. For several years company business in town and abroad had taken priority. He had met and married his wife Jane, a lovely girl whom he had first met at university some years earlier. At that time their relationship had been purely that of friends in a larger group of acquaintances. Then later they had been thrown together on a business trip, their friendship had blossomed and the wedding had followed soon after. They had a son Richard who was now married with children of his own. Regrettably, just before her sixtieth birthday and after a long struggle, Jane had died of leukaemia. Though he missed her terribly Harold had learned to live alone at Edworthy Hall, with a little help from his friends, and frequent visits from Richard and his family who were a joy and delight to him. He would walk around the gardens admiring the plants and shrubs, many of which she had planted years before. They were a permanent reminder of the wonderful life that they had spent together. Occasionally in his dreams, however, he had seen the elfin face and sparkling eyes of the girl by the river and had felt her lips on his.

When some years later she arrived in the village, he didn't at first recognize her. Gone were the elfin looks and short hair, replaced by a mane of flowing raven locks hanging down to her shoulders and beyond. The coquettish smile and laughing eyes replaced by the sensual, more knowledgeable look of a woman who was entirely her own person, knew herself, was proud of herself; a woman who knew how to love and had been loved. She had entered into Harold's life quietly and with no fuss, helping Jane around the house and gardens. She had asked and expected no favours other than a place to park her old bus. When Jane had been taken ill she had helped in any way she could, spending many a night sitting

118

with her when Harold had to be away on business. When the end came she had been there in the background. Her friendship was deep and rewarding. Some times over the years that followed, Harold would spend an evening with her; sitting, talking and sharing a bottle of wine from his cellar. Though these occasions were not that frequent they meant a lot, and the help that they gave to each other emotionally was immense. As the years went by Harold grew to realise just how much he valued their relationship. Although from very different walks of life it never ceased to amaze him how similar their thoughts and ideas were, a fact upon which they frequently commented. Neither of them wished their relationship to be public, particularly Harold who was a very private man.

SEVENTEEN

At the Old Rectory, Giles was getting ready for his visit to the hospital. It was not something that he was very good at, he looked forward to seeing Nancy but once he had been there for a few minutes he didn't know what to say or what to do. He would ask how she was and if there was any thing he could do for her. He would tell her any local news that he could think of. He wasn't very good at that, never having been one to gossip, and he probably forgot all the bits of news that would have been of interest to her. Then there was the hospital itself, it was so impersonal, no privacy either. He had asked if Nancy could have a room to herself, but he was told that the two side rooms were occupied by people with some contagious disease or something, so she would have to stay in the ward with all the others. Nancy didn't seem to mind, but he didn't like everybody hearing what he said to her, so he said less than he really wanted to or should do. He wanted so much to help her and the frustration of not knowing what to do or how to do it made him even more sad. Always in the back of his mind was the thought that he should have been at home, that it wouldn't have happened if he hadn't been away. He knew that it was illogical to blame himself but he did none the less. He had asked the doctor how much longer she was going to be in hospital, but he had said that it was early days yet. Nancy had some complication due to the hypothermia and they had to get that sorted out first. So long as it wasn't one of those horrible hospital bugs that he had heard about, but he had been assured that it was no such thing. Still it was difficult to know what to believe, he worried if they told him anything, and he worried even more if they told him nothing.

He had stopped taking flowers and fruit in to her; there was enough fruit to feed an army and flowers in vases on every window. People from the village had been wonderful, visiting and taking in goodies. Giles would sit there reading the paper to her and eating her grapes, he had had more grapes in those last few days than he had ever had in the whole of his life. At least, that was how it felt. He always took home her nightie to wash and brought in a clean one each day. It always seemed far too hot in the ward, especially to one who was used to the outdoor life of Dartmoor and so lying in bed all day in the same clothes got very hot and uncomfortable. Nancy had always said that if she had loads of money she would like to have clean, freshly ironed cotton sheets every day. It was a small thing but he felt it was a bit of a help.

He finally found somewhere to park, an everyday nightmare, and made his way up to the ward. He had a proposition to put to Nancy and, although they nearly always seemed to think as one, he was unsure as to what her reaction would be. Her recent accident and the stay in hospital had brought home to him just how vulnerable they both were. By rights they should have several more years left together, but even so it was time to do all those things that had to be done before it was too late. The first and most important item on the list was to get in touch with Julian and try to make amends. Just how to get in touch was another problem but nothing was impossible if one tried hard enough.

She was sitting up in bed when he arrived in the ward, smiling beautifully as he walked towards her. She always had a ready smile for him, no matter how she was feeling, and it always had the same effect on him, filling him with a warm glow. He realised just how lucky he was to have shared his life with this wonderful selfless woman. He pulled a chair up beside the bed, kissed her tenderly and sat down taking her hand. He wasn't quite sure how to start so after their usual greeting and small talk he said "I've been thinking Darling, I've been thinking rather a lot recently, I suppose we all do when we're in our own, especially when we're not used to being on our own. I expect that you've been doing the same."

"Yes dear, I've been thinking a lot lying here; it's all I have to do really."

"Well what I would like to do, in fact what I feel we ought to do if you agree, is to contact Julian. It's high time to put the past behind us…."

"Oh yes, yes" Nancy interrupted and tears of joy flooded down her smiling face. Giles moved off the chair and onto the side of the bed. He put his arm around her and hugged her towards him and kissed the top of her head.

"You silly old man, of course I agree, I have been thinking along the same lines myself."

They were both crying now, crying and laughing and looking into each other's eyes.

"When I was lying out there in the woods I was thinking about Julian, thinking that I might never see him again and what a waste that would be. At one point I thought I saw him, but it was only an hallucination, I think I had several of them."

"Well it's high time I put my silly prejudices behind me and tried to make friends. I dread to think of what might have happened to you that night, how much more terrible it would have been for you if you had gone and never seen our boy again."

"It wasn't just you dear; I was just as much to blame. It was all so soon after David's death, it was all too much and we neither of us knew how to cope with it. I've also been thinking a lot about David recently, we don't talk about him very much do we? Oh I know we did at the beginning, probably too much, going over and over the accident and what, if anything, we could have done to have stopped it from happening. I remember you saying that life must not be filled with 'if onlies'. Then almost before we had come to terms with his death we learned about Julian and his being gay. I think our grief turned to anger then and somehow we stopped talking about either of our boys. Probably because it was so painful and we thought that to talk about it would have only increased the pain, for both of us. So sad, so

123

stupid, I know that talking about them wouldn't have brought either of them back, but I'm sure it would have helped us to cope with it all a lot better. I wonder what David would have turned out to be, he was flitting about like a butterfly from one proposed career to another. What would he look like now I wonder? I always thought that he had a look of your father, that same little smile, the way he put his hands together and stared at them when he was thinking. " Nancy broke off looking up into Giles' eyes and, taking a tissue from the box on the locker beside her, wiped the tears from his cheeks.

"I just hope that we can find Julian" said Giles, "maybe we can still find that we can show our love to him and maybe, hopefully it's not too late for him to love us. One of the things that we never considered was Julian's grief for David. He must have been grieving as much as we were but we never made any allowances for him or his feelings. We were too wrapped up in our own emotions to consider him and his pain. I wonder if he will ever understand and forgive us. What fools we were, or should I say what a fool I was."

"I was just as big a fool as you, " said Nancy, as always; ready to take her share of the blame.

"The next problem is how do we contact him, where is he, and more to the point will he want to see us again? After all these years he may not want to have anything to do with us."

"Oh I'm sure he'll come when he hears that we want to see him, when he hears that I'm in hospital. As to how to find him I think I may have the answer. He wrote a letter to me some time ago. Well not to me exactly, he probably doesn't know our address, it was to my sister in Wells. She sent it on to me."

"You never told me anything about a letter, what did it say, what is he doing, is he still with that fellah?"

"Never mind about all that, you'll see it all in the letter, it's in my bible in the top drawer of my bedside table. There's no address, just somewhere in Africa, see what you can do dear. I know I should have told you about it but I was, for once, reluctant to share it with you. I don't know quite why, I suppose I was a bit unsure as to what your reaction would have been. That's not important, what is important is to find him and get him back into the family again."

"Yes dear, you're absolutely right, as usual; I'll get on to it as soon as I get home, Africa eh?" They hugged again and Giles returned to his chair, aware all of a sudden of other people in the ward. It was not like him to give way to displays of emotion in public, something that would normally cause him great embarrassment. On this occasion he just turned and smiled at the concerned faces looking at him and Nancy.

"I think we've made a bit of an exhibition of ourselves, Darling, but for once I don't care, do you?"

"Not in the least, I'm just so happy that we have both decided to do what we probably should have done years ago."

They talked a lot about Julian and his childhood, those happy days watching him grow up, and all the silly little things that, like all children every where, he got up to. The scrapes he got into, and the time that he had to take a trip to hospital after he had broken his arm, he was only seven then. They laughed as they recalled an incident that occurred when they took him back to have the plaster taken off. They had called in at the local garage for petrol and the nice man there had joked with them and had teased him. He had said that when they cut off his plaster they would use the pieces of meat that got cut off by mistake to make pasties. "Best pasties I ever tasted, proper handsome they be."

Julian was upset and said to his mum "They won't really make me into pasties will they Mum?" with that pitiful look on his little face, his bottom lip pushed out and quivering as he fought back the tears.

Visiting time passed only too quickly, an unusual occurrence for Giles, and when he left, he was in a lighter mood, glad to have a purpose, glad at last to have something to do to help his dear wife.

EIGHTEEN

He had only been home a few minutes, had found the letter and had hardly had a chance to look at it when there was a ring at the door bell. It was Frank.

"Come in, come in, take a seat and tell me what brings you here."

"Well first of all Sir, how's your lady wife?"

"Making progress, it's very slow progress but it is progress."

"Good, I'm glad to hear that, I came over straight away when I heard the news from my Mum."

"Are you home for good now?"

"Yes Sir, I intend to start up a business as a local mechanic looking after the needs of the local people, repairs and servicing and so on. If you remember, we spoke a little about it when I was last at home, but I didn't want to say too much just then. I had to go back and think about it for a while. It was a big step to take, a lot of other things involved, so I had to be sure in my mind that I would be doing the right thing. I didn't want to make the mistake of letting sentiment get in the way of sound reasoning."

"Good for you, I think it's a splendid idea. I'm sure you'll do well and I'll be glad to give you my business. It has just occurred to me that you might be able to help me with another matter."

Giles paused, his elbows resting on the arms of his chair, finger tips touching to form an arch his index fingers resting against his nose as he looked across at the young man. Was he doing the right thing confiding in him? There really wasn't much else that he could do, so he continued

"It's a bit delicate though and may not be something that you can help me with."

"Anything at all, I'd be glad to help if I can."

"I need to find our son, and I think that you may have more of the sort of connections that could be needed than I have. I have a letter here from him; not much of an address but it's somewhere in Angola in Africa. By the time I write to him and maybe get a letter back it'll be Christmas. If it is at all possible, I want a result before Nancy comes home. Do you have any contacts in the Bomb Squad or chaps with that sort of expertise? Because that's what our son, Julian is up to, or so it would seem. He's clearing land mines in darkest Africa."

"I didn't know you had a son Sir, you've kept that dark."

"Yes, it's a long story. He was in the services like me, doing well, and then there was this scandal, him and another chap, had to leave before there was too much fuss. Well I couldn't cope with it; I'm not like you youngsters, I could never understand homosexuals. I thought it was just some sort of sexual perversion. But they are still together, so it was obviously a much deeper and more meaningful relationship than I had at first thought. Yes, in fact we had two sons."

"Two sons! What about the other one?"

"Tragic absolutely tragic. He was a lovely boy was David, athletic, strong, always into mischief, always chasing the girls. In fact it might be more accurate to say that they were always chasing him. Round at the house asking for him, he would be out with one and had forgotten to tell the other that he would be out. We had to make excuses for him and cover up for him. It was a bit of a laugh, though more than a little difficult at times. Then he got killed on a motorbike, terrible…terrible…it almost killed poor Nancy. No chance of any grandchildren then, see, that's what all mothers want. Then I went and cocked it all up by saying the wrong thing to Julian. I think I inferred that the wrong son died, unforgivable of me. So he up and left and I haven't heard any thing of or from him till now. Nancy told me about this letter and how she wants me to find him and make peace."

"I think I can understand what you said at the time and why. We all say things on the spur of the moment which we later regret," and as he spoke he couldn't help but remember arguments that he had had with his father; harsh words that he had almost immediately regretted but had been unable to retract. No doubt his father had felt the same.

"Yes, you're not stupid are you, I was though. Any way, what do you think, d'you know

129

of any body who might be able to help me to trace him? It means a lot to both of us but especially to Nancy, as you can well imagine."

"I think I may know some one, he's not in the mob any more, I'll send him an E-mail, that would be the quickest way. If he doesn't know I'm sure he will know of somebody who does. I imagine that those lads are part of a pretty close bunch; all know one another or at least know of each other. I'll get on to it as soon as I get home. Do you mind letting me have that letter? It will have all the details that I need to give my friend to help him in his search. Don't build your hopes up too much though, it may take a time, and I may not have any luck at all, but I'll certainly give it my best shot."

"Take it dear boy, take it, and if there's anything else that I can give you to help just let me know. Only one thing, be obliged of you would keep all this to yourself, if you understand."

"Of course Sir, I quite understand."

"And don't keep calling me Sir; we are neither of us in the 'mob', as you call it, please call me Giles."

"Right ho, Sir." Frank said with a laugh, "I'll be in touch as soon as I have any news." And with that he got up and left.

Once home he got to work on his laptop sending off an E-mail to his friend. What a sad life Giles and Nancy had had, and he thought that he had problems. It would be a pleasure to do this little something to help them. They were such nice people and had always supported him. And what a start to his life in Civvy Street, if it was all going to be like this it might prove to be more interesting than he thought possible. There was still a lot to do before he could set up in business, equipment to be bought and the new workshop to set up in one of the old barns. He also had the farm to tend to, he would take some advice from Phil on that one, maybe reduce the stock a little. But it would be good to keep on the Red Rubies if he could. His Mum loved them and his Dad had been so proud of them, prize winners all. Many of his farming friends had told him that he would have won supreme champion at the Smithfield Show if he had gone. But Stan had never shown any of his cattle. He always said that he didn't need to go to Devon County or any other show, the butchers who bought his bullocks put them in first place and that was what mattered most to him.

He must catch up with his friends now that he was back home for good. His Mum had told him about the village hall fire and Sir Harold's generous offer. The gossip from his own age group he would get soon enough, Jim would put him in the picture there. He would also warn him of any potential bad customers, those who were hard to please and those who were not too good at paying their bills. Perhaps he ought to meet him for a drink tomorrow, that would be nice, or maybe a meal like last time when he was home. That made him think of Linda again, that was another problem. He just hoped that his Mother's philosophy, that things had a way of sorting themselves out, would prove to be true. She also used to say that things always tended to look better in the morning. He hoped that this would also be true for Giles and Nancy and their problem. He knew only too well that in life it's not always possible to put things right once they had gone badly wrong. But they were such a nice couple and deserved the chance to be reunited with their son and hopefully they would completely accept him. So with those thoughts in mind he went to bed.

The next morning having seen to the livestock he spent several hours in the old barn. He needed to clear out all the old bits and pieces of farming equipment. It seemed as though his Dad had never thrown anything away, old tools, small machines and pieces of machines, and a variety of items made of iron, gate hangings and latches and the like. He moved all of these into the old shippon and after a while as he worked an idea came to him. There seemed to be enough to start a small museum, why not? He would see in time just what there was scattered around the farm, he knew that there were several old machines out beside the hedge in the field behind the new covered yard. If he had the time he might bring these in and clean them; get them working again, and then display them. Hopefully some people would be interested enough to want to look at them, it would be educational for the children to see how farming had been in the 'old days'.

After lunch he spent a lot of time on the computer sourcing the equipment that he would need. Then he looked to see if he had any E-mails, particularly a reply to his query of the night before. Sure enough his friend had replied. Some good news some bad, no one had any knowledge of Julian being in the area mentioned in the the letter, however Frank's friend had sent a circular to several of his acquaintances in that line of business giving Giles' address. With a bit of luck someone would be able to pass the message on to Julian and he would then contact his mother. It seemed like a good job done.

NINETEEN

Nancy had had several visitors, she felt very fortunate, almost privileged and spoiled despite the reason for being her where she was. After all she had just had a new hip fitted at no cost to herself. When she thought of how so many of her friends and acquaintances had to wait for months to get a replacement hip she felt that she was almost guilty of queue-jumping. The rest was probably doing her good, she was inclined to be a busy person, generally up and doing all the time. So it was the boredom, the inactivity that she found the most difficult to cope with. To help the time pass she began to take an interest in those around her, the nurses and her fellow patients.

Opposite her across the ward was an elderly lady who like her had fallen and broken her elbow. She was partially deaf, and like all those who suffered in that way, tended to shout. It was a little embarrassing having to listen to her conversation when she had visitors. It was no doubt a lot more embarrassing for her visiting family members.

In the next bed to her was a young girl called Tracy, who it seemed had been in a fight, probably after a night out 'binge-drinking'. She had a broken ankle with complications, mostly caused by her not getting into the hospital before her ankle had swollen so much that little could be done to it until the swelling went down. There were also several lacerations to her face and she had lost two of her front teeth. She was frightened and alone, none of her so called friends with whom she had been drinking had been in to see her. What family she had, Nancy had not been able to discover, certainly none had visited. Nancy was also of the opinion, quite rightly as it later turned out, that the girl was pregnant.

Grace had been in to see Nancy on several occasions, doing her best to cheer her up. She was not the best person to help one get over the discomfort and boredom of a hospital confinement, but she meant well. One evening, when the young girl in the next bed was asleep, Nancy told Grace of her plight and suggested that she might like to help her. This was partly a selfish move to get Grace to direct her attentions elsewhere, but also to help the poor girl who so obviously needed some help. Grace leapt at the idea and the next day came in with the sole intention of visiting Tracy, finding out more about her situation and working out where and how she could help.

The change in both of them was extraordinary. Grace became more human and understanding, almost motherly, she had a purpose and a goal to aim for. Tracy seemed to perk up and start to improve in both health and temper. Maybe it was the first time that any body had offered to help her without wanting something in return. There was no doubt that the worry of her situation had been taken from her to a great extent In a short space of time Grace had arranged a support network for when Tracy was discharged and a place in a hostel in which she would be able to stay.

Nancy was particularly impressed with Grace's behaviour. This little bird-like woman whom most people in the village saw as, at best a joke and at worst an interfering nuisance, had changed dramatically. How Nancy and others had misjudged her. How easy it was, thought Nancy to make that sort of mistake, to judge others without getting to know them properly and find out all the facts. So like the mistake she and Giles had made in their dealings with Julian.

Tracy had realized that Nancy had been instrumental in Grace helping her and had become very friendly and chatty. Although Nancy was the more mobile of the two, Tracy did all she could to help and her lively humour put many a smile on Nancy's face. It turned out that she had run away from home many years before, leaving an abusing father and a drunken mother to fend for themselves. She had had many low paid jobs but had recently lost her latest which had also provided her and her boy friend with accommodation. He had gone up North looking for a job and knew nothing of her plight. Breaking her ankle had been the last straw.

"Can you not telephone him? Surely all you young people have these mobile phones don't you?"

"No, I lost mine when I broke my ankle, and I don't know his number 'cos it's in my phone.

Silly i'n it? He'll come back eventually and hopefully find out where I am. I would like him to be around when I have the baby."

How the other half lived thought Nancy.

TWENTY

Eric was away for the night with a group of his school children. It was one of the nights that they were to spend out on the moor under canvas in preparation for the Ten Tors Challenge. So Linda was having a girl's night in and her friend Beatie was coming over to join her. In fact, as she was not on duty the next day, she was going to spend the night. That meant that they would be able to enjoy a bottle of wine with their dinner. Linda had cooked a pasta dish with a mushroom, garlic and cream sauce to which at the last minute she was going to add some small pieces of cod. She had prepared a small fresh fruit salad to follow and could just imagine them afterwards, curled up in the armchairs with a cup of coffee having a good natter. They always seemed to have a lot to talk about, even though they met up at least once a week, and tonight Linda knew would be no exception, she had plenty on her mind.

There were a couple of loud knocks on the door, it opened and Beatie called out 'Only me' and came through the passage and into the small kitchen were Linda was. She was carrying a bottle and said "Get the corkscrew out Linda; I'm dying for a glass of this."

"Do you want to eat now or shall we have a drink first?"

138

"Oh, let's have a drink or two and eat later. What have you got for supper? Something smells pretty good."

"You wait and see, though it really is nothing special. Let's go into the front room, it's more comfortable."

So taking the bottle they went into the sitting room and flopped down in the comfy chairs. It was a typical cottage parlour, low ceilinged with two small windows and a large fireplace. The original ingle-nook had been updated and there was now a smart wood burning stove with a neat pile of logs to either side. The floor was polished oak boarding with thick home-made woollen rugs. Prints of Dartmoor hung around the walls, two by Southey on the wall opposite the windows, and taking pride of place over the fire, a view of Yes Tor by F.J.Widgery. On a table against the wall stood a vase of flowers and two wedding photographs, one of Linda and Eric and the other of Jim and Pippa, Beatie's elder sister.

"So, what's new?" said Beatie, "you sounded last night as though you had the worries of the world on your shoulders, is anything wrong?"

"Yes...no...oh I don't know...there's so much and I just don't know what's what anymore. My head's in a right old muddle, I'm probably imagining more than I need to and getting myself worked up all about nothing."

"Tell your Auntie Beatie all about it, you may feel better then. And have another glass of wine, that's sure to help."

"Well its Eric, all this after school stuff that he's doing. I know that he was hit bad when we found out that it was down to him that I couldn't have children. As you know he drank heavily for quite a while, then he got over that and started immersing himself in work at the school. Well I was glad at the time, any thing would be better than him drinking. But now it seems to have taken over his life completely, I don't get to see him enough, and he's wearing himself right out. He's always so tired."

"D'you mean… too tired?"

"Well…yes…I suppose I do" said Linda with a rueful grin "It's almost as though he's given up because he knows it's a waste of time trying, but that doesn't mean that we shouldn't enjoy ourselves and each other. Oh I don't know, perhaps I'm getting paranoid, I'm just beginning to feel a bit rejected and as a result dejected."

"You certainly do sound a bit down, and it's not like you. I expect that when all this Ten Tors malarkey is over it'll all get back to normal again. He'll have more time then, time for you no doubt."

"Maybe…but it's been like this for a long time now, it started way before the Ten Tors stuff. Then there's my other problem."

"What's that then?"

"It's Frank, he's been home for over a week now and every time I see him my heart leaps and I get a guilty feeling knowing that I shouldn't feel this way. I'm almost afraid to be myself in case I give him the wrong impression. I can't say

140

anything to him except normal pleasantries. I've no idea what he feels for me, if anything, so I have to treat him almost as a stranger."

"D'you mean to tell me that you think you're in love with him?"

"I don't know, we were in love years ago, least I thought we were. We would walk and talk for hours, up on the moor above his place, listening to the birds and that. We never mentioned marriage, but the way we talked about the future I thought that we would be together for ever. Oh I know we were only kids, we were seventeen, just, but I knew that he was the man I wanted to marry and spend the rest of my life with. The man I wanted to have children with."

"So what went wrong?"

"I wish I knew. He had always had problems with his father. It's sad how fathers, particularly farmers, expect their sons to want to follow in their footsteps, career wise that is. Frank always wanted to be a mechanic; it was what he loved and what he was good at. I know that that caused a lot of the trouble between them and that that was why he joined the army. But then he just walked out of my life, didn't come home for years, and when he did he made no attempt to get in touch with me."

"Did he write to you?"

"Just one short letter at the beginning, didn't say anything about us, just that he was glad to be starting on the carrier that was right for him."

"The brute, he must have known how you felt, did you ever write to him?"

"No, I was too upset, I thought that I would have to wait until I was feeling less bad about it all, and then when I did feel better there didn't seem to be much point."

"Has he got a girl friend, has he had any girlfriends do you know?"

"I did ask his mother once, just casual like in conversation, 'how's Frank these days, where's he to, got a nice young lady has he?' you know the sort of thing. She told me a bit about him and what he was up to, no girlfriend at that time so it seemed."

"Do you think that these feelings that you've got for Frank are making you a bit cold towards Eric and that that's why he's ignoring you?"

"Could be, I hadn't thought of that. I'm still fond of Eric, still care for him, and I don't want to hurt him. I don't want to complicate matters any more, they are complicated enough as it is. Frank coming back has awakened feelings that I thought were buried long ago. Now I have these feelings and it hurts like hell. I'm almost afraid to admit to myself, let alone to you , that I could be in love with him." She started crying, softly at first, embarrassed at showing her grief in front of her friend, but then with heart rending sobs.

Beatie went over and knelt by her chair taking her hands but feeling a bit out of her depth and helpless. She had never seen her friend as miserable as this and knew that there was little she could say that would be of any real comfort.

"Could you have an affair with Frank, that's if he wanted to have one with you I mean?"

"No, I couldn't do that to Eric, it's not what I want at all, and I know that Frank wouldn't. He's a bit old-fashioned that way. Before, when we were together we never got beyond kissing and cuddling, he was very ….I don't know quite what the word is….prudish? And of course we were quite young."

"God, you certainly know how to pick 'em don't you, one can't and the other one wont."

"Oh don't you believe it, Frank would have alright, it's just that he's too bloody well behaved." They both laughed at this and then started giggling and giggling and couldn't stop. Finally Linda said "Come on, this won't do, let's get that supper and some more wine, we could eat in here if you like, on a tray on our knees. OK?"

"Sounds good to me, I'm starving, this Agony Aunt stuff increases the appetite you know. It's just that I wish that there was something that I could do to help or advise in some way. Still, I'm sure that it will sort itself out, these things generally do."

After their supper they got back on to the subject of Frank again, in fact they had hardly been off it all evening.

"The only thing to do, as I see it" said Beatie "is for me to tell him that you're mad about him and see what he says."

"Oh no, you mustn't do that, that could upset everything, maybe even drive him back into the Army. I told you he won't do anything as long as I'm married to Eric."

"Well, whatever you decide to do, I'm here to help you and support you. I'm your friend and I'll gladly do whatever I can."

And with that tears welled up in her eyes and they both fell into each others arms at first crying, then laughing at themselves.

TWENTY ONE

The six boys in the mini-bus were chattering away excitedly, this was to be their first night out under canvas without the supervision of a teacher or guide. When he reached the lower slopes of Kes Tor Eric pulled the bus off the road and stopped.

"Right lads, every body out, this is where the fun begins."

The boys piled out of the bus and then pulled out their huge rucksacks with all their gear, tents, bedrolls and cooking equipment When they had sorted themselves out and were standing quietly Eric gave them their final instructions. "Now, you set off from here over this tor and then on past the standing stone to the corner of the forestry plantation. Your over-night camp will be as arranged at Teighnhead Farm. It's a ruin, as you all know, but it will be a bit more sheltered there than on the open moor. It's only three miles so you should be there in about an hour. Put up your tents first and then get a bite to eat. Don't have a large meal tonight, you may have trouble sleeping if you eat too much, tomorrow morning is when you need to eat well. Then you set off on the route that you have planned, taking in Cut Hill and Fur Tor, and then Hare Tor, Sharp Tor and Doe Tor. I will probably meet you on Brat Tor or Arms Tor. The mini-bus will be at the Fox and Hounds car park.

You have a mobile so you can reach me if you are in desperate difficulty. Remember on the day you will only be allowed to use a phone in a case of dire emergency. Take your time, there's no rush, and work as a team. Are there any questions?"

"Yes Sir. Where will you be sleeping?"

"Oh I shall probably be in the bus, either here or at the Fox and Hounds."

"Oh yes, we all know they do bed and breakfast there, it's alright for some."

"Yes, but remember, I'm not doing the Ten Tors Challenge, you are. Right then, off you go and good luck."

The boys set off up the hill, their heavy burdens not bothering them in their excitement. They chattered and teased each other as boys do as they went along the path up the hill. The weather was fine so they shouldn't have any difficulty that night, and would be fed and bedded down before it was too dark. Eric stood watching them for a while, walking two abreast, laughing and joking as they made their way up to the rocks on the top of the tor. The gradient there was none too steep and they were making good progress. The path they were on was wide and the whole area was close cropped by sheep. They would not find the going that easy tomorrow, still he was fully confident in their ability, he had been training them for weeks now and it had been good to watch them grow in knowledge and understanding of the moor. Sudden changes to the weather were commonplace, it had often been said that on Dartmoor you could experience four seasons in one day. They were all well equipped and as long as they stuck to the rules, and the plans that they had worked out together, nothing should go wrong.

He turned to go back to the mini-bus and saw below him another bus parking. Seven figures got out, collected their gear and stood in a circle round a blond woman dressed in walking clothes. She was giving them their instructions for the night just as he had done a short while before. They were from the girls' grammar school near Bovey and they too were on their first night out. They set off just as he arrived and the two teachers watched them on their way.

"That was good timing Sheila." Said Eric "Where are your lot going to sleep tonight? Mine should be at Teignhead Farm."

"They are going to camp at the settlement on Kennon Hill tonight. Then tomorrow they have to do Hound Tor, Wild Tor, Steeperton Tor and Oke Tor. I'm meeting them in the car park at Belstone."

"Sounds good, so now what?"

"Let's go straight back to my place."

The two mini-buses turned and went back down the lanes, twisting and turning, the drivers hoping that they wouldn't meet any traffic. The new lush spring growth of grasses and wild flowers made the lane seem almost too narrow for their vehicles. It wasn't long before they turned up a rough track that led to an old farm-stead. It was a small farm house with a slate roofed granite porch and a range of traditional buildings surrounding the cobbled yard. Grass was growing out through

147

the stones showing that there had been little or no traffic, either human or animal across the yard, but in no way did it have an air of desolation. It might not be an active farm but the curtains in the windows and the general tidiness showed that it was inhabited. They parked the buses, went in the back door, and almost before it had closed she grabbed him in a tight embrace and kissed him passionately. They stayed locked like that for several moments, then she pulled away and, still holding his hand led him towards the stairs.

"Come on, I've waited long enough for this, we can eat later." An hour later, as they were eating their supper Sheila said, "I can't go on like this for much longer, it's tearing us both apart, we have got to get together properly. I can't stay a mistress for ever; I want to be with you all the time."

"Yes, and I want the same. The trouble is that it's not easy to judge when the timing will be right to drop that sort of a bombshell on Linda. I've got to be fair to her if I can, although I know that what we are doing is by no means fair to her. I suppose no time will be a good time, the hurt to her will be no less whenever I tell her. It's just that if it is at all possible I would like to minimise the hurt to her."

"You haven't got any doubts have you?"

"No, none at all, the sooner I can move in with you the better I shall be pleased. I don't feel that I'm the right man for her, maybe I never was, I don't know. I just feel that I've let her down in a big way and that she would be better off without me. Besides, I don't love her like I used to, and I think she feels the same way about me. In fact I would say that our marriage is dead. We are still friends, but that's all. Perhaps if we split up we will still be friends, maybe even better friends than we are now, who knows?"

"Well you know that I'm here for you whenever you can get away, and hopefully that will be sooner rather than later. I don't need to tell you how I feel, you know that well enough by now. But I mustn't influence you in any way. If you leave her it must be because you want to, not just because I want you to. I appreciate it's a hell of a decision to make, but … I do love you so."

TWENTY TWO

Giles was driving home across the moor, it had been a good visit, Nancy had been in high spirits because they had told her that she would be going home at the end of the week. She had been walking up and down the ward and had also spent a short while on the staircase, where she had managed to go up and down six stairs without too much trouble. It was wonderful to see her so happy with an almost perpetual smile on her face; that quirky little smile that he loved so much. The physiotherapist was very pleased with the progress that she had made and had given her a list of the exercises that she would be advised to do when she got home. Coincidentally, Linda had been in to visit her that morning and had also had a long chat with the physiotherapist. If any therapy should be needed after Nancy came home Linda would be able to come in and treat her in the comfort of her own house. It was all beginning to look so much better as though the worst were at last over.

The setting sun was behind him casting long shadows and giving the moor a copper hue. Many of the moorland ponies had foaled and these were skipping about playfully. One of them in particular caught his eye, a black foal that was unusually marked; it had a pair of white socks on its hind legs and a white bushy tail. Giles felt sure that somebody would want to keep that one for a pet or a riding pony. The foals unfortunately were not yet as way-wise as their mothers, didn't understand the dangers posed by cars, and could step out into the road at any time. It was even more difficult for the drivers of those cars coming towards Giles who had the sun in their eyes. However, he got home safely to find a car parked in his drive. Its door opened and a stocky man got out. He was well tanned with light brown sun-bleached hair, greying at the temples, and a ready smile. He walked over to Giles with an easy stride and holding out his hand said "Am I right in thinking that you are Giles Cameron-Hyde?"

"Yes, that's me, what can I do for you?"

"I'm Ray, I'm Julian's partner, you have been trying to contact him. I understand that your wife is unwell and in hospital, nothing serious I hope. May I ask how she is?"

"She is a lot better thank you; she will be coming home at the end of the week." Giles found himself almost accepting this young man; he was not at all as he had imagined he would be, yet he felt he should be cautious, it was still early days.

"Oh I am glad to hear that, Julian and I were worried, we didn't know what to expect as the only message that we got was so brief, just a general note on E-mail with virtually no details. What was the problem, the reason for her being in hospital?"

"She broke her hip while she was out walking, had to climb over a fallen tree and fell awkwardly. She couldn't get home, in fact she couldn't move very far if at all. She was out all night and half the morning until she was found. Nasty business, it was almost touch and go. In fact if one of the neighbours hadn't found her dog in the river, nobody would have known that she was missing. I dread to think what would have been the outcome then. But come inside and I can tell you more in the comfort of an armchair, and you can tell me all your news."

Giles was half afraid to ask why Julian wasn't there; he wondered if this Ray fellow had been sent down to see what sort of reception they might receive. Maybe Julian didn't want to visit them at all; he could hardly blame the boy if that was the case after the way they had parted all those years ago. They went inside and Giles showed Ray into the sitting room.

"Have you eaten?"

"Yes thank you."

"Can I get you something to drink?"

"What I would really like, if it's not too much trouble, is a cup of tea."

"Certainly, you make yourself at home whilst I go and make it."

It was a lovely warm comfortable room with deeply upholstered armchairs and settee. A row of book cases lined one wall and there were french windows looking out over a lawned garden with large windows to either side making the room bright and inviting. In one corner stood an old mahogany knee-hole writing desk on which there were two framed photographs. One was of Giles and Nancy on their wedding day, with Giles in his Best Blue uniform, his pilot's wings proudly affixed above the top pocket. The other was of a young man whom Ray recognised, from pictures Julian had shown him, as his brother David. He couldn't help but notice that there were no photos any where of Julian.

Meanwhile in the kitchen Giles was feeling more than somewhat uneasy. Ray seemed to be a pleasant enough young man, a warm smile; an open face; a firm handshake; the easy manner of someone who is comfortable in his own skin. It was not difficult to feel friendly towards him, easy to be civil and even welcoming. Both he and Nancy had realised their mistakes of the past and desperately wanted to see their son again; wanted to make amends and become a family again, if at all possible. Yet Giles still felt his homophobic tendencies nagging at the back of his mind. Could he watch his son with this man, sitting together in his house, laughing and joking together, sleeping together? It was going to be very difficult, for all of them, and he would definitely need Nancy's help to deal with it. Maybe she would need his help and support as well. Then maybe he was looking for trouble where none existed, perhaps he should just let it run, go with the flow and let it all sort itself out. Nothing ventured nothing gained, so with a smile on his face Giles entered the sitting room with a tray of tea things which he put on one of the small tables that were around the room saying "Please, help yourself."

"Thank you. You were telling me about your wife."

"Yes, well there was some complication because she had been out in the cold for so long. From what I can understand they didn't want to put her on antibiotics if they could help it, because they not only kill the bad bacteria but also the good ones. That could lower her resistance to other things like C-diff and those sorts of dreadful hospital bugs that we hear so much of these days. So the healing process has taken a lot longer than it might otherwise have done, but she is up and about now and doing well. Now tell me all about Julian and what you have been up to in darkest Africa."

"Well it's quite a long story; I hope you'll bear with me. We belong to a group of volunteers who have for some years now been working at clearing anti-personnel mines that seem to litter the ground in those parts of Africa where there has been civil war. We were working near a small village and had almost finished. In fact there was just one small area left to be cleared that was just outside the village. It was really a wide grassy path leading from their fields towards the jungle. The villagers had returned, it was very important to them to do so because their village was not only their home, their collection of huts where they lived. It was also where they grew their crops and all their food. We had spoken to the head man and through him all the villagers had been made aware of the safe and unsafe areas.

On this particular morning it was rather windy. A small child was playing with a sort of balloon or football made of an animal's bladder that had been inflated. This came blowing across the ground with the child running after it. We didn't see any of this until the child passed us with the balloon in front of him. Julian leapt to his feet and just managed to grab the child and turn around when a mine went off, presumably triggered by the bounce of the balloon. Fortunately it was a few feet away otherwise it could have been much worse. The child was unharmed but Julian was injured in the legs, some shrapnel hit him in the right thigh, and both his legs were very badly burned, the right one more than the left. I did the best I could for him, but my nursing training was not specialized enough to deal with burn traumas of that magnitude. You may remember that I was a nurse in sick-quarters and that was where Julian and I first met. It was obvious that he needed hospital treatment and the sooner the better. Lines of communication out there were almost non-existent and I was very worried as to how we could get him out and to a decent hospital of some kind.

The villagers were wonderful, they realised that he had saved their child without any thought for his own safety, and carried him for miles through the bush on a stretcher. Eventually, to cut a long story short, we got him back to the UK and into hospital in Stoke Mandeville. They have done a wonderful job, though it has taken a very long time, and he, like your wife, has made a good recovery and could be out in a week or two. There will though, be quite a long period of convalescence, but the doctors say that he should make a full recovery. At the moment he is using a wheel-chair quite a lot, particularly when tired, but he has been walking with just a stick yesterday and today, which has cheered us both no end."

Giles sat silently, not sure of what to say, because by comparison Nancy's injuries paled into insignificance. He felt guilty because he should have known all this before. Because of his silly prejudices he had not been where he should have been, where he could have helped his son in a time of need. All he could do was to shake his head and say over and over "I never knew and I should have known." Then after a brief pause he added "I drove him away so it was my fault. As a result I've missed so much of his life, I knew the boy but I never knew the man that he has become"

Both men sat silent for a while, both deep in thought. Giles was struggling to keep his emotions in check, thinking of his son injured and in hospital. What did he look like now, was his hair grey yet, would his injuries leave him limping or disabled in some way? And what were the two of them going to do now, both immediately and in the future? If they came to stay with him and Nancy what would people around make of it all? So many questions, and yet he was feeling elated, almost excited at the prospect of seeing Julian again. But would Julian want to see him?

Ray, meanwhile, was feeling quite at home with this kindly old man. Although Julian had never spoken ill of his father, he had felt a certain trepidation as he got out of his car to meet Giles for the first time. He was accustomed to people's prejudices and occasional antagonism and had expected the worst. It seemed that his fears were

156

groundless. After several minutes silence Giles seemed to perk up and said, "What are you going to do now, are you stopping overnight? You would be more than welcome to stay here; I'll put the electric blanket on and air the bed in the spare room. I'd be very glad of your company if you would, and perhaps you could tell me more about your lives together and all the things you got up to in Africa. "

"Thank you, that would be most kind of you, I'll go and get my bag out of the car." Said Ray, more than a little surprised at the warmth of the older man's welcome. " I wasn't sure if I would be driving back tonight or not, but it would be a lot better to stay over and travel in the morning after a good night's sleep."

So Ray got his bag and after Giles had shown him his room the two of them sat down again and talked until it was time for bed. The conversation was relaxed and easy and Giles found himself beginning to like this young man who had, he realised, spent much more time with his son than he had and probably knew him better than he ever would. There was so much he needed to know, so much time had passed, wasted time that was lost. He and Nancy would have a lot of catching up to do; hopefully they would get the chance now. However he still felt more than a little uneasy at the thought of the relationship of his son and this young man. Would he ever he able to fully accept them as he doubtless would have done if Ray had been a girl? And if he couldn't accept them, was it necessarily his fault, did any of the blame attach to them? No, that probably was unfair, but there were so many questions and no easy answers. Still he would have to try, have to do his best for Nancy's sake, if not for Julian and Ray.

TWENTY THREE

The next morning they had breakfast, the full English. Giles quite enjoyed being the host and cook, and then Ray left with a recent photograph of Giles and Nancy. He regretted that he didn't have one of Julian to leave in exchange, but he said that he was sure that Julian would be writing soon and would enclose some pictures.

"I would like it if you would both consider coming down here for Julian to spend his convalescence. I know that I shall have to square it with Nancy but I can't see her saying no. There's plenty of room as you have seen and you would be no trouble at all."

"Thank you, I'll be in touch, it's a very kind offer and could be very useful too. I'll let you know as soon as we know when Julian will be discharged."

So with that Ray drove down the drive and out of the village, and Giles walked over to the Post Office to get his daily paper. He met Frank in the shop and quietly asked if he had time to come back to the house with him. "I've got some good news to tell you. I'm dying to share it and you are one of the few people with whom I can" he said. Once back at the house he told Frank all about Ray, his visit and all that had happened to Julian.

"First of all I must thank you for helping to find Julian for me, I couldn't have done it myself and I know that Nancy will be just as delighted and grateful as I am. I've been such a fool, such a silly bloody fool. I drove my son away because I didn't understand. I wouldn't let myself accept that those two men could love each other, care for each other and stay together as they have and for as long as they have. How many normal, what do you call it, straight marriages last that long these days. It seems that weddings are all just for show, a big party and a posh frock. The more that is spent on the wedding the shorter the marriage seems to last. However, that's bye the bye, just me on my hobbyhorse. Now, I know I shall have to check with Nancy, but I've asked them to come down and stay for a while. What do you think, good idea, will the villagers accept them?"

"Of course they will, and if there are any that don't they aren't worth worrying about. People should be allowed to make up their own minds about who they choose to be their partners. There's enough unhappiness in the world without putting barriers up between those who love each other."

"It's good to hear you say so; I shall tell Nancy all about this later. D'you know, I'm really looking forward to visiting time today. Did I tell you that as long as there are no set backs she'll be coming home at the end of the week?"

"I'm ever so glad to hear that, give her my best; we all look forward to seeing her soon. Incidentally, do you think that she would like another dog? I know how fond she was of Haig, maybe it's a bit soon to be thinking of a

160

replacement. You see, I know where there is a litter of Jack Russel puppies, only a week old at the moment. If you think that you both would like one, let me know, I can get one for you. It's a good strain of good working dogs."

"That sounds a nice idea, but I'll have to see just how she gets on with her new hip. A puppy might be a bit much."

"It wouldn't be for six or eight weeks yet, so there's plenty of time for you to make up your minds."

"Right ho, I'll mention it to her; it's good of you to think of it. By the way, how is the new business venture going, are you up and running yet?"

"Yes, and so far it seems to be good. The farm keeps me busy for a good bit of the time, but I would far rather have plenty to do. In fact, I'd better be off now."

With that Frank left and Giles went into the kitchen to clear up the breakfast dishes before Rose came. For the first time in weeks he was feeling really happy, as though a cloud had been lifted, and he was humming happily to himself as he worked. Then he went around the house looking in all the rooms to see just what was where and how much space there was for Julian and Ray, if they chose to come and stay for a while. There was a whole side of the house that was hardly ever used; it could almost be converted into a separate flat if necessary. There was even a room that had a sink in it. Without too much work it could be made

161

into a decent kitchen, the water and drains were all there.

When Rose came a little later he was hard pressed not to tell her the news, but he felt that it was too soon and in any case Julian and Ray might not come. Just because it was what he wanted, to assuage his guilt probably, didn't mean that it was going to happen. Better perhaps to say nothing, it might all fall through and then he would feel that he had put a jinx on it. As well as doing the washing up he had also tidied up the spare room in an attempt to conceal the fact of Ray's visit, though it was more than likely that she already knew. There are few secrets in a village, especially from the likes of Rose.

The day seemed to drag by. He read the paper and then walked around the garden thinking of Nancy and Julian. He was amazed that his stupid stubbornness had kept them all apart for so long. Now he realised how wrong he had been and how he had probably subconsciously always wanted reconciliation. His warming of heart had been so effortless, so natural, it had almost happened without him noticing. How ironic that it should take an accident, a near fatal accident at that, to get him to see sense. However, self recrimination wasn't going to help, any more than self pity would. The past was exactly that, and it was to the future that he must look. Just like young Frank, he must start a new chapter in his life. He must think himself fortunate that he still had a few years left. How awful it would have been had he gone to his grave without making amends. It didn't bear thinking of.

At last the time had come for lunch and then he was off to the hospital for what he was sure would be a really happy visit. Nancy was in the day-room when he arrived. He was glad of this because he always felt a little uneasy talking in front of the other patients on the ward. Before he had a chance to tell her of his news he noticed that Grace, the vicar's wife was sitting next to her.

She was busy talking nineteen to the dozen, her little bird-like face pushed as close to Nancy's as the two wooden-armed chairs would allow. News of all the happenings in the village poured out, without any embellishment as Sal or Edna would have done. Most of this news Nancy had already heard but she didn't have the heart to stop Grace, who went on and on, getting more and more animated. Giles was wishing that she would stop, in fact he could have wished her far away. He wanted to tell Nancy the good news about Ray's visit and all the news about Julian, but as long as Grace was there wittering away he just had to wait patiently and quietly. At last she seemed to have suddenly become aware of his presence, because she jumped up saying, "Oh, yes … well I must be on my way…. Good to see you again Giles, I'm sure that you must have lots to say to your wife .. Yes...um …well , goodbye then and God bless." With that she scuttled out of the room.

"Don't look like that Dear, that woman has surprised me of late with all the good she's been doing for the girl in the next bed to me."

163

Giles greatly relieved at her departure was about to launch into a long tale of the events of the previous evening. Before he had a chance to say anything Nancy said "You will have to bring me in some more clothes tomorrow, I've made a list for you; if you can't find any thing I'm sure that Rose will be able to find them for you. Try and get in here by eleven o'clock."

"Yes dear, but why, what's going on?"

"The doctor says that I can go home tomorrow."

"Oh darling, that's wonderful, I am so glad for you. It has been far too long."

"Go on, you've been having a great time without me to keep you in order, down the pub every night I wouldn't wonder."

"Well, I wasn't down the pub last night; I had a visitor, an unexpected and most welcome visitor."

"Really, and who was that then, or should I say who was she?"

"You may joke, my dear, just wait till I tell you."

So Giles proceeded to tell her all about Ray's visit and Julian's accident. Nancy kept butting in with questions, most of which he couldn't answer, because he didn't know. He just had to tell her to be patient and wait for the boys to come down and then she would get all her questions answered. As he had expected, she was as delighted at the thought of them staying at the Old Rectory. She was already making plans as to which rooms they would have and what would have to be done to them to make them nice.

"Steady on dear, they haven't said yes yet."

"Oh but they will, I know they will."

"Well, I hope you are right, I really do. Now there are one or two other things to tell you. First off, Haig, I didn't tell you before I know, and I probably should have done. I buried him under that crimson rhododendron that you like so much, it's just started to flower and you will be reminded of the little fella each year when it comes in to bloom. I hope that I did the right thing there."

"Yes, that's lovely," tears welling up again. So many emotions all on top of one another; Haig's death and the reminder of David's death; the possibility of Julian's return, it was becoming all too much for her.

"Oh Darling, don't cry, thank God that at last we can talk about these things and share our feelings" said Giles as he knelt beside her chair, holding her hands and resting his head in her lap."

"I saw Frank this morning and amongst other things he asked me if you would be likely to want another dog. I wasn't sure, didn't know if it would be too soon. Anyway, he knows of a litter of pups, one week old at the moment. Jack Russels. He said they were a good sort, good working dogs, I said that I would ask you and he said that there was no rush. Very good of him to think of you, then he's a good sort is young Frank."

"Yes dear, yes I would like another dog and Frank's offer of a little Jack Russel sounds just the thing. But I've got too much to think about at

165

the moment to consider another dog just yet. Besides how would I be able to exercise and train a puppy? Maybe later, let's take one step at a time. Lets get me right first, I'll still need physiotherapy and it will be quite a while before I'm fully mobile again."

"Of course Darling, I hadn't thought it through properly, I was just thinking of how much you must be missing Haig. As you say maybe later eh? I'll tell Frank as soon as I see him. One other thing he said that interested me. When we were talking about Julian and Ray and the possibility of them staying with us, I asked him if he thought that they would be accepted in the village. He felt sure that they would, and he also said 'There's enough unhappiness in the world without putting barriers up between those who love each other'. A wise remark which made me wonder if he was alluding to himself and Linda. I think he still feels a lot for her."

"You old softie, Giles, you've been reading too many Mills and Boon while I've been stuck in here, it's making you into an old romantic."

"Not so much of your old, but I won't deny the romantic part. In fact when you finally get home I'll be able to show you just how romantic I can be, old or not."

"Promises promises," said Nancy with a little throaty laugh, and then they both collapsed into a fit of giggles. The relief that the tension of the past weeks was nearly over had suddenly hit them, and they giggled and laughed uncontrollably for several minutes like a pair of teenagers. Finally they regained control of themselves and Nancy wrote another list of things for Giles to do before he came in to collect her next day. She was well aware that it would probably be Rose who did the jobs although she didn't say so. She didn't want to hurt Giles; he had been doing a wonderful job, helping her by visiting every day. She knew how difficult that had been for him to do; knew just how much he hated hospitals. Like many people of his generation he was afraid of hospitals; convinced that you only went into a hospital to die, and although that might not have been the intention it was only too often the usual result. This wonderful strong man, whom she loved with a passion, had his weaknesses. One of his greatest strengths, however, was that he was not afraid to admit to either his mistakes or his fears. Thank God she would soon be at home with him again. She hadn't ever realised just how much she relied on his ever present company even when he wasn't actually with her. It was as though together they were almost one person; whereas apart she felt that she was less than half of one person. It would be good to be whole again.

TWENTY FOUR

It was a quarter past nine and Frank had just come in for his breakfast. He had been up for some time, out in the fields enjoying the fresh early morning air. His new routine was to see to the farm and the livestock before breakfast and then get on with his business as a mechanic. The kitchen was full of the warm smells of fried bacon and eggs. Blanche wouldn't consider anything else to be a suitable meal for a working man to start the day. Frank knew that he would have to watch it a bit, he wasn't taking the sort of exercise that he had when he was in the Army. Blanche was used to feeding Stan who had worked physically very hard all his life and out in the fresh air. He didn't want to seem ungrateful, he realized that his mother was doing all she did out of love for him, but he had seen too many people run to fat when their food intake was too much for their exercise level.

"I've just been on the phone talking to your cousin Cathy, you remember her, from Shepton Mallet. Well, she's just finished her training to be a vet and has applied for a post near here. She would be starting in two weeks time and I said that she ought to come and stay with us for a while.'Twould give her a chance to look around and find out about the area a bit. You could introduce her to some of the folks around here couldn't you?"

"Yes, of course, that would be no trouble I'm sure. I must admit I don't really remember her, its ages since I met any of the family from that part of the world. I seem to remember that they came down here for a holiday, more than once I believe. Was she the red haired one with the freckles or the little fat one with dark hair and buck teeth?"

"She is the red haired one, Ivy is the younger one and she's not fat and she hasn't got buck teeth either. She had to wear a brace for two years, you might be surprised, she's quite a stunning looking girl now, in fact they both are. Any road, I've asked Cathy to come down and stay with us and she's coming on the train tomorrow. I was hoping that you would pick her up from the station, her train gets in at five past two."

"You've got it all worked out then Mum, as usual. I guess there'll be a list of things for me to get in the supermarket before I meet the train," said Frank with a laugh. He knew only too well his mother's ways, once she had an idea in her head the organizing and planning took over. Anything to do with family was her delight and source of great pleasure. It would be a time of cooking and baking, of new recipes and special meals. For Frank, who enjoyed his food and particularly his mother's cooking, it was definitely going to be a pleasurable time. But again he would have to be careful; his jeans were beginning to feel a little tight around the waist.

"You may laugh, she'll be good company for both of us, it's nice to have youngsters about the place. I for one will be glad to have a female companion for a change. I might get the chance to watch something half decent on telly. All you men seem to watch is that darned old football; I don't see anything in it myself."

"Cathy may be a football fan Mum; lots of girls are these days. She may not be into soaps like you."

"Well whatever, 'twill be good to have her here for a few days; company for the both of us. I'll want you to help me turn the mattress in the blue bedroom then I can give it a good airing and fix the room up nice before she gets here, OK? That'll just leave the big double for me to let when the season starts."

"Yeah, I'll be glad to Mum, just give us a shout when you're ready."

"We'll do it as soon as you've had your breakfast and before you go back out to your workshop."

Blanche had already been thinking that if Cathy were going to stay with them for any length of time, which she could well have to, she might not have to bother with the holiday trade at all. It would certainly make life a lot easier for her; she was beginning to feel a lot more tired these days, glad of a little nap after lunch. When she went out in the fields to look at the cattle she liked to sit for a while and just watch them and think. And going upstairs, to make the beds and do the rooms, was more of an effort than it ever used to be. Old age never comes alone, she used to say, and though she didn't like to admit that she was feeling old, she knew in her heart that it was creeping up on her.

"I've got to pick up Linda's car today, she says it's due for a service, so that's my first job. If there are any parts required I can pick them up tomorrow when I'm in town meeting Cathy, it'll save me a journey wont it?"

"If you are going to Linda's you'll be passing through the village. Could you call in at the Old Rectory? I've made a cake for Nancy. Now that she's back home she'll probably be getting a load of visitors and well wishers calling in to see her. She will be glad of something to give them with a dish of tea."

As usual Blanche was thinking that all visitors required the welcome that she would give, no matter in whose house they were.

"No problem, I'll be glad to, I always enjoy seeing Giles and Nancy. Maybe they will have more news of Julian. He could be coming down to stay soon. I reckon he'd be a very interesting bloke to meet, he's led a full and varied life by all accounts."

So it was that an hour later Frank was driving down the road from the farm and towards the village. It was a glorious early-summer morning and already he could feel the heat from the sun. The may blossom was over but the honeysuckle was out in places along the hedgerows, filling the air with its scent. In the village the green was carpeted with the petals from the chestnut tree. There was a van outside the old

171

school, no doubt somebody busy working on the conversion and decoration needed to their new village hall. As to the old village hall itself a lorry and a small digger were doing a grand job of clearing the site. Frank wondered how long it would be before Sir Harold would be able to start building. He hadn't seen anything in the papers about planning permission.

He drove into the Old Rectory and was pleased to see Giles and Nancy in the garden enjoying the sunshine. Nancy was sitting in a large padded garden chair while Giles was standing beside her taking instructions as to what to do in the nearby flower bed. It was a lovely warm domestic scene made all the more lovely by the huge smile on Giles' face. He was obviously delighted to have Nancy's somewhat unusual participation in the work in the garden. It was an area normally left to him to deal with, sometimes with help from Rose. Frank walked over to them, the cake in a biscuit tin held out before him.

"Morning, lovely morning. It's good to see you back home and out and about, how are you?"

"I'm fine" said Nancy "though I would hardly call sitting in the garden out and about. Still it's a first step and I'm making good progress, or so the medical people tell me. I walk with a stick and am getting better each day."

"That's great, Mum sent me over with this cake, one of her specials, and her good wishes as well of course."

"Oh how nice of her, that is kind."

"Do you have any news of Julian? Is he likely to be coming down to stay?"

"Yes" said Nancy, a huge grin spreading across her face "And as we have offered to help him through his convalescence, the hospital are going to discharge him late next week. So he could be here the weekend after next. We haven't been able to do much indoors though, because we don't know exactly what will be needed. In fact we may not have to change anything."

"Nancy and I are getting quite excited, we're like a couple of kids waiting for Christmas" said Giles.

"Great news, I am pleased for you both" said Frank, delighted to see his friends so obviously happy after all their ordeals. "It'll be wonderful for you both to be reunited with Julian; I also am looking forward to meeting him and Ray. From all you have told me they must be a very interesting couple with a lot of fascinating tales to tell. I'd best be off now, I'd like to stay longer but I've got to pick up Linda's car, it's due for a service and she's asked me to do it. By the way, I'm going into town tomorrow to meet my cousin Cathy at the station. She's coming to stay for a few weeks, in fact she's got a position with McGill and Smith, I believe they were the vets that you used for Haig. What I was going to say was, is there any thing that I can get for you while I'm in town?"

"I don't think so thank you. Is your cousin, Cathy did you say, going to be staying with you?" asked Nancy "It'll be nice for your mum to have her company."

173

"Yes for a while certainly, but I'm sure that she will need to find her own accommodation soon. Mind you, I get the feeling that Mum would quite like her to stay for a good while, then she might give up the B&B business and that could only be a good thing in my opinion. Meanwhile Mum thought that it would be a good way for me to introduce her to a few of the local people and for her to get to know a bit about the area."

"You must bring her to see us, perhaps for drinks one evening. I don't think that I could manage a meal just yet. Now, I mustn't keep you any longer; you must get off to Linda's. Do thank your Mum for the cake, its wonderful the way everybody in the village has been so kind to me, both when I was in hospital and now since I've come home."

TWENTY FIVE

Linda was in the kitchen, looking through her cookery books trying to find a recipe for a dessert to be used in a dinner party that she was planning. She was going to ask Jim and Pippa because she knew that Eric enjoyed their company. She was having difficulty concentrating because her thoughts kept turning to Frank. She would love to ask him, but did she dare? Perhaps she could ask Beatie as well, that would make a good mix of six. But after all the confiding in her might, that be too risky, would she let the cat out of the bag? No, it was far more likely that she herself would let her feelings be known, by her body language if nothing else. She looked up and saw through the window Frank's car coming in through the gate. Her stomach churned, her heart beat faster, and then she thought 'this is silly, I'm behaving like a soppy schoolgirl. Pull yourself together Gal.' so she went and opened the door to be met by Frank's warm smile.

"OK to take the car Linda? I'll leave you mine in case you need to go anywhere. I should have it finished by this evening; if there are any problems I'll ring you."

"You'll be needing these then" she said, handing him the keys, and as their hands touched she felt her heart racing and a flutter in her stomach. "Thanks a lot, I'll see you later" she said, turning swiftly indoors in an attempt to hide her emotions and the blood rushing to her face. Back indoors she kicked herself for not asking Frank in for a cup of tea or coffee. He must have thought her very rude but how could she have hidden her feelings, as strong as they were at that moment? Now she realized how difficult it would have been if she had asked him to join them for dinner.

She turned to the stove and made herself a cup of coffee, time to sit and think a bit. Her thoughts were all over the place since Frank had come home again, it was time to try and sort them out. She was still fond of Eric, still cared for him, but did she really love him any more? Come to think of it had she ever really loved him? Had she ever loved him in the way that she had loved Frank, and felt that she still loved Frank? Eric was a good man, kind and thoughtful. He didn't drink any more, or if he did it was to have not more than one drink. That had been a problem for a time, but it was understandable, it must have been a huge blow to his male ego to find out that he was incapable of being a father. He must have felt very inadequate. She thought that she had reassured him on that point, she had told him enough times that she wasn't worried about not having children. Now they seemed to be growing further and further apart. He seemed to be staying at school late every night, almost as though he preferred work to home.

Did he still love her? She really didn't know, she had just assumed that he did, but they certainly didn't have much contact of any kind

176

these days. She had tried talking to him, asking him if anything was wrong, anything troubling him, but he would just say no, he was fine and then walk out of the room.

She found herself thinking of Frank as she so often did these days. What she felt for him was of little consequence, what mattered was what Frank felt for her. She had absolutely no idea; he had given her no signals or any hints as to his feelings. More than likely he looked upon her as a good friend and that was all. In fact he probably had a girlfriend from his army days, tucked away somewhere. It seemed like Beatie was right when she jokingly had said 'one can't and the other won't'. Trouble was, it left her in the middle with nothing. If only she knew how Frank felt, but she definitely couldn't ask him. And she unfortunately wasn't the sort who could flirt with him to see what reaction she would get. However, when he came back with her car she would ask him in, give him a cup of tea and pay his bill. Then just maybe she would get the strength from somewhere to talk about old times, times when they were kids and boy friend and girl friend. The good times they had had together, the dreams they had had for their futures and the plans they had made. Plans that were really no more than hopes, nothing written in stone, but none the less the serious aspirations that most teenagers have at that stage in their lives. She would have to be careful though; it wouldn't do to sound too pushy or desperate. Hopefully memories of those happy times just might get him to say something that would tell her how he was feeling.

It would be worth a try, so long as she had the nerve to do it.

But then if she knew what Frank was feeling, that's if he had feelings for her, would that not make matters worse? It could just lead to more problems, and supposing he ran out on her again, went back in the Army or something. Why did life have to be so difficult?

Two hours later the phone rang, it was Frank and immediately her heart was in her mouth at the sound of his voice.

"I'm afraid your car won't be ready today" he said "There are some parts I need to get for it, but I'm going into town tomorrow and I'll get them then. So I should have it finished and back with you in a couple of days, will that be alright?"

"Yes that's fine, thank you, is it anything big that's wrong?"

"No, no, it's just brake pads and a washer or two, nothing serious."

"Oh good. By the way, how are you going to get into town, you left your car here for me to drive?"

"I know, that's alright, I'll take Mum's car."

"I'll see you in a day or two when it's ready then. Bye" And with that she hung up, her heart still pounding.

TWENTY SIX

It was Tuesday and Jim was in Hatherleigh market. He was there to meet a potential customer and he had always found that farmers were most at their ease when they had just done some successful business. The farmer that Jim wanted to see had brought a bunch of steers to be sold. If the sale went well there was a good chance that Jim might be able to persuade him to become one of his customers.

The cattle ring was surrounded by farmers, leaning on the rails, talking to one another over the noise of the cattle roaring, the drovers shouting and the auctioneer's sing song cry. As each animal came into the ring it was appraised by the watching crowd, heads would go together and comments passed as to the merit or other wise of the beast. Often at the same time the merit of the owner would also be commented on.

Jim caught sight of the man that he wanted to speak to in earnest conversation with what looked to him to be a dealer. They were on the other side of the ring so he would be able to keep an eye on them and not miss the farmer when he left. After a few minutes a pair of well presented steers came into the ring, bidding was brisk and the price rose to above that which had been the norm until then. Two more followed and then a final two. The murmuring around the ring was of general appreciation as the onlookers recognised quality when they saw it. A few congratulated the farmer and he left, making his way through the market towards the town. Jim crossed over to meet him. "Nice bunch of bullocks, Mr French, they sold well. I would think that you have topped the market today. Now that you are in a good mood I was hoping that I could persuade you to put your feed business my way."

"Oh it's you Jim; I always gave you my business when you were travelling with that firm from Newton. Who are you with now?"

"I'm on my own now, I set up nearly two years ago and I need to expand if I can. That's why I came out here to see you."

"Well I like your cheek and I always liked the way you looked after me before, so yes, call round at the farm, day after tomorrow and we'll do some business."

"Thank you very much, I'll see you then." And with that they parted and Jim made his way back through the stalls towards the car park. He had passed through the covered area, with the stalls of cleaning fluids and bin bags and cheap plastic goods, and was outside again looking at a stall selling chicken coops and the likes made of wood. They were on a flat bed trailer and looked to be well made if a trifle rough. He was about to ask of the vendor if he would consider selling any of them through his shop, when through the goods on the trailer he saw Eric. With him was a sporty looking blond and they were walking hand in hand towards the plant stalls. Jim watched them for a while; they had quite a long chat with the stall holder and then moved on after friendly laughs and goodbyes. Once they were out of sight Jim went over to the stall holder, whom he knew, and said "Hello there Graham, how's it going?"

They exchanged a few pleasantries and reminisced about the days when they had both worked for the same company. Then Jim asked "Who was that blond you were talking to just now, was it any one I know?"

"That's Sheila Caunter from over Chagford way. Her parents had a small farm but they died a while back. She doesn't farm, she's a teacher, but she still lives in the farmhouse and lets the land as far as I know. Why do you ask?"

"I thought that I recognised the bloke with her, that's all."

"Oh, that's Eric, he's always around with her, they've been together for some time now, at least a year I would say if not more."

"Really, thanks Graham, I'll see you around." And with that Jim left, went back to his car and drove back to his office deep in thought. His earlier suspicions about Eric were correct; he was having an affair and had been for some time by the sound of it. Although Hatherleigh was out of his area, so to speak, he was nevertheless quite open about it. It was almost as if he wasn't afraid of being seen, even wanted to be seen. Now he wondered what he should do. What could he do, should he tell Linda and if so how and when? She would be the last to know, that was usually the way. Would she thank him if he told her? And how exactly would he tell her? He couldn't just blurt it out. But if he only hinted at it; well he'd been doing that for some time now, she wouldn't take him seriously. Perhaps the best thing would be to keep quiet; after all it might be quite innocent, they being so open about it and all.

It kept on niggling him all day, and when he got home that evening he decided to tell Pippa, after all they had no secrets and shared everything. Besides, she would know what to do; when it came to awkward matters of the heart it was better to leave it to a woman.

"I saw Eric today dear, when I was in Hatherleigh market."

"Really, what was he doing there, showing a bunch of kids where their food comes from? It would be a good thing for teachers to do. There are far too many children nowadays who haven't a clue on matters like that; think that milk comes from Tesco's and meat comes in little plastic boxes covered in cling film."

"No, he was walking hand in hand with a blond girl, a Sheila Caunter from near Chagford. I got all the information from Graham, you know, he used to work with me. Well he has a stall there selling plants and things, and Eric and this Sheila woman were talking with him for quite a while. So I went over to ask who the girl was and he told me that they have been a couple, so to speak, for over a year now; sees them about together quite a lot. I wasn't sure what to do, I didn't speak to them, in fact I don't think that they saw me at all. It would have been a bit embarrassing to say the least."

"Well, you've been saying for a long time now that you thought that he was playing away, now it looks as though you were right. It does sound a bit brazen though, walking around Hatherleigh market together hand in hand."

"Yes, but what to do, I don't know that we can do anything, I certainly don't think that I can tell Linda. I don't like to do nothing, but I don't know really what should be done in a case like this. "

"Perhaps I could talk to Beatie, they are best of friends. If Linda already has her suspicions she would have confided in her. It really isn't our business but Linda's such a nice girl I would hate to see her hurt. Of course, Beatie may not know anything and then what could I say, nothing? No, I'd have to say something because I would have already let the cat out of the bag."

"It's difficult, you can't do right for doing wrong, let's sleep on it. It beats me why Eric should want another woman, what's wrong with Linda?"

"I know, it beats me too, but nobody knows what goes on behind closed doors. Some couples live a miserable life in private but in public their marriage appears to be perfect. Others seem to be desperately ill matched and we can't understand how or why they stay together, yet they do, and probably are far better suited than any of us realise."

"Which category do we fall into, or is there a third one for those who get on in private as well as they do in public?"

"You old tease, you know very well that I'm totally besotted by you, it's just that I'm afraid to show it too often in case I wear you out!"

Jim jumped off his chair and made to grab Pippa but she was too quick for him, she was already off her chair and halfway into the sitting room. She threw herself onto the settee where he fell beside her and took her into his arms.

"Now who's the tease?" he said.

TWENTY SEVEN

Frank had always liked railway stations. It was not that he was a train spotter; he didn't particularly like the modern diesel electric trains. They didn't seem to have the majestic power of the old steam trains, with their hissing and puffing and the smell of coal fired boilers. Nor was it that he had always wanted to be a train driver as a child, being far more interested in tractors and cars. It was the crowds of people that fascinated him. On his leaves whilst in the Army he had travelled through many countries and often by train. He would people watch at stations, imagining where every one was going, making up stories in his head about their journeys; the reasons for their travels. Who they would meet along the way and what sort of reception they would find at their journey's end. Now he was watching the few passengers getting on the London bound train. Two business men, one old with a well travelled briefcase; a raincoat folded over his arm with a newspaper tucked in the pocket. The other much younger in his obviously new suit, pale blue shirt and yellow tie with a far too large knot. He could be going for an interview or starting a new job. Then there was the small family, mum and dad and two children, probably off to see the sights of the big city. The girl was holding on to her mother's hand hopping from one foot to the other in her excitement. The boy, who looked to be a few years younger, probably eight, was misbehaving as all boys of that age do and giving his dad a hard time. He imagined them taking a ride on an open topped bus, going to the Tower, Madam Tussaud's and riding on the London Eye. There was also a rather anxious looking, middle aged woman who repeatedly looked at her watch as though willing the train to arrive, and when it finally did she was the first to board . Could she be off to visit a sick or even dying relative? Just as the doors were about to close a young couple came rushing down the stairs past Frank, their coats flapping and arms waving frantically. The man, who was carrying the only bag, managed to reach the train door first and held it open while his partner caught up with him. Why is it, thought Frank, that so many people don't leave enough time for their journey and the unexpected incident that so often can crop up and delay them?

The shopping and the journey into town had taken longer than expected. There had been a few quite heavy showers that morning and, as so often happened, this had brought more people on to the roads and in to the town. It was a good job that he had left early.

There was a pause of a few minutes and then the west-bound train pulled in. Frank had positioned himself on the footbridge above the platforms from where he was able to see all the passengers as they got off the train and walked towards him. He could also see through the station out onto the park on the opposite side of the busy road. There the council gardeners had been hard at work creating a wonderfully colourful display of flowers in the beds amongst the green lawns. It was good to see such brightness in the brick and slate of the town.

He had very little idea as to what his cousin looked like; all his mother had said was that she was small, red-haired and stunning to look at. The people alighted; some were met by those waiting on the platform below, greetings exchanged and the usual questions about the journey. One elderly lady with a wheel-chair had to get help from a porter. He had been well trained and the job was completed quickly and without fuss and with smiles all round. It warmed Frank's heart to see this little display of service with a smile. Then he saw Cathy. He wouldn't have called her small, more like petite, or even tiny, dragging her wheeled suitcase behind her, a holdall in her other hand and her handbag on a long strap over her shoulder . She looked more like a girl coming home from boarding school for the holidays. Her dark red hair was cut short in an urchin style and she was wearing a light jacket over a white blouse, dark jeans and boots with a good heel. Her face was lightly tanned and there was no sign of the freckles of her youth. Frank ran down the stairs to meet her and was welcomed with a slightly questioning smile.

"Frank?" He nodded and smiling awkwardly said "You must be Cathy, I'm afraid I would never have recognised you if we had passed each other in the street. All I could remember was your wonderful red hair. Here, let me take your bags, we have to go over the footbridge and then the car is just outside."

"Well, you look just as I remember you, except perhaps a little bigger, but your face hasn't changed. How's your mum? I was sorry to hear about your dad and also sorry that I couldn't get to the funeral. I was busy with exams at the time."

"Mum's fine, least I think she is. It's hard to be sure really, she may be just putting on a brave face, but I do think that she has come to terms with it. I see her looking off into space from time to time but most of the time she is pretty good, thank you. It may have helped to know that had he lived any longer he would have suffered a lot more. I know that that helped me."

"I'm sure that your coming home from the Army helped a great deal as well. It would have been a very lonely life for her, the nearest neighbours being over a mile away and all. I suppose if you had stayed in the Army she might have had to sell up and move into the village or even into town?"

"I don't think Mum would have moved into town, and I can't imagine her selling up, she loves the place and the Red Rubies too much."

They got into the car and drove through and out of the town. The roads were beginning to dry in places and the sun had come out, though it looked from the heavy clouds to the West as though there were more showers to come. They chatted as they went, she asking him about his new life now that he was no longer in the Army. He asked her all about her training to be a vet. He couldn't keep himself from asking whether her height, or lack of it, would be a problem with some of the larger farm animals that she might have to deal with.

"Not really" she said "I know I was the smallest on our course but I never found it to be a problem, In fact there were times when it was a distinct advantage to be small. I'm sure I'll manage, besides, a lot of the work is to do with pets like cats and dogs and not so much with the larger farm animals."

"Well, it will be good to have you stay for a while; I know Mum is greatly looking forward to having a bit of girly company."

He stopped the car on high ground so that they could look at the view before dropping down into the valley and on to the farm. Ahead of them, on the other side of the valley, the patchwork of small fields were looking their best in a myriad of shades of green. The rain had given it all a freshly laundered look. Beyond, the moor stretched away into the purple distance with the points of the tors jutting up sharp against the skyline. Cathy could only vaguely remember her visits to Dartmoor as a small girl. Then it had just been a place of steep hills and ponies on the roadsides. Of narrow lanes between stone walls where passing another car was none too easy and often required one or other car to reverse a long way. Now she noticed the wildness and the grandeur of the rock topped tors. The colours and the patterns of light and shade as the clouds raced across the sky. The little farms with their small fields nestling in the valleys; seemingly sheltering from the dark and forbidding moorland beyond. She remembered a phrase she had heard her uncle use, 'going up moor', and she could now see the significance of it.

Frank pointed out some of the landmarks and the lie of the land. He didn't expect her to take it all in, he knew that the only way she would learn the layout of a new area was to drive or walk it herself. While they were sitting with Frank pointing to things, leaning across Cathy at times, Charlie and Sal Blundell drove by. Frank smiled to himself, knowing full well that Sal would be dying to know who his companion was. What she didn't know she would doubtless make up and spread around the village with help from her friend Edna. He drove on and eventually they turned up the small road that led to the farm where Blanche welcomed Cathy with a warm embrace and her customary "Come in I'll make us a dish of tea. My word, haven't you growed up since I last saw you? I do like your hair done that way, it really suits you. You've got your mother's eyes too, come here and give your old Auntie a hug."

So they went into the warm homely kitchen and had a cup of tea and some home-made cake. Though it had changed a little, a modernizing touch here and there, it was just as she imagined it would be. Particularly the smell; that sense that was so evocative where memories where concerned, completed for her the mental picture that she had carried. The heat from the Aga, the freshly baked cakes and the singing of the kettle all made her feel so comfortable and welcome. And her aunt's welcome almost warmer than the Aga.They sat, and the cat was soon up on her lap, rubbing the side of its head against her hand asking to be stroked and made a fuss of. They drank their tea while Cathy told Blanche about her journey and in answer to questions gave a full update on her family and their goings on. Afterwards, Blanche showed Cathy to her room and said "When you'm settled perhaps you'd like to walk around the farm with me."

"Thank you, I'd like that."

"Have you got any boots with you, for outdoors I mean? I could lend you a pair of wellies if you like. They you've got on are hardly fit for field work."

"No, it's alright Auntie, I've got my walking boots with me. I was hoping to go up on the tors a bit while I was here; perhaps Frank could show me where to go for a good walk. It's all so beautiful around here and so different from at home where it's all so flat."

"I'm sure he'd be only too pleased, there's nothing he likes better than walking on his precious Dartmoor. I'll see you downstairs when you're ready then."

She unpacked her few belongings, hoping that she had brought enough for her stay. The trouble was that she had no idea how long that would be, but she felt so comfortable already that she was in no hurry to move on. And her Auntie Blanche seemed to be willing her to stay; it really felt good, almost like coming home. So she changed into clothes more suited to the farm and went downstairs. Her bedroom window overlooked the farmyard, so going downstairs she went out to get a better look around.

She spent a little while trying to remember the places where she had played during her holidays there. The brook turned through ninety degrees at that point heading away from the farm and upstream. On the opposite bank was a grassy area and a small stand of magnificent old beech trees. She recalled how they had taken a picnic over there one day on a previous visit and how excited she had been at crossing over on the stepping stones with a basket of food. A few ponies were now standing under the trees, half asleep with their heads down and their tails swishing lazily at the flies. A grey wagtail was on one of the rocks, its tail constantly bobbing and the bright yellow feathers on its breast reflected in the water. Every now and then it darted up to catch one of the flies that formed a little cloud over the water swirling gently by; the stream being a good bit wider and slower moving at that point.

Blanche came out to join her, shrugging into an old anorak, and they walked out over the fields, admiring the Red Rubies of which Blanche was so proud. Most of the silage harvest was over, but Frank had cut one late field and the sweet smell of new-mown grass filled their nostrils. They stopped for a while at the hedge against the open moor, listening to the skylarks singing way up high and the stonechats chittering their warnings from the tops of the gorse bushes. She watched a wheatear fly from rock to rock, looking so smart in his grey frock coat, pale creamy yellow waistcoat and with that rather severe looking black horizontal stripe through his eye. The bell heather was just beginning to bloom and there were odd patches of deep purple here and there. Up at the top of the valley the bog cotton formed a sheen of silvery white, almost like snow amongst the rich green of the moss and grass growing in those permanently wet places. Cathy realised that as a child she had never properly taken in the beauty of the place and its multitude of wildlife. There was so much here to see and do.

They talked a lot, mostly about Cathy's ambitions for her job, why she had chosen that career and the training that had been involved. Then Cathy asked Blanche a bit more about Stan, his illness and subsequent death and how she was coping with it all. Blanche found herself opening up to this girl in a way that she hadn't been able to before. Though unable to tell her the details of Stan's illness and death she was able to talk about how it was affecting her. She was surprised that a young thing like Cathy could have such an 'old head on young shoulders'. Then she realised that she was judging the girl by her size, forgetting that though tiny in stature she was a grown woman. Perhaps it was all the more easy to talk because Cathy was, though related, almost a stranger compared to her friends locally. She knew nothing of the recent history and so she was seeing it all with fresh eyes. Yes, it certainly was good to have the company of this charming and lively young woman to stay with them. However, she realized that she mustn't get too attached; Cathy would no doubt want her own place and would be moving on as soon as she could. She would just have to make the most of her visit while it lasted.

TWENTY EIGHT

A good crowd had gathered in the village hall, Phil had called a meeting and invited any one who had an interest in the goings on in the village to attend. As a result some thirty or forty people were sitting in rows facing the stage. In the front row as usual and fitting their self appointed stations were Sal and Edna. Sal couldn't wait to tell her friend, in a stage whisper, about the pretty young girl she had seen with Frank. "Parked up they was, in that lay-by at the top of the hill overlooking the village. He was leaning across her, could have been pointing out something, though he could have been giving her a kiss. 'Twas hard to tell really."

"D'you know who she was then?" said Edna.

"No, no idea, I expect she is a girlfriend from his Army days or something like that. I've never seen her before, not that I know of. Mind you, I didn't get that good a look at her 'cos Frank was leaning over her. She has red hair, I can tell you that."

"Oh we'll find out soon enough, I've no doubt."

Two rows behind them Linda was sitting with Beatie and had heard the whole conversation.

Neither of them said a word but they both were thinking the same thoughts.

Phil German mounted the stage and called the meeting to order by ringing the old school bell that had been unearthed during the renovations.

"It's good to see so many of you here tonight. I thought that we had better have a meeting as the work of converting the old school into a village hall is now all but finished. There are a number of things that we have to discuss, the first being what to call this building. I had thought that we might quite properly call it The Edworthy Hall, in recognition of Sir Harold's generosity. However, he tells me that on no account may we do that. He doesn't want his name on it, he is a somewhat shy man, though he does appreciate our feelings and he is touched. There seem to me to be a few good options; The New Hall, The Old School, The School Hall are those that spring to my mind. What do you think? We'll have another go at it later this evening after we've had time to think about it a bit more.

We also need to set up all those organisations and activities that usually take place and any new ones. This building is a good bit bigger than the old one so we have more scope. It had occurred to me that we might use the larger of the two side rooms here as a snooker room, it would be a good form of evening entertainment for the youngsters, and those of us who are not so young but feel young. The main thing I wanted to discuss though is that we ought to have a sort of opening ceremony of some sort. What do you think, what form should it take? Lets have some ideas from you folks; I don't want it all left to me."

There was a general chattering in the room for a few minutes and then Charlie Blundell said "Why don't we have a dance, a Midsummer Ball? We had to put off the summer variety show because of the work that had to be done, so let's have a dance. A dance is something that we can all join in."

"Yes, make it a square dance, we could ask that group from Moreton, they're pretty good and have that lady caller to tell us what to do." said a voice from the back of the room.

"Will the younger people like square dancing?" asked another.

"Play some disco records in the interval, and then every body will get a bit of what they like. Anyway from what I saw at my friends wedding, they had a square dance and after they got the hang of it you couldn't keep the kids off the floor. They loved it, and they all joined in proper.

"Well, that seems to be settled then" said Phil "Can I leave it to you Charlie to organise the music side of things? We will need to know if they can come and on what date. Then we will be able to set our date."

"Certainly, but I don't want to have anything to do with selling tickets or anything."

"Why don't we make it a fancy dress ball? That would add a bit of fun to it, and there could be a prize for the best costume, if we could get anyone brave enough to be the judge." This suggestion was from Rose Stapleton who was sitting at the back with Giles and Nancy.

"And I would be only too pleased to give the prize" said Nancy, "It would be my pleasure after all the kindness that the people of this village have shown to me these last few weeks. In fact, I'll even be the judge if you'll have me."

"Oh, we'll have you all right and thank you Nancy." said Phil.

At this point Edna uncharacteristically spoke up saying "I'm not so sure that fancy dress is such a good idea. It's not that I don't want people to have their fun, but it might put the wrong emphasis on the evening. Besides, it could make it very difficult to dance properly and easily and that would be a petty."

"I agree," said Sal, emboldened by her friend's outburst, "Why don't us have a fancy dress competition for the little children?"

"Yes," said another voice from the back of the hall. "And make it an afternoon do for the little ones, with games and things like that as well. Then the dance in the evening can be for grown ups and big children only."

"That sounds like a good idea to me," said Phil.

The meeting continued in good mood for another hour. The various activities and their respective organizers were arranged. Frank, who was sitting at the back of the room with Blanche and Cathy, had agreed to organize and run the young persons side of things, table tennis, snooker and badminton. It had been suggested that Eric might do the job but Linda had said that she felt sure that he would be unable to do so; he was always so busy with school things these days. Linda was asked if she could run a yoga class. Rose suggested an art class, when asked who she had in mind to run it she said that she would be happy to do it. Not many apart from the Cameron-Hydes knew of her talent as an artist. Nancy had a fine painting of Giles sitting in the garden that Rose had done; and Giles had asked her to do a portrait of Haig from a photograph, as a surprise present for Nancy. Charlie and Sal would run the winter whist drives as usual. The mother and toddler group and the short mat bowls team would be able to start up again after their enforced break.

"One final thing" said Phil, "Because we received a fair sum from the insurers we do have enough money to purchase equipment for the various groups, so don't stint yourselves, we can afford to do the job properly. As to the name, the most popular choice from you all seems to be, The School Hall. If I don't see you before I'll see you at the midsummer ball. Goodnight and thank you all for coming." And with that he rang the bell and the meeting closed.

Phil may have closed the meeting but, as was so often the case on occasions like this, people were in no hurry to leave. They stood about in small groups chatting and gossiping and going over the events and decisions of the evening. Farmers had a chance to chat with their neighbours and compare notes. Most had finished silage harvesting by that time though some had a few acres left to do. Teenagers were talking about their forthcoming exams and young mums about their families. They had all missed the opportunities for socialising that the village hall and its organizations offered. By the time that Linda reached the door Frank was gone. She turned to Beatie saying "Would you like to try a drink in the pub before we go our separate ways?"

"I'm a bit whacked tonight Linda, could we make it another time?"

"Sure, tell you what, why don't we meet up in town this weekend? I want to get a small present for my sister Marnie. She's expecting her second child soon. We could do a bit of girlie shopping and have a bite of lunch somewhere."

"That sounds great, I'm on an early shift on Saturday, I could meet you at about twelve if that's OK with you?"

"Perfect, we could meet by that fountain thing where we usually do, twelve o'clock. I'll have my mobile with me so if there's any change to our plans you can ring me. See you then, bye"

They parted and went out into the night, both of them thinking of what had happened that evening and of their proposed shopping trip. But most of their thoughts were of the conversation that they had overheard between Sal and Edna. Neither had mentioned it but Beatie had sensed Linda stiffen beside her and had felt for her. She wanted to say something to her friend to comfort her in some way but also to warn her not to let her emotions run away with her and get her into deep water. She had been there before and been hurt.

She would have liked to put her arm around her and told her to take no notice of the silly gossip, but she couldn't. It was too public and besides, it was only Sal and Edna and they were notorious for gossip that was well wide of the mark. What was it her mum used to say? Eavesdroppers never hear good of themselves. One of these days Sal and Edna would say something that would get them into deep trouble, but she wasn't going to hold her breath. Their sort always seemed to get away with it.

TWENTY NINE

Nancy had hardly slept at all, it was not that she had had a restless night, she certainly hadn't tossed and turned, she just had been unable to sleep. Thoughts of being reunited with their son Julian had been so overwhelming that her brain had just been unable to switch off. In the bottom drawer of her desk she had a box containing some of the paintings that he had done while still at school. These she had been looking through that afternoon. Most of them were landscape scenes of Scotland, from when they lived at Lossimouth. One in particular, of a loch through the trees, the mountains behind so perfectly reflected in the still water, captured the majesty and the wildness of that area. It took her right back to those days when she and the boys went walking, David would usually accompany her and their dog, leaving Julian busy with his brushes and easel. Rose had offered to take that particular painting; she had something in mind for mounting and framing it and would bring it back to hang in the lounge in time for Julian's arrival. Nancy's only concern was that it would be done in time, as she felt that it was important to show to Julian that their welcome was not only warm but based on a love that had never died despite their lack of understanding.

She remembered how he used to take photographs of some of the subjects that he wished to paint and then work from them. He used to say that the mood could change too quickly for him to capture before it disappeared, and with his sketches and photos he might get it right He really was a good artist, or was it just the wishful thinkings of a mother. Maybe he would take up painting again, possibly as a profession. There was plenty of scope around where they lived, Dartmoor scenery and all its wonderful and varied wildlife. Perhaps that combined beauty could give him the inspiration to take up his brushes again.

As a boy he would have been in his element here. She remembered how he and David had always loved exploring and camping. The first time had been a disaster; they had pitched the tent on their lawn and had gone out to spend their first night under canvas. It was fine to begin with, but as the night went on the weather worsened, it rained and it blew and by eleven o'clock two pathetic little faces had appeared around the curtain of the French window. They spent the rest of that night camped under the dining room table. On another occasion, when a school friend had let him down and was unable to join him at the last minute, he had stormed off in a huff with his tent and all his equipment on his back and set up camp in the garden of a family friend. It was very fortunate that he had stayed there because whilst cooking his breakfast the next day his little gas stove leaked gas and almost caught the tent on fire. Luckily he wasn't hurt, though his eyebrows were singed to nothing, the friends helped him and rang Nancy and all was restored to normal. Later he developed his love of wildlife and was always bringing home injured animals to be cared for and later released if they survived.

Then she had wondered whether things would have been different if he had gone to a village school, like the one here, instead of a boarding school. Not that they had much choice in the matter, with Giles being posted all over the world, the boys had had to go to a boarding school. It was the only way that they would get any stability and continuity in their education. But it also had meant that their only friends were those from school. Yet David and he had been so different, a fact that both she and Giles had been proud of, so it was nature not nurture. She had known exactly how to treat them and what each of them liked and responded to. It was, she realised, a long time ago and his life had changed so much since she last saw him, his tastes had probably altered too. There was so much that she just didn't know about him. Although she felt sure that inside he was still the son she had nursed and watched grow up, she knew that life had a way of playing nasty tricks on those who expected a predictable future. He had left because he felt that there was no way that his parents could accept his sexuality. Maybe one day he would be able to talk with her about it and explain his feelings to her. Although they certainly hadn't thrown him out it would have been far too difficult for him to stay. At first she had felt a certain amount of bitterness, not so much at him but at fate for dealing them all such a lousy hand. First David's death on that motorbike of his, and then Julian being gay, it had been all too much. Giles, who didn't say a lot or show his feelings much, had been as devastated as she was at the thought that they would never be grandparents. The worst part had been that they had never spoken about it after Julian had left and the longer it had gone on the more difficult it had become to bring up the subject. Even now, though they were both full of emotion and almost bursting to talk about it, they were still hesitant, still almost afraid in case putting their thoughts into words might hurt the other.

Her accident and subsequent stay in hospital, though not particularly pleasant, had done a lot to loosen their tongues. They had always been able to talk about anything that was troubling them, their worries about the future, health problems and the likes, but strangely never about Julian. She remembered how Giles had talked about Ray the day after his visit. He had been positively enthusiastic about the man, much to her surprise, and had answered all her questions about him in a manner that showed to her that he had accepted him. Did this mean that he would accept Julian with an equally enthusiastic welcome? She would know the answer to that question in a few hours, hours that seemed like weeks at the moment, they dragged so slowly by. Giles snorted, said something unintelligible and turned over; he seemed to be having a restless night too. Then she must have dropped off for a minute or two because it was light outside now, almost full daylight and the birds were singing in the garden and the woods beyond. Giles turned violently and almost shouted "Oh no, oh god no, you poor boy" and then turned again burying his face in his pillow. A moment or two later he woke and turned to Nancy saying "Are you awake dear?"

"It seems like I've been awake most of the night."

"I've just had an awful dream."

"I thought you must be having a nightmare, you were thrashing about so."

"Yes, well I dreamed that Julian had just arrived. He got out of the car from the driver's side, which seemed odd, and came towards us. He was on crutches, he had only one leg, and his face was so horribly burned and disfigured that we could never have recognized him. It was awful, absolutely awful."

"It was only a dream Darling," she said, catching hold of his hand. "He's fine, you said yourself that Ray said he was going to make a full recovery."

"I know, it just seemed so horribly real, quite frightening really."

"How extraordinary, I was just thinking of the time when he was camping and his gas stove caught fire and he came home with his eyebrows singed almost to nothing."

They paused for a while lost in their thoughts, and then Giles said "I could do with a cup of tea, would you like one too or is it too early?"

"I'd love one; I almost got up to make one myself an hour ago."

"No, I'll go, no point you getting out too soon with your hip, we'll have a nice cuppa in bed and then when we're properly awake we'll get up."

It was just after ten thirty when Rose arrived, a good bit later than usual, which had had Nancy worrying. Giles kept saying the boys wouldn't arrive until lunch time and that there was plenty of time but secretly he was just as worried as she. Rose came in with the painting under her arm wrapped in brown paper. She had put it in a simple mahogany frame that matched the furniture in the lounge perfectly. The three of them had then gone into the lounge and decided to hang it in pride of place over the fire. Nancy had also removed the picture of Giles and herself that had stood on the desk and replaced it with a photograph of Julian, taken just before he left school.

Upstairs she and Rose had made ready two bedrooms, one with a double bed and one with twin beds, because they had no idea what their sleeping arrangements were.

They were sitting in the lounge when they heard the car arrive. Nancy almost ran to the front door with Giles not far behind. They stood in the porch waiting for Julian to get out of the car. He seemed to take a long time but finally the door opened and he got out and stood half leaning against the car. Nancy felt that he looked

207

surprisingly relaxed and comfortable in his check shirt, beige chinos and desert boots. Tall, tanned, upright and smiling, that quirky smile that all the boys in the family had, he looked so like he had done before he left. He may have been several years older though he didn't look it, or was that a mum's wishful thinking. His hair was lighter than before, probably bleached by the African sun, but still thick and no sign of grey. Nancy could wait no longer and was across the drive, one hand held out towards him the other working her walking stick. Julian pushed himself off the car and stepped towards her. She threw away her stick and fell into his arms where they stayed for several minutes.

"Thank God you're home safe and well, it's been far too long."

"It's good to be back Mum."

They stayed for a few more moments in each other's arms saying nothing. He released her briefly to introduce Ray who had come around the car to stand beside him. Giles watching from the porch was aware of a passage from the Bible that was running through his head, 'this my son was dead and is alive again, was lost and is found'. Yet he realised that it was not his son that had been lost, it was he, Giles, who had lost his way and very nearly lost his son into the bargain. He stepped forward, a little hesitantly being somewhat unsure as to what to do. Julian released his hold on Nancy and came towards him saying just one word, "Dad." That one word, with the expression and feeling that he had put into it said it all, said more than a thousand words could say. Giles found himself instinctively throwing his arms around his son, something that he probably hadn't done since Julian was a small boy. They stood locked in an embrace, as Giles said "Welcome home Son." He was glad that his head was over Julian's shoulder, for some reason he felt embarrassed at the tears of joy that were streaming down his cheeks. He needn't have worried; both Julian and Nancy were crying too, crying and laughing as only deep emotion can make people do. Then they walked up to the house together, Julian in between his parents with their arms linked. Exactly who was supporting who was hard to tell; maybe the excitement of the moment had meant that neither of them needed their sticks. A few paces behind, Ray was following them carrying their suitcases.

Once inside the house in the lounge they all sat and, for quite some time, just looked at one another. It seemed as though words were hardly needed, and in any case there were so many thoughts running through their heads that it would have been hard to talk coherently. Though it felt so natural and normal, at the same time they were all finding it hard to believe that they were really together again. Then little by little the questions started coming out, first from Nancy and finally all of them were talking, questions and answers pouring out. Initially the questions were to do with Julian's injury and just how the recovery process was going. Then they wanted to know all about their work in Africa and other places where they had been. Nancy, like her husband before her, found herself liking Ray instantly and was fascinated by the stories he had to tell. There would be plenty more tales to hear later and of course the boys would want to know all about Nancy's accident and all the other things that had occurred in their lives over the past twenty years.

"I don't know about you chaps but I could do with something to eat" said Giles.

"Rose said she would be leaving a salad in the dining room for us, we can have something more substantial later" said Nancy, "and then we can show you around afterwards."

Giles got to his feet and led them from the room. Despite the warmth of their reunion he still couldn't help but feel a little uneasy about Julian and Ray's relationship. Perhaps as he got to know them both better his worries would pass. In any case, so far the homecoming had passed without a hitch; in fact it was rapidly beginning to feel as though they had never been apart.

THIRTY

Linda was a little late, she hated being late but the traffic across the moor had been particularly heavy and as she drove into the Park & Ride car park she saw a bus just pulling out. So although she had left in what she thought was plenty of time, it was nearly ten past twelve when she arrived at the fountain in the middle of Plymouth. There seemed to be more than the usual amount of people milling around, quite a number of whom were watching a pair of jugglers performing. As a country girl she didn't particularly like Plymouth, it was too busy, too noisy and with far too much concrete for her taste. However she did like the occasional shopping trip.

"Have you been here long? I hadn't allowed for the holiday traffic, sorry."

"Don't worry" said Beatie, "I haven't been here that long, besides I quite like 'people watching'. It's amazing the antics some of them get up to."

They went into Dingles, their senses immediately assailed by the smells from the beauty counters.

"I thought I might get Marnie some perfume, what do you think?"

"Sounds good to me, do you know what she likes?"

"Yeah, Miss Dior, but we could sample a few others while we are here. I might just get myself a bottle."

They spent a good bit of time at the perfume counters, trying the various scents available, and noticing how they smelled so different on each other. Finally they bought Marnie's present. Linda found that the scents of some brought back many a memory. She considered buying some Anais Anais; it was the perfume that Frank had bought her for her seventeenth birthday. If she had been wearing it the other day when Frank had returned her car would it have evoked the same sort of memories for him? Why was it that her thoughts kept returning to Frank? Normally these shopping trips with Beatie were such fun, laughing and joking as they tried different perfumes and clothes. But this time she wasn't able to give it or Beatie her full concentration.

"Let's go and have a look at the clothes up in the fashion department" said Beatie, bringing Linda back from her reverie. So up they went to the ladies clothes department for a good look around. They rummaged about, looking at a number of items and having a laugh at some things that they wouldn't be seen dead in. They were in and out of the fitting rooms, asking each other's opinion, and laughing hysterically at some of the more outlandish items that Beatie always managed to find and for a short while this lifted Linda's mood a little. They were such good friends that they relied on the other to give an honest opinion.

Beatie settled on a daring little dress that they both thought would be ideal for the forthcoming dance in the new village hall. Although she tried, she couldn't persuade Linda to buy anything, she obviously was not in the mood for retail therapy, and in fact she seemed to be more than somewhat preoccupied.

"D'you want to see any more here or shall we go and eat?"

"Let's go and eat, I'd like to try that little pub down on the Barbican, they say it's very good" said Linda.

So they went to the pub and found a nice quiet table in a corner. With their food ordered and a drink in front of them Beatie said "What's up Linda, you've been like some one who's dropped a quid and found sixpence?"

"I know, I'm not good company at the moment, I just don't know what to do."

"Still this business with Frank, eh?"

"Yes, I'm so confused at the moment; I don't seem to be able to think of anything but Frank, since he came back. I know that I shouldn't be thinking like this, I'm a married woman, though I probably wouldn't say a happily married one, but married none the less. And I do care for Eric, but I fear that I'm in love with Frank, as much in love as I was when he left if not more so. Was I ever truly in love with Eric? Or was it just that I was on the rebound? I suppose that's what it could have been, although it was several years after Frank had gone that we married. Or is it because my relationship with Eric isn't too good at the moment and I'm in need of affection and TLC, in need of the sort of closeness that I used to have with Frank? I wanted to talk to him the other day but it was no use, I just get all tongue tied. I can't be pushy, it's just not me. I need to know if he still feels anything for me, like it was when we were young. I've got a feeling that he does and won't admit to it. But then there's this girl that's staying with them, who is she and what is she doing there? What can I do, how can I move on, or do I have to live with this for ever?"

Beatie could see the tears welling up in her friend's eyes and reaching across the table she took her hand and said

"You poor thing, this is really getting to you isn't it? I'm a bit worried that you may be getting carried away. Just because Frank is back it doesn't mean that its all going to be like it was all those years ago. You may be letting your hopes run away with your feelings, I'd hate to see you let down again. I just wish that there was something that I could do that would help. Would it do any good, d'you think, if you went away for a while? You said that you were planning on spending a day or two with Marnie after the baby comes, why not go and stay with her for a couple of weeks? It might help to get all these thoughts out of your head for a while. You'd be busy with babies and nappies and things, and you wouldn't have the constant reminder of Frank being around, you wouldn't keep bumping into him, would you?"

"No, and I wouldn't keep on bumping into him with that girl of his, whoever she is."

"You haven't discovered who she is then?"

214

"No, I've heard all sorts of stories, but I don't suppose that any of them are right. She could be a girl-friend that he met while in the Army, a relative staying with him and Blanche or a paying guest. I don't know and I don't really want to ask him. But that's a good idea of yours, I could take a couple of weeks off and stay with Marnie, in fact she did sort of ask me back along if I would. Yes, I'll give her a ring and set that up. She's only got to give me a call when she goes into labour and I can be there in a few hours."

"Is she having it at home then, or in hospital?"

"Oh, at home, she's got a wonderful midwife, and she had such an easy and straightforward birth last time, she thinks that a home confinement would be best."

"No two births are the same, still she may be right and I must say that I would rather have mine at home if I were having one."

"That's good coming from an NHS nurse who works in a large hospital; have you no confidence in the system then?"

"Oh it's not that" said Beatie "It's just that I would rather be at home with my family around me, especially if the midwife was as good as Marnie's seems to be. There's only one drawback, and I am now wondering if I should have suggested it in the first place."

"What's that then?"

"Well, will being with a toddler and a new born baby make you all broody for one of your own again?"

"No, I'm not too worried about that any more. Of course I would have liked to have had a family if it was possible, but it didn't break my heart when I found I couldn't. For me, having babies was never the big deal that a lot of people seemed to think it was. They always said that I didn't need dolls to play with, 'cos I was always pushing my younger brothers and sisters around in a pram. What people didn't know was that I had to do that, I didn't have a choice. After Dad died, Mum needed all the help she could get, and as the oldest child, I was the one that got roped in to do it. I didn't mind, I loved my kid brothers and sisters, but it was a job not a game."

"I never realised that, you never said before."

"There wasn't any reason to, and you never asked."

"So you'll do that then, go in with Marnie for two weeks?"

"Yes, when I get home I'll give her a ring and fix it up. As you say, it'll give me a break away, and maybe if I don't keep seeing Frank I won't keep on thinking about him. I don't know quite how soon it will be before Marnie starts, it may be only a day or two. On the other hand it may be a couple of weeks."

"What about Eric, will he be able to cope while you're away?"

"Oh yes, he's quite capable in the house, I don't have to worry about that, thank God."

"Well I know what I'm going to do when I get home; I'm going to ask Mum if she knows who this mystery woman is that's staying with Frank. She may already know, but I'm sure that she will ask Blanche if she doesn't, and then I can tell you. It's obvious that you're dying to know."

"Thanks, I'm not sure that I want to know, but I won't rest until I do, silly me. And thanks again for listening to my woes and for trying to sort me out."

The two girls left the pub and walked up to the bus stop in the centre of town. Beatie's bus was the first to come and after she had gone Linda turned and went into Dingles and bought a bottle of Anais Anais perfume. She tried to persuade herself that she was buying it for herself and that that was the only reason. But she knew in her heart that she hoped that Frank might smell it on her and it would remind him of the days when they had spent all their free time together.

THIRTY ONE

After she got home Linda started preparing their supper. It would have to be something that could be warmed up because Eric was away at a cricket match or something, and there was no knowing when he might be back. All she knew was that as long as the weather stayed fine he would be late. So she set to and made a large pan full of chicken curry. With the new fast cook rice it would only take a few minutes to get a meal when he got home, and if he didn't want any thing nothing would be wasted. The circumstances of her childhood and the way that her mother had always managed had taught her well, there was no waste in her household. She sat down and ate hers alone as she so often found herself doing these days.Then she rang Marnie and offered her services for two weeks if required. Marnie was thrilled and said that she had better pack her case as she was already six days past the due date. Linda spent the next hour packing and then ringing her clients to tell them that she would be away for the next two weeks, maybe more, and that she would 'inform them when normal service would be resumed'.

At half past eight the phone rang, it was Marnie to say that she had started.

"You're joking, we were only talking an hour or two ago."

"I know, but believe me it's true. There's no need to rush, I've called the midwife and she'll be here soon. You don't need to be here before morning really, if that would be easier for you."

"No that's alright, I'll see to Eric's tea first and then I'll come over. In fact I think he's here now so I shouldn't be too long. Bye love"

Eric came in looking a bit glum, Linda guessed that the match hadn't gone too well, so without saying anything she got his tea and put it on the table. He sat down and ate silently until the plate was empty. He was thinking of what he had to say to Linda, it wouldn't be easy, he had been putting it off for far too long which only made it more difficult. Their relationship had been any thing but good for a long time and it was really only cowardice that had stopped him from telling her before. Linda meanwhile had brought her suitcase downstairs and seeing it Eric said somewhat anxiously "What's on, why the suitcase, where are you going?"

For a moment his guilty conscience made him wonder if she had found out and that she was leaving him.

"Marnie rang as you drove in to say that she had started her labour. I had offered to go in and help, as you know, but I've decided to stay for two weeks. I could do with a break. It's hardly a holiday I know, but it will be a change and that's supposed to be as good as a rest. You'll manage

I'm sure and you can always ring if you do have any problems."

Eric's mind was in a whirl, he didn't know what to say. He had been about to tell her about Sheila and his affair with her. But now that she was about to go away, would this be the right moment? No moment would be right for what he had to say. She was going in to help her sister with a birth, what should by rights be a joyous occasion, telling her now would put her in completely the wrong frame of mind maybe. Yet if he didn't tell her and it came out later, while she was away for instance, that would probably be worse. She would only ask why he hadn't told her before. No, it had to be now, he had psyched himself up for this confession all the way home in the car. He had told Sheila that he would tell Linda this evening, he had to do it and the sooner the better.

"Before you go there's something I've got to tell you."

"Really, what's that?"

"Sit down a minute please; this isn't going to be easy." He paused a minute to collect his thoughts, his heart pounding. Linda sat down opposite him, a puzzled look on her face.

"I can't go on living a lie any longer; it's been too long already. I've found someone else; I've been seeing someone else."

"You mean, you've been having an affair?"

"Yes, I'm sorry."

"Really, and how long has this been going on, weeks, months or is it years?"

"Since before Christmas. I am sorry, truly I am, and I never wanted to hurt you. You have never done anything wrong, and I don't and can't blame you in any way. We drifted apart and I did nothing to stop it, though I still care for you and your well being. I fell out of love with you."

"And in love with someone else I presume."

"Yeah, something like that."

"Do I know this person; may I ask who she is? I presume it's a she."

"You don't know her, least I don't think you do. She's called Sheila Caunter, she lives near Chagford, she teaches at the girls' grammar school."

"I see, and what do you two propose to do now?"

"I would like, that's to say we would like it if I moved in with her. She has a farm that she inherited that she lives in, though she doesn't farm it, she lets out the land."

Eric wondered why he was telling her so much, perhaps he felt if he kept talking she would have less chance to vent her anger on him. But Linda said nothing, she had gone cold, she sat staring across the table at the man she had been married to for years and realized that she probably didn't know him at all. She also thought that he probably didn't know her either, they certainly hadn't spent much time together of late and had never talked deeply about anything much. She stood up and taking her case moved towards the door.

"I'm off to my sister's now; will you be here when I get back in two week's time?"

"No, I'll leave now probably. I'll take a few things in a bag and come back for the rest later. I don't want anything more than my own personal things, you can have the rest. I know that there will be a lot more sorting out to do but I hope that we can do it all without any rancour."

"I don't know what to say, I just don't know what to say. You can end a marriage just like that, no warning, no discussion, nothing?"

"Discussion would only have led to a fight and I didn't want that, I hoped that you didn't want that either. I almost thought that you might be a little bit relieved that I was going, seeing as we hadn't been exactly a loving couple for such a long time."

"Now you're trying to put the blame on me, are you?"

"No no, far from that, I take all the blame. Look let's not get into an argument, I probably shouldn't have told you now that you are off to help Marnie. I just want as clean and uncomplicated a split as is possible. I'll get my things and go, and we can talk about the details after you come home."

Eric dropped his head, looking at his hands on the table. He was quite calm now, his pulse rate back to normal, his anxiety passed. He was resigned to accept whatever Linda might throw at him. As it turned out she surprised him. She walked around the table to stand behind his chair and put her hands on his shoulders. She knew him better than he realised, far better than he could ever know her.

"Thank you" she said quietly "Thank you for being honest with me, it must have been difficult. We were both aware that things weren't good between us. There were even times when it crossed my mind that your staying away so much could be with another woman. But I persuaded myself that it wasn't so; put it to the back of my mind because it was so much easier to deny it. "

She paused, trying to control her emotions, not wishing to explode into anger or descend into floods of tears. Eric remained quiet, still with his head down, looking at his hands.

"I think its best if I go now, saying anything more now would be a mistake. I need time away, time to think. I was planning on staying for two weeks with Marnie, that may give me the time I need to try to come to terms with the situation. There'll be a lot more that we need to talk about later; there will be a lot of questions that I need to ask but now isn't the time."

She picked up her suitcase and walked to the door. As she turned to say goodbye she suddenly felt very alone.

He heard her car start up and drive away and he pushed back his chair and went upstairs to their bedroom. He threw a few things into a couple of sports bags, collected his toilet things from the bathroom and then sat on the bed. He looked around the room, the room in which they had slept together for all of their married life. A room full of memories, memories of love and of despair; of lovemaking and of heartbreak. Of hopes and dreams for the future that unfortunately hadn't materialized. He had messed it all up. At first he had blamed his sterility, but only because he had to have something to blame. Then he had taken to drinking, though that had done him more harm than good. When he had finally pulled himself together, mostly with Linda's help, he didn't stay with her. He should have thanked her for all her help and understanding. Instead he made out to himself that it was all her fault, that she wanted to have a child more than she wanted him, and so he had looked for solace elsewhere.

Eventually he had found it in Sheila. They had taken their time; they both wanted to be sure that what they felt for each other was real and lasting. Then, once they were both sure, they had consummated the relationship. Now, now that they were certain, had absolutely no doubts, finally he had plucked up courage and confessed to Linda. At first he had felt a feeling of relief, a weight was lifted off him, and he was no longer living a lie. Then there was a moment of panic when he realised what he had said and feared for what Linda would say in return. But Linda hadn't shouted at him hadn't even questioned him much. She had just walked out and said 'thank you' as she left. There were tears running down his cheeks now, he wasn't sobbing, he wasn't really even crying but there were floods of tears as he went down the stairs, through the kitchen and out to his car. As he switched on the ignition the radio came on and a girl was singing 'love hurts'.

"Too bloody right" he said as he drove away.

THIRTY TWO

Linda drove through the village and once out on the main road she pulled into the first lay-by. She too was crying and had to pull herself together before driving on. There was no doubt that it had come as a shock to her, despite her occasional doubts. Their relationship had seemed to be alright. There had been no arguments, no cross words; they had just got on with their lives quietly. Quietly and separately and perhaps that was it. They had been living independent lives, in the same house maybe, but not as a couple. She started talking to herself.

"What did I do that was so wrong? He never wanted for anything; I always kept the house clean and tidy; there was always a meal on the table when he came home. I know that he felt bad when he found out that it was down to him that we couldn't have children, but I always said that it didn't matter, that it wasn't the end of the world. When he went on the booze I never criticized him, I did all I could to help him off it and eventually we succeeded. Was it that I didn't show my love for him enough, but I couldn't put on an act? I don't do that, that's not me. Should I have noticed, were there little signs that I missed? If there were why didn't I notice them, was I too busy with my own life? Should I have tackled him, questioned him when I spotted those signs? Was it really because I have been thinking of Frank so much that subconsciously I have neglected Eric? One thing I do know, I mustn't tell Marnie, I've got to act as normal as I possibly can while I'm with her. She will have enough on her plate without my troubles."

She wiped her eyes did a quick make-up job using the car mirror and started on her way again. But it was no use, she was feeling let down, jilted and generally miserable. She pulled in again and rang Beatie. "I've got to talk to you, can you spare me a few minutes?"

"Of course I can, whatever's the matter?"

"Eric's leaving me."

"What do you mean, leaving you?"

"As I say, he's leaving me, he's got another woman."

So Linda proceeded to tell her all about the events of the evening. After a while she began to feel a little less sorry for herself and stopped crying.

"Well, I reckon it's a good job that you're going in to stay with Marnie for a while, you need to get away now more than ever. I'll drive over to see you tomorrow sometime; I'll want to see Marnie and the baby and it will give us a chance to talk properly."

"Thank you, I'd be so glad if you would, this has been a helluva knock to my confidence. I know it's stupid, but I can't help thinking that in some way it's my fault and that I've failed."

"Of course it's not your fault, stop trying to take the blame, these things happen. Maybe this was bound to happen, after all you said yourself that you were probably not well suited. Go and enjoy your time with Marnie, ring me when there's any news, and then wet the baby's head with a glass or two of wine or a G and T. I'll see you soon, OK?"

"Yeah, and thanks, you're a real friend, I don't know what I'd do without you, I couldn't go through this on my own."

"Don't be silly, you're the strong one, always were, but I'm here and glad to help in any way I can. Don't worry so, I'll be in to see you more than once or twice while you're there."

The conversation ended and Linda, more composed now, drove on to her sister's and the excitement of a new baby.

Beatie went down from her room to join her parents in the lounge. Phil was reading the paper and Elaine, her mother, was reading a magazine. Beatie lived at home and had her own bed-sit upstairs, but that room, she felt, was for when she wanted to entertain friends. So it was, that most evenings after dinner when she was at home and not working, she would go downstairs and spend time with her parents.

"Mum, who's that girl staying with Blanche? I've seen her quite a lot lately in Frank's car."

"If you had asked me this morning I wouldn't have known. I saw Blanche this morning in the shop and she told me all about it. The girl, as you call her, is Blanche's niece, Cathy, from Somerset. She's been training as a vet for the last I don't know how many years. Now she has got a job down here starting next month I believe. So she has come down here for a bit of a holiday and to get to know the lie of the land, so to speak. I think Frank has been taking her round and introducing her to the area and some of the local farmers. He brought her here this afternoon, all apologetic like for not having brought her here before."

"So is she going to live at Wistworthy?"

"Oh no, that's just a temporary measure until she gets her own place, as I understand it."

Phil looked up from his paper and said "She seems a very nice maid, not at all pushy, knows her stuff alright, though nothing beats experience. Whether she can handle dealing with bullocks or not remains to be seen."

"Why do you say that Dad?"

"Well she's only a little slip of a thing."

"Good things come in small packages, or so you always told me," said Elaine, who was by no means a big woman. Phil laughed; he stood a good foot taller than his wife and had always called her his pocket Venus.

"I wondered if she was Frank's girl friend, some one that he knew from his Army days."

"You've been listening to those two gossipers, Sal and Edna I suppose."

"No, it was just a guess on my part and I reckon they guessed the same. After all it was a fairly obvious supposition to make. Nobody has seen much of Frank for several years, we don't know what he's been up to, he could have a wife and three kids for all I know."

"Well according to Blanche, Frank is as single as he was the day he went into the Army.

THIRTY THREE

Nancy had persuaded Giles to accompany her to the Post Office to get their papers and one or two other items. She was determined to show her face in the village, not just so that all could see that she was making good progress, but to boost her own self confidence. So with stick in hand, just in case as she said, and with Giles beside her, she had made the journey across the village green. Giles tried hard not to appear worried, which he was, as he walked beside her. He felt that Nancy was trying to run before she could walk, and in fact had said as much. But she had replied that the nurses had told her that she was to do as much as she could without over doing it. When she had asked how she would know if she were over doing it, she was told to stop when she felt strained or tired. So she had told Giles that if she got tired he would just have to carry her home, at which he had laughed and said that it would give him great pleasure so to do. As it turned out the trip was uneventful and they reached the shop without mishap. Sal Blundel was there, most solicitous in her enquiring and Nancy felt relieved to have told her of her progress. Now at any rate the rest of the village would know before lunch, though probably with a fair amount of embellishment. On the way back she sat on the seat under the chestnut tree in the middle of the green. It wasn't that she needed a rest, more that she wanted to watch the world go by. In the heart of a village there are always people coming and going, people to watch and people to talk to. Although she could have stayed in the shop and met several there it was somehow more private out in the open under the tree.

Elaine German stopped and chatted for a few minutes which reminded Nancy of how Phil had organised the search party that had found her after her fall. She asked them to come around for drinks one evening, they would check their diaries and she would contact them later that day. Then Frank came by and with talk of drinks still in her mind she asked him when he would be coming for drinks with Cathy, as they had discussed a few days earlier.

"How about tonight?" said Giles.

"That would be fine; I don't think I've got anything on, though I can't speak for Cathy. If there's any reason why we can't come I'll give you a ring before lunch."

"We look forward to seeing you; about seven o'clock be alright?"

"Yes, that will be fine, thank you. I'll see you then." And with that he was off with a cheery wave and his usual smile. Nancy and Giles continued their return and as soon as they were indoors she sought out Julian to tell him of the drinks party they had just arranged. He already had been told of the part that Frank had played in reuniting them, and was naturally looking forward to meeting him. "Who's this Cathy that he's bringing with him, is she his girl friend or what?"

"She's his cousin from Somerset; she is down here partly on holiday. She has just qualified as a vet and has landed a job locally. Frank is showing her around the area and introducing her to some of the local farmers before she takes up her position."

"Not a girl friend then, does he have one?"

"That's a difficult one to answer" said Giles "and I would rather not be the one to try. It's a long story, goes back a long way, and those of us who count Frank as a special friend wish and hope that the situation will eventually be resolved and that he will find the happiness he deserves."

"Wow Dad, you really have aroused my curiosity, tell me more."

"I can't, not now at any rate, maybe later, in a year or two. I certainly can't say anything without talking to Frank first. I'm sorry that I said anything, you'll just have to bear with me."

"What your Dad is trying to say is that there is a history of unrequited love where Frank is concerned. For a very good reason he couldn't marry the girl, not through any fault of hers, and so he went off and joined the army. The trouble is, now he's come back, and she is still in the neighbourhood. I've no idea what she feels for him, if anything, but I know that he is still very fond of her. As far as I am aware, from what his mother has told me, he has never had another girlfriend."

"My God, it sounds just like a Dickens novel or a TV soap. Does the whole village know about this? I suppose they do, it would be difficult to keep things secret in a place like this I would imagine. Ray and I have met the lovely Sal and Edna, so we do have some idea."

"No," said Giles "We are two of the few who do know and we hope to keep it that way."

"Well you can rely on us to keep it to ourselves. But I'm glad that you told us a bit about his situation, it saves us from dropping a clanger or making some silly insensitive remark."

Nancy got up from her chair and said "I must go into the kitchen, perhaps Rose can help me to make a few nibbles and vol au vents for tonight. I'll leave you men to sort out the drinks; I do so want it to be a special evening."

THIRTY FOUR

It was just after seven when Frank and Cathy arrived. Giles met them at the door and took them through to the sitting room. Not surprisingly Frank's thoughts went back to the night when Giles had asked him to help in finding Julian and had revealed the fact that he had had two sons. Realizing that this was not common knowledge Frank had not told Cathy about David until they were in the car and on their way. He had told her about Julian and Ray as he realised that they would both be introduced and felt that forewarned was forearmed. However he hadn't told her much about their recent past, as he was hoping that Julian would regale them all with tales of mine clearing in Africa.

Nancy was sitting in one of the deep armchairs and Julian was standing beside her.

"Do come in and sit down, you must be Cathy, it's nice to meet you. Frank has told us a little about you, not a lot, he's not one to gossip. This is our son Julian, recently back from Africa."

Introductions made they sat while Giles got them their drinks. Then Ray came into the room with a tray of nibbles and further introductions followed.

"Mother tells me that you have recently qualified as a vet and have a post that you are going to take up here in this area." said Julian.

"Yes, it's all very exciting, first job and all that. Frank has been showing me around the area a bit and introducing me to some of the local farmers. I don't know just how much of my work will be with farm animals, it may be mostly small domestic pets that I have to deal with."

"Have you specialised in any particular field?"

"No, not really, though I must say that if I have a preference it would be to treat the larger animals."

"So will you be staying at Wistworthy?" asked Nancy.

"No, not for ever, although it's very nice there and Auntie Blanche has made me most welcome and says that I can stay as long as I want, but I really think I ought to get a place of my own."

"I expect she's glad of a bit of female company" said Giles "Will you be hoping to buy a place out here, or nearer to town?"

"Having seen the countryside around here I'd love to find a place in this area. The trouble is that prices are rather high up here on the moor although at the moment elsewhere prices are falling. It might be wise to rent a place until I can see better what is happening in the property market."

"Prices are always high up here" said Nancy "It's because there is no more building allowed up here in the National Park; supply and demand. Then because of that, people from 'up country' with plenty of money buy anything that comes on the market. To them, no doubt the properties seem cheap. They do them up and make them even more expensive. I wouldn't mind so much but so few of them stay for more than a year or two. I know we are newcomers, but we've been here for several years now and I'm delighted to say that we've been accepted. My recent stay in hospital and the visits that I had whilst I was there showed me how kind the local people are. Yes I think I can safely say that we've been accepted."

Frank had been looking around the room and his eye rested on the picture above the fireplace. "That's a lovely picture you have there, I don't think I remember it from my last visit."

"It's a view of Lochindorb that Julian painted many years ago." said Giles proudly. "We were living near Elgin at the time, I was stationed at Lossiemouth. Nancy and the boys used to go out into the country, walking and picnicking, and Julian used to paint. Always had a good eye, you know."

"It's beautiful. Do you still paint?" Frank asked, turning to Julian. "I would imagine that there are lots of places around here to give you inspiration."

"Perhaps you could introduce Julian to some good spots," said Nancy. "After all you probably know the moor as well as anybody; you were born and raised here."

"I'd be pleased to," said Frank "but what I might think of as a good view and what Julian would like to paint would probably be totally different."

"Well for the moment it would have to be fairly close to the road, I'm still not too good on my legs yet. Hopefully in a few weeks I'll be able to go out onto the wilder parts of the moor."

"Well there are some lovely bridges around here, any of them might do.Postbridge is a bit busy with tourists at this time of year, but Bellever Bridge with the trees beside the river is pretty. Then if you want a wild, wide open place there's Whiteworks. There are old tin mining remains there, a row of cottages and the expanse of Fox Tor Mire and the Devonport Leat."

"That sounds great; I must make a note of those places. I think we'll probably just drive around a bit and stop when we see something that might make a good picture."

"Do you paint as well?" asked Cathy turning to Ray.

"No, but I would be pleased to go along because I like bird watching and I can do that while Julian does his painting. From what I've seen so far, there are lots of birds around here so I shan't get bored. In any case, the walking is so enjoyable in countryside like this that I may not even have time to look at the birds."

"There are also several reservoirs" said Frank "If you like painting expanses of water. I have a map I can let you have and I'll highlight a few places on it that might be of interest. I could drop it in tomorrow if you like."

"Thank you very much, that should start me off on the right lines so to speak."

"Did you do much painting when you were in Africa, or was that not possible?" asked Nancy

"No, somehow it didn't seem appropriate amongst all that devastation and despair. To indulge my hobby when people all around were virtually struggling to exist would be wrong. In any case, even if we had the time I had no equipment or facilities."

Then Julian and Ray told them a little about their lives in Africa and the work that they had been involved in. They were obviously passionate about it and had a way of describing everything that brought it all very much to life for those listening. For Frank who had visited other parts of the continent as a tourist it was an eye opener. The others found it totally fascinating.

"Would you give a talk in the village hall on your lives and work in Africa? I'm certain that it would be very well received. A few photos would help if you have any."

"I do have a number of photos on disc, if I can get a means of projecting them I'd be glad to show them." said Ray.

"There you are" said Giles "You have a double act ready to go, and if you wished, any profit raised could go to the charity that you were working with."

They all talked for some time about the possible show and other events that regularly took place in the village. Then Nancy said "You must come to the square dance that is going to be held next month, it is being held to celebrate the opening of our new village hall. I shall be going even though I certainly wont be fit enough to dance"

"Well if you are going, Mum, then how could I refuse."

The conversation turned to Cathy and her family and her early life in Somerset. Then seeing that it was nearly ten o'clock Frank felt that it was time to go, he was wary of making Nancy overtired. So they got up and bade their farewells promising to drop in the next day with a map for Julian. Once in the car Frank turned to Cathy and asked "Well, what did you think of them?"

"Giles and Nancy are lovely people, he's a real sweetie. As to Julian and Ray I have to admit that I was more than somewhat surprised. I suppose that I, like so many, had pre-conceived ideas about gays, and they are so unlike what I was expecting."

"In what way?"

"Well, apart from being two extremely likeable men, they just seem to be so normal. There's nothing camp or effeminate about either of them. In fact they look and seem more like a couple of rugby players."

"You've had many dealings with rugby players?" asked Frank with a grin.

"There was a strong rugby team at veterinary college, we used to go along and cheer from the touch line" said Cathy somewhat defensively. Then seeing the look on Frank's face she realised that he was only teasing her and started laughing.

"I wonder how long they are proposing to stay down here. Nancy is so obviously delighted at having them around, and with their advancing years she and Giles may soon need somebody nearby to keep an eye out for them."

"Yes, it's a problem that affects us all eventually, I suppose that that is one of the reasons that I came home to these parts. With Mum left all on her own and the farm to run, somebody had to make changes. It seemed to me that if I could make a home and a living here it would help more than just me."

"But who's going to look after you when your Mum dies? You'll be a crabbed old bachelor with just a few cows and some old rusty farm machinery." It was Cathy's turn to leg pull. "Or perhaps you have some special lady tucked away somewhere that I haven't heard about."

"I wish" said Frank with a rueful grin, his thoughts miles away. Who exactly was going to look after him after his mother died, or before that even? When would he start getting the symptoms, if at all?

"Well I am going to go to this dance next month, maybe with you and Auntie Blanche, and I shall be watching you closely to see who you pay most attention to. I can't believe that with all the talent there is around here a smart chap like you is still single" Cathy drew him back out of his contemplations.

241

"And what about you? I can't believe that a little cracker like you hasn't got an army of admirers beating a path to your door."

"Enough of the mutual admiration society, I do have a special friend from college, but I don't think that either of us is ready to make a serious commitment. We are just good friends, as they say. It may lead to something more in time and it may not. I certainly don't intend to rush into any thing."

"Very wise, on the other hand, it can be a mistake to keep your feelings hidden. If your fellow doesn't know what and how you feel for him he may think that you don't really care. Then he may go off and find someone else and you'll have missed the boat and that can be very painful."

Cathy was silent for a while, she realised that Frank had almost told her something, something to do with a relationship that he had had maybe. She wasn't sure if she should pursue it or not. Did she know Frank well enough for that? Maybe because she was not of the immediate area and his circle of acquaintances he might be able to confide in her as his mother had done, that's if he wanted to.

"I sense that there is something that you want to tell me, if there is I would be happy to listen. I wouldn't presume to give advice; I'm far too young to be an agony aunt or even an agony cousin. But sometimes it helps to talk to someone who is outside the problem so to speak."

"Thank you; you're not just a pretty face are you. I may take you up on your offer, but not just now. I have a strange feeling that something has changed or is about to change. I'm not quite sure what; I must wait a while and see if I'm right."

"Maybe you need to take your own advice and show the lady your feelings."

"Yeah, maybe I will, if I get the right opportunity."

They had arrived at Wistworhty and Frank pulled the car into the yard. There was a light on in his mother's room. Perhaps she was already in bed but Frank felt sure that she would be downstairs in her dressing gown before they got indoors. Sure enough as they entered the kitchen she was there with her usual "Will I make us all a dish of tea?"

"Thanks Mum; that would be lovely."

"Let me do it" said Cathy, "I'm sure we didn't mean to get you up out of bed again."

They sat for a while in the friendly warmth of the old kitchen, drinking their tea and talking about the evening they had had and the people that they had shared it with.

Eventually they went up to bed and Frank lay for a long while thinking about Linda; not an unusual occurrence. He felt sure that it would not be right to tell her of his feelings for her, at any rate not just yet. But there had been something about her manner the other day that made him think that she wanted to say something to him. Of course it might have been to tell him to leave her alone, that she was married and out of bounds, which was the very reason why he had kept his feelings to himself. But her manner hadn't been cold or aloof. Far from it, she had been warm but almost nervous, and she had blushed like an embarrassed schoolgirl when she had given him the keys to the car.

Then there was what Jim had said to him about Eric. Was he really playing away as Jim put it? Just because he spent a lot of time after school hours helping with activities and things didn't necessarily mean that he was having an affair. Even if he was it wouldn't mean that Linda was free. She could well love Eric and be prepared to fight to win him back. The last thing that he wanted to do was to split up a happy marriage, or for it to be thought that he had done so.

And still in the back of his mind was the fear that he might have inherited his father's disease. If so it would be totally wrong for him to father children or to subject a wife to looking after him through an awful and early death.

"Let's hope Mum is right and things do have a way of sorting themselves out, maybe they will look better in the morning." And with that thought he drifted off into sleep.

He awoke with a start at half past two, he had been dreaming though he had no idea what had awoken him. However he was, in a way, glad because the dream had been unsettling. In it he had gone to see Linda on Cathy's advice. In fact she had gone with him. When he knocked on her door instead of Linda his father had opened it saying. "Why are you here and what's she doing with you?"

244

"I've come to speak to Linda, I want to explain things if I can. I want to tell her how I feel."

"Well you'd better come in, but I don't think it will do you any good."

They had gone through into the kitchen, except that it wasn't Linda's kitchen but their own one at Wistworthy. Linda was there with Beatie. They were standing over a pram and cooing over the contents.

"Look Frank, look at Linda's lovely baby" said Beatie.

Frank had gone over to look but instead of a baby he saw a cow's head on the pillow in the pram.

Then for some reason they were all out in the yard and Cathy was pushing the pram out of the gate saying "Well if you don't want this baby I'm going to keep it, it's just what my boy friend always wanted."

Frank had gone to run after her but his father had stopped him saying
"It's no good son, they would never let you keep a baby in the army, it's against Queen's Regulations I don't doubt."

"But whose baby is it? I thought Eric couldn't, you know…."

"It's a wise child that knows his father" this from his mother who had suddenly appeared. Then "I'll make us all a dish of tea."

It was at that point that Frank had woken up and he lay thinking about the dream for a while. Where on earth did these strange thoughts come from and was there any credibility that he should attach to them? He doubted it, he had never been one for that sort of thing, was scornful of star signs and the like. Nevertheless it had upset him and caused him to think a bit. So it was quite a while before he managed to get off to sleep again.

THIRTY FIVE

It was two days after the drinks party and Julian was sitting on the bank of Burrator Reservoir busy painting the scene before him. It was a day of sun and cloud with a light breeze blowing. Parts of the lake were rippled by the wind, yet where the water was sheltered and still the reflection of Leather Tor and Sharp Tor was like a mirror image, clear and crisp. Across the tors that were the backdrop of the picture, the shadows made by the clouds formed ever moving patterns of dark and light. Julian was engrossed in his work, revelling in the view, the fresh air and the sights and sounds around him. The light was perfect, the colours vibrant, so many different shades of green and brown and purple. The sky a cool light blue with the soft white clouds, so different it seemed from the brassy, burning hot skies of Africa. He and Ray had driven around looking at some of the sites earmarked on the map that Frank had given them. Bellever Bridge had attracted them with the old partially complete clapper bridge and the tall fir trees beside the river. But there were workmen doing something to the stones beside the road so they left, hoping that perhaps another day would be better.

Ray was off somewhere with his camera and binoculars looking for birds and any thing else that might interest him. He was gone for some time, climbing through the arboretum and up onto Sheeps Tor. At one point he was delighted to see a mother wren taking her brood of fledglings on their first outing. She would fly a distance of two or three paces and then call to them to follow. One after another, with a certain amount of hesitation, they would take off and follow her to her next perch. Then off she would go again, calling to them to follow. It was amazing how loud a voice such a small creature had, but as Ray reflected, the same could often be said of small people. Beyond the tor he found a fascinating collection of four concentric stone circles. He found it difficult to photograph them because he couldn't get high enough to see the effect of the rings properly. When he returned he stood behind Julian for a while looking at the image on the easel.

"You've captured that beautifully. I am constantly amazed at the way you are able to get the atmosphere of the place on canvas."

"I think it needs a bit more work on it but I can do that when we get back. My back's aching from sitting on this stool; I shall have to get something better, something with a bit more support."

"You liked the scene then?"

"Yes, in a way it reminded me of Scotland, the water and the trees and the hills beyond. It's not as majestic as Scotland but it has a wild charm and it's so accessible which helps. I want to get out off the road a bit further and into the heart of the moor. It's the wild beauty of this country that I feel myself drawn to."

"Drawn in what way, as a person or as an artist?"

"Both I think, I feel curiously at home here, even I might say at peace. I think I'd go so far as to say that I'd like to stay here, live here I mean. I know that it's early days and I mustn't let my heart rule my head too much, but I really think that I'm falling in love with this place."

"Good, because I've been feeling the same and I've been thinking a lot about it while I was walking. I didn't really want to say anything because I didn't want to influence you. You have your parents to think about and consideration of them must be influence enough. But I do feel that I could settle here, we've been accepted, whole heartedly it seems, and especially by your parents. That must be a great joy to you after all the years apart. They are a lovely couple. I don't know why I should be surprised at that, after all they created you and I've loved you for years, ever since that first day in Sick Quarters."

"Well I'm glad you feel that way too, I didn't want to pressure you either After all you have family living in another part of the country and you might well have wanted to live closer to them."

"Oh, they're not that far away. As I see it there's nothing to stop us living here, I'm sure we can make a living here. I could go back into nursing and you could paint and maybe run art classes for those who want to walk on the moor

249

and take back a more personal memento of their visit."

"I think we ought to look for a place of our own though. Although it's very nice living with my parents it could be a bit stifling. Mum I know would love it if we were to stay with her for ever, but even though the house is big enough we would be tripping over one another in no time. No it would be better if we were in our own place not too far away. That way we can keep an eye on them, surreptitiously so to speak, and later when they can no longer manage living on their own maybe we would move in. What do you think?"

"It sounds fine to me, I have no idea how easy it is around here to rent a place, we'll have to start looking. I just hope that Cathy isn't after the same place as we are."

"That could be a problem, she's a nice kid, I was pleased to meet her and Frank. He's a great guy, a real down to earth, honest country man. I look forward to walking with him; we could learn a whole lot about this area from him."

"What about this dance, are you going to be up for it?"

"I am certainly going to give it a try; my injuries are feeling less of a problem every day. As to our relationship, it's a square dance, you don't have to have a partner necessarily, there's bound to be girls like Cathy there who are unattended."

"Even so, I doubt if this village is quite ready for us to be seen dancing the last waltz together."

"No" said Julian with a laugh "I think perhaps you're right there, we'll just have to wait and have the last waltz when we get home."

Still laughing they packed up their things and drove back across the moor to the village that they hoped would soon be their new permanent home. For a couple who had been living out of kitbags for almost all of their lives together, the thought of settling down in a permanent home was somewhat strange, even a little frightening and yet appealing.

How things had changed in the last few months, and all because a little dog had chased a mother duck and her brood of ducklings.

THIRTY SIX

Beatie was in the kitchen preparing the evening meal for her parents and herself. She enjoyed cooking, it was, she found, a good way to wind down after a day on the wards. Tonight's dish was to be a simple fish pie with a mashed potato topping with fresh vegetables from the garden. She had just put the pie in the oven when there was a knock on the door. It was Jim who had come round with some catalogues for Phil. He left them on the small table in the hall and followed Beatie into the kitchen.

"Are Linda and Eric away on holiday or something? I passed there last night and there were no lights on and no cars to be seen. Then as I came by just now there was a magazine or something sticking out of the letter box. I stopped and went in to see what was up. There was nobody about, so I pushed the magazine through so that it didn't show. It was a bit naughty of the postman to leave it sticking out like that, makes the place look unattended, an invitation to burglars. I had a quick look around the back, calling out as I went; nobody there that I could see so I presumed that they must be away. I thought that you would be bound to know, so as I had to come here I thought that I'd ask."

"Linda's gone away for two weeks to stay with her sister Marnie who's just had a baby. She's been away for over a week now, I'm going over to see her again tomorrow. I'll tell her what you said about the house looking deserted."

"Is Eric with her?"

"No, she went on her own, he would only have been in the way, it's not a very big place y' know."

"Well he was out last night when I passed."

"You know Eric, probably engaged in some after school activity or other, he's often late home."

"After school activity or a bit of overtime, nothing would surprise me where Eric's concerned. I should think it might have been a school trip away for a night or two, his car wasn't there this morning when I passed and I was middling early today."

"Well I really wouldn't know" said Beatie. "All I know is that Linda is in with her sister and she should be coming back in two or three days."

"Tell her I'll keep an eye on the place, I'm passing there most days, quite often twice a day."

"Thanks, I'll tell her, I'm sure she'll be glad to know that."

"Bye then, I'm off for my tea. The smell of your cooking is great, I don't know what it is, but it has certainly sharpened my appetite."

Beatie turned back to her preparations, her head in a whirl. Jim had obviously sensed something or maybe he even knew something. That comment of his about 'a bit of overtime'. She knew full well what he was alluding to. It wasn't the first time that he had suggested that Eric was being unfaithful. She knew that Linda didn't want their split to be public knowledge until she was ready, but perhaps it would be no bad thing if it were out in the open whilst she was away at Marnie's. That way maybe most of the gossiping would have died down by the time she came home. Whatever happened there was going to be talk around the village because it would seem to most people to be so unexpected. But give it a week and they would have found something or someone else to gossip about, it would be just a nine day wonder like so many other incidents.

Well, she was going in to see Linda tomorrow, she would tell her what Jim had said, his suspicions about Eric and about the house looking empty, and maybe even suggest that Linda ought to tell all now. It was bound to be difficult, people would take sides. Some would blame her and others would feel sorry for her and all would talk about her and Eric and make up their own theories as to what had gone wrong.

"I wish I were on duty tonight, I wouldn't have time to think about this all night which is what I'm probably going to do now."

The next morning Beatie was up late. She had hardly slept at all until the early hours and was feeling like death warmed up. Still, after a shower and a cup of coffee and some toast she felt a little better and set off to town to see Linda.

Marnie and the new baby were asleep, they still hadn't decided on a name for her, so Linda had put the toddler, a boy called Joe, in his push chair and they all set off down the road to the park. There were swings and a slide and a sort of see saw for children to play on. Few people were there apart from them. Beatie and Linda sat on a bench while Joe obligingly played on the grass. His new game was to fetch a ball, if it was thrown for him, and return it to be thrown again, rather like a dog would play. At any rate it gave the girls a chance to talk which was what Beatie was dying to do.

"Jim was round last night. I think he knows or has guessed. He sees that the house is empty and, bless his heart, is worried that someone might break in so he's going to keep an eye on it for you." She proceeded to tell Linda all that had been said the evening before. "Would it be such a bad thing to let every body know what has happened now, while you are here, away from all the gossip? Then by the time you do have to face them it will be old news and there won't be so much whispering behind their hands every time people see you. In any case Eric is the one they will have their knives into surely, after all he's the one that's gone off and 'committed adultery'."

"I don't think that that will make much difference, there are bound to be those who think that I drove him away, drove him into the arms of another woman. You know as well as I do how some of the men in the village think, no man can ever be wrong. It's always the woman's fault; she's always got a headache or some such nonsense as that."

"Don't be so negative Linda; people aren't as daft as that, in any case Eric has admitted it was all down to him. If he was honest enough to say as much to you, there's no reason why he shouldn't say so to the rest of the village."

"It's not just what other people think; it's what I think that hurts. He has left me, I let him down; I was no good as a wife; a failure who obviously couldn't satisfy him properly."

"Don't be ridiculous, you were a wonderful wife. I remember you telling me, in one of your unguarded moments, what a good sex life you had. Don't tell me that was all talk; that you were lying to me. It certainly didn't sound like it at the time. And all that time when he was on the booze and you stood by him and did every thing to help him to beat his demons, as he called them. No no no, you've got nothing to reproach yourself for."

"That's not what he thinks, otherwise why would he have felt the need to go elsewhere for love or sex or whatever it was that he wanted? OK, so he admitted that he was at fault, it still doesn't make me feel any better. He's still gone and the house is empty. We may not have had a perfect marriage, not much of a marriage at all, but I wasn't completely alone. I am now."

She started crying, quietly at first and then with heart rending sobs. All the emotions that had been pent up inside her for the past few days came flooding out. Beatie let her sob; she realized that this was the best way that Linda would get rid of some of the pain. She remembered how when she was younger, her kitten had died, been run over by a passing car, and she had almost been afraid to cry. She was fourteen at the time and probably felt that she was too old for that sort of emotional display. Her mother had said to her, 'don't be ashamed to cry, it's nature's way of washing away the pain'. So she put her arm around Linda and said nothing, just pulled her towards her, put her head against hers and kissed her on the cheek several times.

Little Joe had no idea of what was going on but he knew that people who cried were sad and when he was sad he liked to have a cuddle. So he toddled over to Linda and put his arms around her legs, it was all that he could reach, and his head on her lap.

"You're not alone, you've got me and lots and lots of good friends, and look, little Joe is trying to comfort you."

"Yeah, I know, I've got a lot to be thankful for, a lot to thank you for too."

They stood up and started walking back to the house, Joe valiantly trying to push his push chair. When they got to the house they had a cup of tea and after a long silence Linda said "Alright then, you tell them what has happened, but don't slag Eric off, I don't hate him and I don't want everybody hating him either. I leave it to you how to do it and then when I come back, in three days time, hopefully the dust will have settled a bit."

"You'll get over it Gal, you are stronger than you may think. I've never mentioned this to you or any one else for that matter, but I know a bit about affairs. I know it from the other side so to speak."

"Why, what d'you mean?"

"I had a fling for nearly eighteen months with a doctor at the hospital; a married one. It was wonderful and exciting, probably because it was dangerous and wrong and we were afraid of getting caught. Of course he was never going to leave his wife; they never do, although of course he said that he would. Then I saw her one day, she looked absolutely gorgeous, or she had been. There were lines of old age on her face, a young face too. I asked another of the nurses who she was and she told me. She also told me that she had a serious drink problem, brought on because her husband was having an affair. That was all I needed, I dumped him right away. He stayed with her, helped her a bit with her drink problem and everybody thought he was a hero. Now I understand he's having a fling with another doctor. He's a right shit, but still every one seems to think he's wonderful. There's no justice. So don't worry about Eric, he'll come out of this alright don't you worry, you just concentrate on yourself."

"My, you are a dark horse. Who would have thought it, you having an affair? I never even knew you to have ever had a steady boyfriend. In fact, there was a time when I thought you were on the other bus."

"What, me a lesbian! No way, I like men, it's just that I've never managed to find one I have really liked who isn't already taken, and the longer time goes on, the less good my chances are going to be. Any way I must be going, I've got lots to do, spreading the news. I think the first people I must tell are Pippa and Jim. He'll say 'I told you so'

I've no doubt. Then I had better tell Mum and Dad and then hopefully they will tell the rest of the village quietly and discreetly. Dad's pretty good at that sort of thing. Mind, once Sal and Edna get their teeth into it look out. I once heard Edna say that she never spread any gossip; it was the people that she told who did the spreading. And she believed it too."

She got up and kissed her friend. "Give my love to Marnie, I'll see her another day."

"Bye then, thanks for everything, I'll see you at home in three days time."

THIRTY SEVEN

Beatie didn't go straight home, as she left town it occurred to her that Jim's place of work was not that far away. So on impulse she turned and drove over to see him. The yard was busy, farmers' land rovers and trailers being loaded up with feed stuffs and wire netting and the like. A group of women were discussing the merits and otherwise of some bedding plants that were on sale near to the door. A large woman smelling of horses and carrying a big bag barged out past her, nearly knocking her down. A gruff 'sorry' and she was gone, striding over to her muddy old four by four. Why did everybody have to be in such a hurry these days? She strolled into the shop, which was even busier inside than it was outside, and had a look around. When she saw someone wearing a sweatshirt with the company logo doing nothing, she asked if it would be possible to speak to Jim Blundel.

"I'm afraid you can't today, he's out on a visit somewhere, is there anything I can do?"

"No thank you, I'll catch up with him later, it wasn't important."

Out into the car again; well it had been an impulse, she was sure that she would find him at home tonight. If he wasn't there she would tell

Pippa, which might even be better, it might be easier girl to girl. She and her sister had fought like cat and dog when they were small, but as soon as they were both in secondary school things had changed and they had become really close friends. There were few things that they didn't share; clothes, make up, books, records and best of all confidences. Things had changed again slightly when she and Jim had got married, but that was only to be expected, they were no longer living under the same roof.

She had never told Pippa about her affair with the doctor, they had often discussed boy friends but that was different. She felt sure that her sister would disapprove, probably because she herself would have disapproved if it had been the other way round, Guilt can be a funny thing, she thought. Some people were more affected by it than others. Any time that she was with her lover she felt that it was alright and that she was doing no wrong. It wasn't just that passion took over, he was a good and generous lover, but also he made her feel special and wanted. And he gave the impression that his marriage was over by mutual consent. But then as soon as she left him and went home to friends and family she felt guilty, even dirty. Many a time she said to herself, 'that's it, no more, I'm not going to see him again, I'm going to break it off.' But she didn't, it took the shock of seeing his wife and the state that she was in to finally bring her to her senses. Then she was so glad that it was over, all the secrecy, the lies, the pretending. The most difficult thing had been

261

trying to be in two places at once, impossible really. Pretending she was at work or somewhere when in reality she was with him. More than once she had nearly been caught out, it was too easy to say the wrong thing, especially as to her whereabouts.

Did Eric feel any sense of guilt, she wondered. The affair had been going on for quite some time, since before Christmas according to Linda. It had probably been a lot longer than that if she knew anything about men and affairs. He must have fallen out of love with Linda to be able to start an affair. He couldn't have fallen in love with this other woman and still have been in love with Linda. Maybe he had never truly loved her. She felt sure that Linda really only loved Frank, always had done and always would do. Eric was only second best, and maybe he had realised that, and that was why he had looked elsewhere. Without either of them realising it, Frank coming back had just been the final straw. Linda's thoughts had been of him, she hadn't been over bothered at Eric's absences in the evenings, and he had probably felt unwanted. It was impossible to apportion blame solely to either one of them, if she were honest they were both guilty, they were just not really suited.

Once she had reached the moor she pulled the car into a lay-by to stop and think some more. She felt desperately sorry for Linda; she could understand that her confidence had been badly knocked. It must have made her feel a failure and unwanted, unwanted by others, not just Eric. She had done her best to reassure her, to tell her that all her friends loved her and would stand by her. She hoped that she had got through to her. Towards the end of their talk it did seem as though she might have. But what she couldn't say, though she badly wanted to, was that Eric's leaving was possibly the best thing that could have happened to her. Now the way was open for her and Frank wasn't it? She remembered only too well the conversation in her cottage that night. Remembered too, how strongly Linda obviously felt for Frank, now that he had come back to live in the area, and how her gut feeling told her that he felt the same way about her. But it was far too early to mention that, even though they had talked about her problems with Eric some time ago when he was paying her no attention. Could she persuade Linda to come to the dance with her? The rumours and speculation should have died down by then, and she would be able to show her face to the world, show that she was OK.

She sat for a while longer, looking at the wonderful view of Dartmoor, the familiar row of hills and tors. The best view in England her dad used to call it, it certainly was pretty good. There was permanence, a reliability about it. Looking at it she realised, not for the first time, that her problems and those of her friend would be forgotten in a very short while. Next year they would be sitting drinking a glass of wine together, laughing and wondering what all the fuss had been about. She started up the car and drove down through the village and on home.

Once indoors she went straight upstairs to her room and then took a shower and changed. Suitably refreshed she went down to the kitchen and made a pot of tea for her parents and herself. It was odd that she felt nervous about telling them about Linda; it was almost as though it was she that was having the problem. Such is friendship.

"Mum, Dad, I have some news for you, sad news. Eric is leaving Linda; he's been having an affair with a woman from over Chagford way."

"Oh no, how awful, poor Linda, how long has this been going on?" Elaine put down her cup and went over to sit beside her daughter, only too well aware of the close bond that existed between her and her friend.

"She must be devastated, poor thing. Well we'll do every thing we can to help, wont we Phil? She would be more than welcome to come and stay here for a while if she would like to."

"Who is this woman, do we know her, does Linda know?"

"She's Sheila Caunter, a teacher I believe."

"I knew her parents, had a small farm somewhere between Chagford and Gidleigh I think. Nice people, from what I can remember of them."

"Well as you know Linda is over with her sister Marnie helping with the new baby. Marnie's husband will be home in a day or two for three weeks, so Linda will be coming home then. I felt that it might be best if the news about Eric were out, so to speak while she was still away. Linda agreed and asked me to tell a few people, particularly you and Jim and Pippa of course."

"Yes of course; it'll be a nine day wonder, these things always are as far as those outside are concerned. It'll be something that lasts a good deal longer for Linda no doubt."

"She doesn't want people bad mouthing Eric, I think she feels that it can't have been entirely his fault. She obviously feels guilty and is racking her brains trying to see where she went wrong. I kept telling her that she mustn't blame herself, these things happen."

"Well she can count on our support in what ever way she wants," said Elaine.

"Well I'm off to tell Jim and Pippa now; I'll leave it to you to tell your friends."

She walked over to her sister's, it was a lovely late afternoon the lanes were full of scent from the honeysuckle and the yarrow. A tractor was purring away in the distance and down the road a pair of riders came clip clopping towards her, a perfectly normal scene.

She didn't beat about the bush, after a few pleasantries and the expected questions about Marnie's baby she told them both about Eric. Contrary to her expectations Jim didn't say 'I told you so'. In fact he was very quiet and left it to the girls to voice their opinions. It was Pippa who finally said

"Jim told me several weeks ago that he had seen them together at Hatherleigh market."

"Really Jim, why didn't you say?"

"What could I have said, and what good would it have done? We talked about it and decided that the only person we could tell was you and that would be just passing the buck. We didn't think that that would be fair to you. Besides, we didn't know any details, the only evidence that we had was just one sighting by me and what my friend Graham had told me. We felt that it would be best if we left it and waited until we knew more definite details. After all it could have been something perfectly innocent."

"Yeah, like what. You had often said that you thought he was playing away, you were right all along."

"Maybe so Beatie, but that doesn't alter the fact that their marriage is over and Linda has been hurt. What we need to do is help her and support her. You say that she has decided that she wants it known now while she's away, well I'll see to it don't you worry."

"If Sal and Edna get hold of it, it will be all round the parish in a matter of hours, if not minutes. God knows what gory details they will add to make it sound better."

"Don't worry, I'll tell Uncle Charlie, he'll see to it."

THIRTY EIGHT

And so it was that two days later Edna called on Sal saying excitedly "Have you heard about Eric leaving Linda? I bet there's some juicy information there that we've missed, what d'you think?"

"What ever it is, we know nothing and we say nothing."

"Why, what's got into you Sal, it's not like you to turn down the chance of a good gossip?"

"Never mind about that, Linda's a nice maid, and this is one occasion when we keep quiet. It's for the best; you take my word for, it OK?"

"Well if you say so, you've lived here longer than I, you know these people better than I do."

Jim had obviously been right to tell Charlie.

Elaine had told Blanche; she had made a point of going up to Wistworthy and was rather glad to find that Frank was not at home at the time. She knew a little of the history from Phil and knew that Blanche would be the best one to tell Frank.

"It's going to be a bit difficult knowing what to say the first time we see her. The last thing we want is to have to tip-toe around her, take out our words and look at them first."

"The easiest way to do it is to act as though it happened a month or more ago; as though we've known for ages and its old news" said Blanche. "That way we don't need to talk about it at all, unless she wants to and then its she that brings up the subject."

THIRTY NINE

Linda came home to an empty house; it even had the smell of a house that had been unoccupied for several days, a sort of hot stale smell. Every where was tidy, the dishes had been washed and put away; even the ironing in the flasket had been done. Probably, thought Linda, because he needed the clothes to take with him. There was an envelope on the table and inside was a letter;

'I have taken all my clothes and personal things. Also the CD's that I think were mine and the two pictures that the boys at school gave me. If I have left anything behind that you don't want let me know and I'll come and collect it.
If you want a divorce, and I've no doubt that you will, I won't contest it, also if there is any cost involved I will be happy to cover it. It is my fault, mine alone. Though I am no longer in love with you and probably haven't been for some time, I still care about you and your wellbeing.
I am truly sorry that I am putting you through all this pain.
Love   Eric'

She read it through twice and still she felt nothing, just a sort of numbness. Perhaps she was all cried out, all emotion gone. She walked through into the sitting room; all was just as tidy there. Her eyes came to rest on the picture of them on their wedding day, they both looked so happy then, their plans for wonderful future ahead of them. That did it, that brought it all back again and she burst into tears, sobs racking her body. She threw herself into an armchair and cried for several minutes. Not for Eric or for losing him, she was almost used to the idea of that by now, but for herself. That's all there was now, just herself to think of and care about. She went up into the bedroom and like Eric had done two weeks before, she sat on the bed and thought briefly about their past together. Then jumping to her feet she said out loud "This wont do, its no good looking back any more, I've got to get on with my life, my new life. I have got to be strong, brave, brave enough to meet people without worrying. But first of all I'm going to make myself a nice cup of tea, and then I must stop talking aloud to myself." And with that she went downstairs, put on the kettle and phoned Beatie.

FORTY

Grace was quite excited as she entered the hostel. She was going to meet Tracy's young man Jeff for the first time. More to the point, she had what she felt sure was good news for them. She had found a job with accommodation that she felt would suit them perfectly. They were in the rather crowded, smoke filled day room, sitting on a small wooden-armed settee. Tracy jumped up when she saw Grace and running and hopping over to her, as best as her nearly healed ankle would allow, introduced them saying "This is my Jeff, Mrs Russel."

Jeff appeared to be a smart enough young man, clean shaven, about twenty five with long hair pulled back and tied in a pony-tail. All around it seemed were sad-looking young mothers chattering away to each other and crying babies

It was a lovely sunny day and Tracy suggested that they went out for a walk in the nearby park where they would be able to talk. Grace was glad to get them and herself out from the depressing atmosphere of the room.

"Now" she said, thrusting her face up under Jeff's chin, "I think I may have found just the thing for you two youngsters. There's a job for you Jeff and part-time work for you Tracy with accommodation. That is in a small annex off the main house. Kitchen, living room bathroom and two bedrooms; well one bedroom and a box room would probably be more correct. It may not be exactly what you would like, but it's a start. It's in a nice friendly village out on the moor near to where I live." She went on to describe the village and some of the activities there that might be of interest to them. To her surprise and Tracy's also Jeff flatly turned down the idea.

"What's up with you Jeff? You always said that you liked it up on the moor, and that you always wanted to live up there. Well now's your chance, so what's wrong?"

"Nothing wrong with going to live on Dartmoor, it's just that village; I don't think that I could live there."

"Why ever not?" said Grace "I'm sure that you and Tracy would be most welcome and would settle in in no time."

"I'm not so sure" said Jeff "I think I've been there and if I'm right I may not be welcome back, to say the least."

"Why, wha've you done, wha've you been up to?" said Tracy turning on her man with her eyes blazing. "Have you been in trouble again and not told me about it?"

Jeff looked a bit sheepish and kicked the ground with his toe, just like a two year old would do. "Well I dunno if I can say really, fact is I dunno if 'twas my fault or not, see"

"What ever are you talking a bout Jeff, have you been breaking the law or something?" said Grace

272

"Promise you wont say anything, cos if 'twas down to me I certainly didn't mean it."

"Well I don't know that I can promise, but if you have done something silly it may be that we can help you."

"I stayed in your village a few weeks back; least from what you've been saying I think it was your village. You were having a jumble sale in the hall at the time. I slept in the toilets of the hall that night, broke in and kipped down on a load of old boxes on the floor. I was woke up at about three o'clock, the whole place was on fire, so I just scarpered out the window and ran away. I don't know if the fire was caused by me or something that I had done, but I heard on the news later that the fire had totally destroyed the village hall. So I doubt if I would be welcome back there, see? That's why I can't take the job."

"Oh is that it, well I think I can set your mind at rest there. The villagers may have lost their old wooden hall but they now have a much better one in the old school building. In fact some might say that you did them a favour, that's if it was you that started the fire. They said at the time that it was caused by an electrical fault. Anyway, I'm not going to say to anybody that you were there at the time; it would serve no useful purpose so to do. As far as I am concerned the matter is over and shall never be mentioned again."

"There see Jeff, there's no reason why we can't take the job, it would be a wonderful chance for us and the baby to have a new beginning in the country side. Say yes, go on, please."

273

"Oh alright Tracy, we'll take a look at it, and thank you for all your help and understanding Mrs Russel. You're a real diamond, to give up your time and help us like this, there's not many would have done so."

"Not at all Jeff, it's been a real pleasure to have been able to help you and Tracy in this small way. If you would like we could go up there now in my little car and you could then meet your prospective employers and possibly have a look round."

"That would be brill, wouldn't it Jeff?"

And so it was that a few days later Jeff and Tracy moved into the annex of the big guest house that Jeff had passed as he walked around the village looking for somewhere to sleep all those weeks ago.

FORTY ONE

Phil and Elaine were sitting in Giles and Nancy's sitting room enjoying a drink and discussing the forthcoming square dance. It was due to be held in three week's time and would celebrate the opening of the School Hall.

"I wish that we could give Sir Harold something, a small gift, a token of our appreciation and gratitude for all that he has done for this village." said Phil.

"Its very difficult to know what to give to a man who has, quite obviously, got all that he needs and probably ever will need." said Elaine.

"There's always something" said Nancy "Some little thing, it doesn't have to be big or vastly expensive to be meaningful."

"Have you been up to his place much?" asked Phil. "Can you remember what he has in his house; it might just give you some idea as to what he likes, ornaments, pictures whatever?"

"He's got some fine pictures up there" said Giles "I can't claim to be an expert on art, but there are definitely a couple of lovely moorland scenes by Widgery and other paintings of this area."

Rose, who had come in at that moment with a tray of goodies to go with the drinks said, "Why don't you give him a painting then?"

"Yes, but what painting and by whom, there are so many Dartmoor artists, and it would have to be a print. Suppose we got one that he already owns?"

"Yes Giles, and he probably would have the original."

"Get your son Julian to paint one" sad Rose "He's brilliant. That way it would be really special and an original too."

"We would have to pay him of course, we couldn't expect him to do it for nothing." said Phil. "That is if he's prepared to do it."

"Well you only have to ask him, I expect he would be flattered to be asked and would love to do it for you." said Rose.

"Do you have any particular location in mind?" said Nancy.

"Yes I do, I think I know what could be just the spot. I could take Julian there and if he could and would be prepared to do it, I think it might be just the thing. If you like I'll have a word with Julian; we might even go there tomorrow, if the weather is right."

"Have you any recollection of the paintings in Sir Harold's house Rose?" This from Elaine who had been sitting quietly, listening.

"Oh I think so, I was in and out of the house quite a lot when Jane was ill."

"Of course yes," said Giles "I was forgetting that. Well that's settled then, we've got three weeks until the dance, let's hope that we can get it all done in time."

"Do you think we should have an alternative plan in case Julian can't or won't oblige?" asked Elaine.

"I trust Rose's powers of persuasion to pull it off. You are quite confident aren't you?" said Giles turning to Rose.

"I will be very surprised if he doesn't say yes" said Rose.

FORTY TWO

So it was that a couple of days later Rose took Julian down the lane to the area that she had been thinking of. They had to walk a little way but he was a lot stronger now and said that he would happily have walked twice the distance. Beside them was a small stream, and almost hidden by the willow and alder trees that grew along the banks, was a delightful little clapper bridge

"Go out onto that bridge and sit for a moment. I want to do just a quick sketch or two with you on it.

She went and sat on the bridge, her legs crossed, her elbows resting on her knees with her face cupped in her hands gazing into the water.

"Great" he said, "You make a fabulous model."

A few minutes later she rejoined him to see four quick pencil drawings, two of her head and shoulders, one of the bridge and one larger sketch of the whole scene. It was astonishing how much he had captured in just a few lines.

They went on another hundred yards or so and then she sat him near the river, with the trees to his right on the opposite bank, looking downstream across the meadow to the tor beyond.

"What d'you think?" she said "D'you like it? Will it make a good picture?"

"It's great" he said, "I love it."

"I'd like you to do something else for me, something special. It will require a bit of imagination, OK?"

"Fire away, at worst I can only say no."

"Well, you see that big rock over there at the base of the hill. Can you put three figures there around a fire, having a picnic?"

"Yes I should think I can. It's a good idea, it will tell a story, help to bring it to life and that's always good. You'll have to go over and sit or crouch, or stand as though bending over a fire. It's just so I can get some idea of scale, proportion and perspective."

Rose went over to the spot and stood as though tending to a pot on the fire. Then turning towards him, she sat cross legged for a while. Then she sat with her back to him, half-kneeling with her legs to her left and her weight partly supported on her right arm. After few minutes she went back and looked at the few sketches that Julian had done.

"That's great; I'll leave you now, if that's OK by you. I'm going for a walk I'll be back in about two hours. You have every thing that you need, have you?"

"Yes thanks, I'm fine, I'll see you later."

Julian was in his element, the light was perfect, there had been a shower before lunch but now all was clear. The clear afternoon sunlight threw interesting shadows and put a golden glow on the meadow. At the base of the hill the bracken was a deep dark green with the odd patch of russet where a frond or two had already turned. Above it the bell heather was a rich purple with an odd splash of bright yellow from the autumn gorse. To his right a small stunted thorn tree beside the river gave foreground interest, while to the left at the far side of the meadow was a rowan tree, its berries still not yet quite ripe.

Rose set off and walked down the river towards Dartmeet. She passed above the restaurant and the little bungalow and walked up the hill, crossing the road after a while. The bracken was tall and the scent of it was hot and summery. The path was steep and she was glad to sit for a while on the 'coffin stone' where so many others had paused and set down their tragic burden to rest as they struggled up the long hill. Butterflies were every where and there were crickets singing in the grass all around. Once over the brow of the hill she turned left and made her way up through the heather and gorse covered slope of the tor to the rocks on the top. She sat there for a while drinking in the scene, enjoying the feel of the sun on her back and thinking of that day many years before.

It was a good bit more than two hours later when she returned. The weather was warm with only a few small clouds in the sky, so very like the day when she had last been there, it was uncanny. She called out to Julian as she approached, she was unsure as to whether he would want her to see the painting just then. He might prefer to take it home and put some finishing touches to it first. But he sat back with the picture open for her to see.

She was staggered, amazed, the light was perfect, the whole scene was perfect. Instantly she was transported back in time. The figures, though they were in the middle distance and in no great detail, had life and movement. Three girls around a fire; a little wisp of smoke, hardly visible rising in the warm air. Whilst the shadows from the trees fell across the water and gave it interesting patches of light and dark, warm and cool. It was a truly fabulous picture.

"Just one thing" she said "and this isn't meant as a criticism in any way, you've done a wonderful job. It's the girl standing, bending over the fire; could you give her a short, faded blue dress?"

"Yes, of course I can." And taking his brushes with a few deft strokes he did as she asked.

"That's it, its perfect, oh Julian …."

She was crying now, unable to speak so filled with emotion.

"It's not that bad is it?" he said, trying to lighten the mood a little.

"No, it's beautiful, absolutely beautiful, thank you so much. Sir Harold will love it I know."

"Although I understand it's supposed to be a gift from the people of the village, I don't think that it's a gift from them at all."

"No?"

"No, this is a gift from you, a very personal gift I think. Am I right?"

"Yes, but please don't tell the others. There are special memories attached to this place, special to Harold."

"And you, if I'm not mistaken."

Rose said nothing; she stood looking at the scene that he had just painted so beautifully. It was incredible how vividly he had depicted that moment from her youth and brought so many memories flooding back. She dried her eyes and turned to help him as he packed up his things. As they walked to the car he said "Its alright, your secret is safe with me. Just one more thing though, does it have a title?"

"Yes, but it must be put on the back."

"OK, what is it then?"

"Trout for tea."

FORTY THREE

It was a beautiful morning, one of those mornings when it felt totally wrong to stay in bed. Linda was up early, out through the lanes and up onto the open moor by half past six. For the first time in several days she felt alive and happy with herself again.

"This is the first day of my new life," she said to herself striding along with a spring in her step, "Eric and the old life are gone and I can start over again. I'm a young woman in good health with a good business and good friends. I have no worries financially, a roof over my head and food in the larder, what do I care."

There had been quite a heavy dew and all around the low early sunlight was causing each dew drop to sparkle like a rainbow; particularly eye catching were those on the gossamer spider's webs on the gorse bushes, the colours making them look like Catherine wheels. She kept to a wide path where the grass was short and less likely to get her boots soaking wet. Then taking a sheep track she climbed up to the rocks on the top, where she sat and looked around. Each valley had a layer of mist filling it, giving the tors the look of islands rising out of a light grey sea, but it was a mist that was soon gone as the heat from the sun became stronger. Purple grey horizons stretched away one after another to the edge of the moor. Nearby on the next ridge, overlooking the head of the Redacre Brook, she could just make out the flat rock that Frank used to call 'the curlew rock'. They had often sat there watching and listening to the birds as they talked. Teenagers' talk of likes and dislikes; hopes and dreams of what they might do in their future lives. It was always so peaceful up there, their own special place which though out in the open still felt very private. She must go there again one day, maybe….

In a stand of beech trees below her a young buzzard was calling to its parents to come and feed it, its plaintive *kee-ah kee-ah kee-ah* cry ringing out over the moor. It had probably left the nest a few days earlier, but the parents would have to keep feeding it for several weeks until it learned how to hunt for itself. The parent birds would mew occasionally as they soared on the thermals, looking down several hundred feet for their prey on the ground below; the youngster would cry incessantly all day.

The crying stopped abruptly, perhaps food had arrived; Linda smiled and thought of Marnie and of how her baby would stop crying when she was put to the breast.

The feeling of peace and happiness that came over her was overwhelming. She remembered how Frank had always talked of the peace that he got from being on the open moor. He used to call it his church and she was beginning to understand why, and also a little of how he must feel.

She stood up and started down the hill taking a different path from the one up which she had climbed. In the gorse bushes she heard a *tsick tsick,* the stonechat's angry warning call. She gave a similar call in reply and was amused to hear the little bird answer her; they had quite a conversation for a while. Then across her path a furry caterpillar was slowly walking. It was probably that of a fox moth or tiger moth. She remembered how as children they had called them *fuzzy bears.* All around her she realized that the natural world was carrying on its life as usual; reliable, never ending and unstoppable. It was just in her world that things had abruptly changed but the changes didn't have to be solely bad. She could make good from them she felt sure.

As she reached her front door she heard the phone ringing, she fumbled for the key and in her haste dropped it. She felt sure that she wouldn't get in before the ringing stopped but she did get there just in time. It was Eric, who after a brief greeting said

"I was wondering if it would be alright to call round this evening."

"I suppose so, why?"

"Well I thought that perhaps we ought to discuss and maybe decide on where we go next."

"What exactly do you mean, what is there to discuss?"

"Well divorce and so on, maybe there are belongings and things that I have left that you would rather I took with me. I can understand that it is difficult for you. I can understand if you are bitter, it's only to be expected. But I do hope that we can be civilized and still maintain a friendly relationship while we sort things out."

"That may be difficult; still, I see no reason why you shouldn't come around this evening, say seven o'clock."

"Thank you, that'll be fine, I'll see you then."

She hung up and went upstairs to take a shower. The good feelings that she had been experiencing during her walk were gone. No, she didn't feel bitter; she felt a bit cross because his call had spoiled her mood. So she showered, dressed and made herself a bit of breakfast and was then ready for her first client.

Eric was late as usual. School did obviously keep him late from time to time, it wasn't always Sheila. He apologised which only irritated Linda, still she invited him in and said "Have you eaten? I'm having spag bol, there's plenty if you would care to join me."

"No thank you, it's very kind of you to offer but I mustn't hang around too long." He was standing awkwardly, just inside the door, his hands held together in front of him almost protectively, not stuffed casually into his pockets as he would normally have done. His head was slightly bowed and he was being uncharacteristically polite, talking as though they were strangers, which in a sense they were because their situation was certainly strange and new to them both. Whilst there was nothing to be gained by arguing and

286

rowing, there was no need to tip-toe around each other all the time.

"Don't be silly, we can eat while we talk."

"Well OK then, thank you."

She drained the spaghetti and almost without thinking served it and the Bolognese sauce into two bowls as usual. Then they sat down as they had done in the past to eat their meal. It was weird, in some ways they were the couple they had always been and yet they weren't.

"I've put a few things over there that I think are really yours, that little table that your mother gave to you and some books. I'm sure that there are more things that you should take, you really ought to go through the cupboards and check."

"Thanks, what I really wanted to know was do you want to start divorce proceedings now? As I said in my note I won't contest it and I am prepared to pay all costs."

"I really hadn't thought about it, I've thought about a lot of other things to do with our new situation but not that. Is that what comes next, I've no idea? Do I have to see a solicitor to find out just what I have to do? It's not something that I know anything about. I don't want any fuss; I don't want any trouble or argument, can we not sort this all out for ourselves?"

"I really don't know either, I felt sure that there must be some legal things that can only be dealt with by a solicitor. Would you like me to make some enquiries?"

"Yes, if you don't mind."

She watched him forking spaghetti into his mouth and couldn't help but wonder what sort of meals Sheila made for him, what sort of a cook she was. Was it all out of the freezer and into the microwave, all ready cooked from the supermarket? Perhaps not, she was a farmer's daughter after all and no doubt had been brought up to cook good home grown produce in the traditional way. She reached for the wine bottle and topped up her glass.

"Would you like a drop more wine? I know you're driving,"

"Thank you, no, I'd better not. This is lovely spag bol." There was a pause in the conversation as they finished their meal. Then Eric said "There's one other thing, no rush at the moment, and I'll see to it if you like."

"What's that?"

"The tenancy of this place is in my name, I'm sure that Sir Harold will be quite happy to transfer it to your name, it's just that it's another job that has to be done. If you like I'll go and see him about it. I didn't want to do it without checking with you first, I don't know just who knows what our situation is, from your side, so to speak."

"That's alright, its common knowledge now, but thank you for thinking of me like that. Yes, you can see Sir Harold if you like; it'll save me a job. Like you said on the phone this morning, it would be nice if we can be civilised about it all. I know that at times it's going to be difficult, for instance the first time that I meet Sheila. Oh, you may do your best to keep us apart, but it's bound to happen some day. I just hope that we can all be grown up enough to handle the situation"

"I do too, in fact if we keep talking like this I see no reason why we shouldn't. Thank you once again for the supper and the chat. I'll take those few things and be on my way. Don't be afraid to call if there is any thing else that I can help with or that you feel I ought to do." And with that Eric collected the things that Linda had put out for him, said goodbye and was gone leaving a small card on which were details of his new address.

Linda took the dishes to the sink and started washing up. It was strange she thought, there had been no animosity from either of them, and no warmth either, just a cold sort of nothingness. Even with a total stranger there would have been more warmth. Here they were, two people who had been in love, married, had spent several years together and shared a life together. Now they were strangers, worse than that, they knew each other only too well but were treating each other as strangers. It was probably because they just didn't know how to react to this new situation and were desperately trying to get through it without fighting as so many people did. It all felt totally unreal, rather like a dream.

Eric meanwhile was driving to his new home and thinking how glad he was that it had all gone so smoothly. He had half expected Linda to have berated him, called him an adulterer and worse, and told him that she hated him for what he had done. Heaven knew he deserved it, but no, she had been cool and calm. It made him feel all the more confused and sad; all the more guilty and conscious of the hurt that he had caused her. But it would have been dishonest and even more hurtful to have continued with the marriage. He no longer loved her; in fact he had not been in love with her for some time. When Sheila had come into his life he had felt no guilt at going out with her. Perhaps that was because he no longer felt that he belonged to Linda. Of course he knew that that was wrong, and now that they had finally split up he felt very sorry for the pain that he was obviously causing her, but guilt? No, not really. If he felt anything it was relief. Selfish relief.

FORTY FOUR

Frank called in on Giles and Nancy on his way home from delivering a car that he had been servicing. They were all out in the garden, on the other side of the house playing croquet. He was pleased to see both Nancy and Julian getting on so well, no sticks in sight anywhere. Ray was the first to spot him and said, "Hello Frank, what brings you here, d'you fancy a game?"

"No thanks, it's good to see the two former invalids doing so well though. I've come to see Nancy, if she's got a minute."

Nancy turned from the game and walked over to him, "Certainly Frank, what can I do for you?"

"I was wondering if you had come to a decision about that pup I offered you. I can't expect the owner to hold it much longer, so I thought that I'd better come and see you. Besides I'll be seeing him tomorrow morning."

"Oh Frank, I am sorry, I meant to get in touch with you before but it quite slipped my mind, what with all the excitement of Julian and Ray coming. It hasn't been the same without a dog about the place, but I was just a little worried as to how we would cope. Yes, we'd love to have it, is it a dog or a bitch? Not that I really mind. I know Haig was a dog and that worked well, but I do quite fancy a bitch, they are sometimes more biddable."

"As far as I know it's a dog, at least my friend always calls it he. But then, come to think of it he calls most all of his animals he, so it could be either."

"That's lovely; when can I go and see it? I don't really care what it is, I know I shall fall in love with it the moment I see it."

"I'll take you there myself if you like, would tomorrow evening do?"

"Yes please, that's very kind of you. What time about?"

"Seven be alright?"

"Wonderful, you must come in for a drink with us when we get back. I certainly feel well enough to look after him now, and with Julian and Ray around it will be no trouble at all, will it boys?"

Julian, who had just finished his game, joined them at that moment to hear the last bit of the conversation, laughed and said to Ray, "There you see, we haven't been here five minutes and she's got a hundred and one jobs for us to do, and I'm supposed to be convalescing."

"You great fraud" said Nancy "You went for a five mile walk yesterday, there's not a lot wrong with you. I'm delighted to say that you are a lot fitter than I am, thank God."

"OK Mum, but that doesn't mean that I'm prepared to run around after a ten week old pup all day, cleaning up its poo etcetera."

"It won't do you any harm, you'll love it really."

"Right Oh then, well I'll leave you to sort out the doggy domestics and I'll see you tomorrow," said Frank. Then with a laugh and a wave he said his goodbyes. As he drove across the village green he met Jim, who had just pulled up outside the pub.

"You coming in for one? I could murder a good pint."

"Sounds like a great idea to me, it's been a long hot day," said Frank, so the two of them walked into the bar and having got their drinks sat at a table under the window.

"You've heard about Eric I take it."

"Yes" said Frank "I couldn't help but think of our conversation a few months ago. I remember you saying that you thought he was 'playing away'."

"Well I was only guessing then, but later I saw the two of them at Hatherleigh market, walking around hand in hand like a pair of sweethearts. I asked a friend of mine, who has a stall there, if he knew anything about them and he said that they were often there together. Of course he didn't know that they weren't married, so he didn't think anything of it. The trouble was that I didn't know what to do. I couldn't tell Linda, could I? Pippa and I talked it over and decided that we just had to keep quiet and see what happened. If it got any more noticeable we thought that we might have to mention it to Eric, let him know that we knew what he was up to, so to speak.

293

Of course we also thought and hoped that it might be just a brief affair that would fizzle out and die and then no one would have been any the wiser. I understand that he told Linda himself, clean breast and all that."

"Yes, that's what Mum told me, sad job though."

"Maybe he's done you a good turn Frank, maybe you can renew the relationship that you had with her before you went in the Army."

"I wish it was as simple as that, in reality I'm back to square one again."

"Well that's good, isn't it?"

"No, not really, but it's my problem and I'll have to sort it out the best I can. Enough of my problems, on a lighter note I've just been in to see Nancy and we've arranged to go and see a pup for her tomorrow."

"That sounds a great idea, she must be lost without a dog; she always had that little highland terrier with her. What sort of pup is it, another of the same?"

"No it's a smooth coated Jack Russel, comes from good stock, should be just the thing for her. I offered it to them while she was still in hospital, it was too soon then for them to make a decision but I'm glad to say that they are now well enough to say they want it. 'Course it will still need to have some of its jabs I've no doubt, but that shouldn't be a problem."

"Not with a vet in the family, which reminds me, how's that cousin of yours Cathy, has she started work yet?"

"Yes, she's been working for a week now, loves it."

"Is she still living with you and Mum?"

"For the time being, she's still looking for a place to buy but I think she is hoping that if she waits a little longer the prices will have fallen even further. It's good to have her around the place, she's not only company for Mum, but it means that Mum doesn't have to do bed and board for holiday makers any more."

"So if she is still with you I take it that you will be bringing her to the dance next week, with you and Mum that is."

"Oh, I'm not too sure about that."

"Go on, it'll do you good, I understand that Bob here has a license so we can have a drink together even if you don't want to dance. But if I remember rightly you are a pretty good dancer, you always used to go to quite a lot of dances."

"I'll think about it, but now I reckon I'd better be getting on home. It's been good having a chat; I'll see you around, OK?"

"Yeah, at the dance."

The two men walked out to their cars and set off for their homes. Jim was a little puzzled at Frank's attitude; he had expected him to be a bit more positive where Linda was concerned. There was something there that didn't make sense, something that seemed to be stopping him or them from getting together. That bit about 'back to square one'. It almost sounded as though it was the same thing that had made Frank leave home and go into the Army all those years ago. Yet he knew that Frank cared a lot for Linda. 'Maybe Pippa knows, I'll ask her when I get home', he thought. But she was as much in the dark as he, although the girls were good friends.

"I don't think even Beatie knows, and she is a lot closer to Linda than I am. You are probably imagining it; besides Frank is too much of a gentleman to rush in now. He will wait until they are properly divorced I expect."

"Yeah, you could be right, that would be his way, true enough."

But he was still thinking about it when he got into bed and it was still a mystery that he couldn't solve.

FORTY FIVE

So it was that at half past five the next day Frank and Nancy drove over to the next parish to collect her new pup. The area was just off the moor and the growth on the hedges fuller and more luxuriant than they were used to. After what seemed like forever driving down a twisting tunnel-like lane they came to a small cottage on a corner surrounded by beautiful old beech trees. Nancy had been wondering what they would do if they met any one coming the other way, there seemed to be so few places where they would have been able to pass. The cottage was of stone with red brick surrounds to the windows. It was set a little back from the road with a small untidy garden in front. They pushed open a rickety old wooden gate and went up the path to a front door badly in need of a coat of paint. Nancy couldn't help but hope that the owner looked after his dogs better than he did his home. As if reading her thoughts Frank leaned over to her and in a quiet voice said

"Don't worry, Jan knows more about dogs and breeding them than anyone I know." With that the door opened and a little man of indeterminate old age stepped out. His thinning grey hair hung down over his ears surrounding a smiling wrinkled face that looked like well tanned leather. His eyes were the bluest that Nancy had ever seen, darting this way and that taking in every thing in sight.

"You'm 'ere then."

"Yes, and this is the lady I told you about who is having the pup."

"You'd best way come in then." And with that he turned and led them in through a dark passage into a room that was tidy and clean, much to Nancy's surprise.

"Sit yourselves down an' I'll get the pup" he said waving towards the chairs. He disappeared into the dark passage and soon returned with the pup in his arms and its mother running beside him looking up at him all the while.

"Yere art then" he said putting the pup down in front of Nancy, "What de think of 'n, proper booty in 'er?"

Nancy was thrilled with the pup, it was a bitch as it turned out, mostly white with a brown tail and a very pretty brown and white head beautifully evenly marked. It was suitably boisterous, as a pup should be, and also to a great extent house trained.

"She's lovely," said Nancy taking her purse from her bag. "I must pay you and then we will be on our way, I can't wait to show her to the others when I get home. I just know that they will all fall in love with her."

So with the deal completed and after a few more pleasantries they left, Nancy happily cradling the pup in her arms ignoring the cardboard box that she had been offered.

Frank could see from her expression just how much Nancy loved the little creature and it gave him great pleasure to have arranged it for her. All the while when she had been in the hospital she had made little fuss of her own predicament, but he could tell that the loss of Haig had been a cruel blow. Perhaps this new pup would help her continued recovery; it would certainly give her something else to think about.

"I think I'll call her Peggy, after the girl in Swallows and Amazons. There were two sisters called Nancy and Peggy. Any way she looks like a Peggy to me."

"Well that's all that matters" said Frank, "I'm so glad that you like her, it's always difficult choosing for someone else."

"I'll get onto the vets when we get home to fix up for the rest of her injections. I might even ask for Cathy to be our regular vet, now that she's joined the practice."

"I'm sure that she would be delighted if you were to ask for her specifically, it will make her feel all the more at home here."

So they drove back through the leafy narrow lane, which strangely didn't seem so long as they drove back home. Nancy was stroking and talking to Peggy all the while, who seemed to be most interested in all that was going on outside the windows of the car.

Once home in the Old Rectory Nancy jumped out of the car and almost ran to Giles who was waiting in the doorway. She was like a kid with a new toy, it was lovely to see.

FORTY SIX

Two evenings later Blanche was out and Frank and Cathy were enjoying their supper in the old farm kitchen. Cathy had been telling Frank about her first few days working and was saying how she had been to see Nancy. "That Peggy is a dear little pup isn't she, almost as sweet as her owner. We had a nice long chat, Nancy and I, she thinks a lot of you."

"I hope she didn't let out too many dark secrets."

"No, far from it, she was most discreet, too discreet in fact. It is very plain to anyone who knows you that you are unhappy about something. She seems to be one of the few people around here who knows about your real reason for going away to the Army. She knows that it wasn't just to get the training that you wanted, or to get away from a father who wanted you to stay at home on the farm. She mentioned the phrase 'unrequited love' but she wouldn't be drawn to explain further no matter how hard I tried."

"No, she wouldn't, she and Giles are the only two who know, and they only know because I trust them to tell no one."

"Would I be right in guessing that it is to do with Linda? I've seen the way that you look at her and the way your face lights up when she's around. It's the same when you or somebody talks about her, other people may not see it but I do. It's obvious that you are in love with her, so what's the problem? Why don't you do something about it, tell the poor girl?"

"I wish I could but it's not that easy."

"It may not be easy, but until I know what the problem is I won't be able to help you, easy or not. So give me the chance to help, tell me what this is all about. I told you that I was willing to be your 'agony cousin'. You can rest assured that I will respect your confidence."

"Well it's a long story so I hope that you won't get bored by it. I suppose it all started at school. You're right in thinking that it is to do with Linda, we became mates and then boy and girl friend. It was all innocent stuff, walks on the moor, bird watching and stuff. Kissing and hugging but no more than that. We never spoke of marriage, although we did talk about our hopes and ambitions for the future. She always wanted to be a physiotherapist and I wanted to be a mechanic. Well Dad wasn't too pleased about that and so to avoid too many arguments I decided to go into the Army and follow my chosen career there. By the way, how much do you know about Dad's death, has Mum told you anything?"

"No, not really, I didn't like to pry, I thought that she would tell me what she wanted me to know and if there was any more, she would tell me when she was ready."

"Well, like I say, I was going to go into the Army and then Dad discovered that he had Huntington's Disease. That did it, I read that it's very often hereditary and so I panicked; I couldn't put Linda through that, I love her far too much. I could pass it on to any children that we might have and apart from that she would have the dilemma of looking after me when I got ill. Knowing what Mum had to go through with Dad in those last months; I now feel even more strongly that I can't put her through that."

"Can you be tested for it, are you sure that you have it, or the gene or whatever that it is carried on?"

"Yes, there is a test."

"Well have you had the test? Obviously not or you wouldn't be telling me all this. So if not why not?"

"Scared I suppose, frightened silly really; and in any case when I got back from the Army Linda was married. So I just let things slip I suppose."

"And now that she is splitting up with her husband and will be free again the problem has resurfaced, is that it?"

"Yes, that's it in a nutshell. So what do I do now, I did think of going away again."

"Would that solve anything?"

"No, I don't suppose so, I don't know; I just don't know what to do for the best."

"Well I'll tell you. The first thing that you've got to do is get yourself tested. You may find that you haven't got this terrible disease. Meanwhile I'll look on the net and see if there's any new information, a new treatment maybe. The other thing that you've got to do is take me to this square dance. I've never been to one so I'm dying to go. It'll take you out of yourself and do you good. It'll also give me a chance to get to meet some of the young fellas around here. It won't do either of us any harm to get out and enjoy ourselves, OK?"

"God, I hope so, I'm sure that you're right." There were tears in his eyes as he said "Thanks for listening to me, it's just …"

"I know, you've been bottling it up for far too long, it's too much for one person to have to carry." She had come around the table and was beside him with her arm round his shoulders.

"I do love her so; I love her so much that it hurts. The trouble is that I think she has feelings for me too and I daren't say anything, even now, because I don't want to lead her on. It just wouldn't be fair to her."

"You're right, absolutely right, and that's all the more reason for having the test done, and the sooner the better. Once you know what the extent of the problem is, you will know what to do and how to cope with it; that's if there is a problem. There's another thing that you don't seem to be considering. If Linda loves you as much as you obviously love her she may still want to be your wife. You don't have to have children, and she may be prepared to help you through the bad times at the end"

"Oh I don't know, that would be too much to expect."

"Maybe, maybe not, now I'm going to have another glass of wine, are you going to join me, or would you rather have a whiskey or something?"

"I'll join you in a glass of wine, perhaps we ought to make it two, we deserve it or at least you do. Thanks once again."

"Don't be silly, I'm only too glad to help in any way I can. I remember how good you were to me when I came here to stay on holiday as a little girl. I know that I was a lot younger than you but you always treated me as an equal, not as an annoying little kid which I'm sure I was."

Frank laughed at the memory. They took their glasses and sat in the easy chairs either side of the Aga and spent a while reminiscing about childhood days on the farm. The sun had always shone then, they had explored the moor together, mostly Frank showing her all his special places. And they had had fun helping at harvest time, although most of the work was too much for Frank, let alone for Cathy. Still they had felt that they had been a useful part of the team and had gone to bed every night tired out. They talked and talked and slowly Frank's mood lightened.

It wasn't long before Blanche came home and they all had a cup of tea and then went to bed. Cathy lay for a long while thinking about Frank and his dilemma; she felt sure that she would be able to find out some more information. Although most of her contacts were vets she did have a friend or two who were doctors, they might be able to give her some advice. It would be worth a try.

FORTY SEVEN

It was the afternoon of the dance. It had been decided to have a party for the smaller children in the afternoon organized by the mums from the pre-school groups. The hope was that they would not come to the dance in the evening which could very easily spoil it for the grown-ups. So a fun afternoon was in full swing; there was a merry-go-round and swinging boats outside, together with a few stalls selling second-hand toys and children's clothes. Inside at one end was a bouncy castle that was being run by Rose's son Jimmy, while at the other end Ray was about to put on a magic show. He would be Mr Cagim, oriental conjuror, suitably disguised and wearing a turban. It was an act that he had performed in Africa many times. He was not only very good at it but the children loved his silly humour, so his act was part clown part conjuror. There had been so many children out there who needed some laughter in their lives; children who had lost their father or mother; children who had lost a limb to a land mine or were other wise blighted by the ravages of civil war. A bit of tomfoolery and magic made them laugh and helped them to forget, if only for a few moments.

Rose and Julian were doing face painting, something that he had never attempted before, though he was definitely very good at it. There were several children going around roaring and looking like cheetahs or baboons and the likes, much to the amazement of their parents and friends.

When the magic show was over tea was served, mostly cocktail sausages, mini pizzas and cheese straws followed by cakes and jellies washed down with fizzy pop. Then the mums gathered up their kids, the hall was swept and the furniture arranged for the evening. Rose was in charge of the décor, it was to be a simple theme reflecting the area in which they lived. However she was very cagey as to what exactly she was going to do, sending everybody out of the hall except Jimmy, who was to be her assistant.

FORTY EIGHT

Beatie had rung Linda to say that she would be coming round a bit early for a girlie time getting ready for the dance. They had already decided that she would spend the night there.

"I'll bring a bottle and we can have a few drinks and nibbles before we go."

So she had duly arrived with a small case of clothing and a large bottle of white wine. They had had a shower first and were sitting in the bedroom in dressing gowns doing their nails whilst slurping and nibbling.

"I don't know what I'm going to wear;" said Linda, "I don't want anything too formal do I? Perhaps my white jeans would do for a start?"

"They would be just the thing I reckon, what would you wear with them?"

"I don't know; a blouse or something?"

"No, you want something off the shoulder, it's a warm evening and you need to show off those lovely arms of yours. Have you got any strappy tops?"

"No, I haven't."

"Well it's a good job I brought over a few with me; here try one or two of these on." And Beatie took out several little tops from her case which she put onto the bed. "Put your jeans on first and then we can see what goes best with them."

Linda put on first one then another; several were tried on more than once until finally Beatie said "That's the one, that's just the ticket, you look fabulous in that."

It was a light turquoise silky, slightly see-through top with thin straps, and it hung free from below the bust and moved as she did.

"That really shows off your figure to perfection. If I remember rightly you've got a turquoise necklace that would go perfectly with that. Then all you need are some strappy beaded sandals to add the finishing touch."

"Yeah, I've got a pair of them; I bought them for a party, one that we never went to in the end."

"Well that's you sorted out. Now it's my turn," said Beatie as she took from her case the dress that she had bought that day they had been shopping together in Plymouth. Slipping it on she said "I don't know if our village is really ready for this, and I need you to help me to lace it up at the back, if you will."

Linda had not really seen the dress before, on the day that they had shopped together in Plymouth her mind had been elsewhere. It was chocolate brown with white polka dots. It had no straps or sleeves, finishing above the bust and fastened across the back with straps in a bootlace fashion. This left a V-shaped part of her back showing almost down to her waist. The A-line skirt finished just above the knee.

"It is a bit daring, but I think you look great in it, if you don't pull in that dress I'll be amazed."

"The trouble is, the only ones I ever fancy, the good looking well turned out ones, are always gay."

So, laughing and joking they finished their preparations and made to leave. They each looked a wonderful picture of health, a pair of stunningly good looking young ladies; Linda tall and statuesque with her dark wavy hair and summer tan; Beatie slightly shorter and fuller of figure with her short light chestnut hair and slightly lighter skin tone. Just as they were about to open the door Linda said "I've forgotten something, I wont be a minute," and with that she ran back into the bedroom, picked up her bottle of Anais Anais perfume and put it in her bag. Then shutting the door behind them the two girls walked the few hundred yards to the hall.

FORTY NINE

Rose's dressing of the hall was a work of art. The walls had been painted white so she had a perfect blank canvas to work on. Her theme was Dartmoor and, to set the mood, on either side of the stage in large grey granite-looking tubs was a huge bunch of heather and gorse. Every where the theme was continued with purple, gold and green ribbons festooned around windows and any other protuberance. There were a few tables and chairs near the door, and each of these had a small be-ribbonned grey pot containing a bunch of heather and gorse.

There were several people already in the hall when Linda and Beatie arrived. In a small room inside the entrance Bob Peters had set up a small bar, plastic glasses only, and several of the local young lads were taking advantage of the facility.

"I'm not sure," said Linda "Its years since I walked into a room like this on my own."

"Well you're not on your own, you're with me, silly, and I'll look after you. Anyway, every one here is a friend of yours; you've got nothing to worry about. Besides, you look a million dollars. Come on."

"Oh, alright then, I suppose so."

They entered the room to see several groups of people sitting or standing around the walls. In a corner near the stage was a group consisting of Giles and Nancy and their two boys. Beside them were Blanche, Frank and Cathy. Linda's eyes were instantly drawn to Frank, looking very smart in a pair of tight jeans and a white shirt.

The first to greet them was Sal, who came over to them and said "My word, you two girls are a picture of loveliness, I do like your top Linda, the colour suits you so well. What do you think of the hall, hasn't Rose done a splendid job with the decoration?"

"Yes, it's very good,"

"And it's so good to see you here, both of you." And with that she was off into the room at the side to help with the setting up of the refreshments.

"That was nice," said Beatie "I didn't expect that from her."

"Yes it was somewhat unexpected, but she couldn't help but say, 'it's so good to see you here.' Then as an afterthought, 'both of you' She'll be out the back I bet, telling all the other gossiping old dears that I'm here, without Eric and looking like I couldn't care less."

"Well she would be right, you couldn't care less, and make sure that you show them all."

It was all very well saying that, thought Linda, the trouble was she did care. It was so difficult not to care. Her husband had left her because she wasn't what he wanted, wasn't good enough, so how could she not care. But perhaps Beatie was right, the people in the hall that night were her friends, they cared for her and she must put on a brave face and show them that she was strong.

They moved to sit at the side and were joined by Jim and Pippa who had just arrived.

"Good crowd here, I reckon it's going to be a real fun evening," said Jim, "I don't know much about square dancing, still I'm told that they have a caller who tells us what to do."

"Yes, our parents used to go to square dances a lot, so I expect they will remember the steps and put us all to shame ," said Pippa.

"If they can remember," said Beatie with a chuckle.

At that moment the drummer gave a roll on the drums and the caller stepped up to the mike to start the proceedings. The band was called The Pixielanders. They consisted of a fiddle player, guitarist, accordionist, drummer and a lad who seemed to be able to play anything; banjo, mandolin penny-whistle or flute. Like so many youngsters they were wearing jeans and T shirts. On the front of the shirts was printed a picture of a pixie. Their music was a mixture of country 'n western and hillbilly, with more than a hint of rock. There was no denying their talent as musicians and the effect on the audience was palpable. Few could resist getting up and taking part in the dancing, so infectiously toe-tapping was the rhythm. They started with a fairly simple dance where all the dancers formed a large circle, ladies and gents alternately. As the evening progressed the dances became more complicated with square

312

sets of eight and dances such as 'Strip the willow' and 'Cumberland gap'. Every body was enjoying themselves, those who had never tried that sort of dancing, or in fact any sort of dancing, were beginning to realise that they had been missing a lot of fun. During a pause between dances Beatie whispered in Linda's ear "What did I tell you? The two best looking fellas in the room are Julian and Ray. It's always the same!"

"Oh go on with you, there's plenty of talent here besides them, what about that blond chap at the far end, he's OK isn't he?"

"Have you been up close to him? You wouldn't think he was OK if you had. Besides he's had too much to drink in my opinion."

"Well I think you would be right to concentrate on Julian for tonight at least, he's a good dancer, light on his feet and a real gentleman. You may not be able to pull, but you'll have a great evening," said Linda with a giggle.

At half past nine there was a break for refreshments and the sale of draw tickets to those who hadn't already bought any. People sat around in groups, laughing and joking, many of them very warm from their exertions, and glad of a rest. Linda and Frank found themselves together in the queue for food and he said "Great evening isn't it; every body seems to be having a good time. How about you, are you alright?"

It was an awkward moment; Frank hardly knew what to say though he felt that he must say something, preferably something reassuring. He

313

was as usual concerned for her feelings, putting his own into the background.

"I'm fine thanks, I wasn't sure at first if I would enjoy it, in fact I wasn't even sure that I wanted to come, but I'm here and having a surprisingly good time."

"I'm sure we'll get the chance to dance together before the evening's over, but I would like to book the last waltz with you, if I may. My god, that sounds awfully pompous and old fashioned doesn't it. It just shows how out of touch I am with the dating game."

They both laughed at this and Linda said "Of course I'd love to have the last waltz with you, and you're not the only one out of touch, I've not had that much practice myself lately. I suppose I ought to have said 'get your coat, you've pulled' I think that that's the modern phrase."

They laughed some more, partly with relief at breaking the tension that they both had felt at this encounter. Linda unsure as to Frank's feelings, if any, towards her; and Frank worried that she would be feeling raw and rejected after Eric's recent departure.

Then after three quarters of an hour for eating the band struck up and they were all up and dancing again.

In a corner the Reverend Quentin Russel was in deep conversation with Phil. "Wonderful evening, so good to see the community together enjoying themselves like this. And this music is so lively I can hardly keep my feet still."

314

"Yes it certainly is catchy" said Phil "It would be good if we could do this on a more regular basis."

"I quite agree, maybe we can."

"There's one favour I would like you to do for us if you will Vicar."

"Yes Phil, what's that?"

"We have a gift for Sir Harold, I wonder if you would mind presenting it to him at the end of the evening?"

"Delighted to, you just let me know when and I'll be only too pleased."

"We are going to have pause for the draw before the last waltz. Then I will call on you to make the presentation, maybe a little thank you speech or something and that will be that, OK?"

"Yes I'm sure I can do that. May I ask what the present is?"

"It's a landscape painting, Julian has done it for us, according to Rose it has some significance for Sir Harold, but she won't say what. We haven't been allowed to see it. She organized it all, and based on the few paintings that I have seen that Julian has done, I am sure that it will be good. He is without doubt a very talented artist."

"Certainly something for us all to look forward to, by the sound of it."

So it came to the time for the draw and Phil got up onto the stage.

"I can see that you have all enjoyed yourselves this evening, would you like to do this more often, perhaps two or three times a year?" There was a chorus of assent from the floor. "Well, if we can persuade these boys to come and play for us again I know that I for one will be delighted. They are definitely one of the best bands I've heard in a long time." At this there was a cheer and some body at the back of the hall shouted 'Three cheers for the band, hip hip…' a resounding 'Hooray' filled the hall followed by two more.

"I think that that says it all chaps," said Phil, turning to the band.

"You'll have to book early, we can get a bit busy, I'm glad to say" said the lad who played the fiddle.

"I'm not surprised" said Phil. "Right now; let's get on with the draw."

The winners of the ten prizes having been drawn and the prizes presented Phil took the stage again.

"Before you take your partners for the last waltz I do have a few things to say, people to thank. First of all I must thank the entire band, whom we have already mentioned. Next the ladies who provided us with an excellent spread of refreshments, and Bob Peters, our local pub landlord, for providing the bar. Then I'm sure you will all agree with me that the decorations are magnificent, and for that we must thank Rose. And finally we must thank Sir Harold, because without his outstanding generosity in giving us this building, none of this would have happened. We have a small gift for you, Sir Harold and I call on our vicar, the Reverend Quentin Russell to come up and make the presentation."

Both men approached the stage and Phil passed to the vicar a large flat package wrapped in green paper and tied with purple and yellow ribbons.

"There's not a lot that I can say or add to what has already been said, both here tonight and on many occasions and in many homes around this village. Thank you just doesn't seem enough. This small gift comes with gratitude and affection from us all." And with that he passed over the package.

"Now it is I, from whom 'thank you' doesn't seem enough. I expect you want me to open this now, well I can assure you that my curiosity is as great if not greater than yours." With that he tore the wrapping off to reveal Julian's painting. Sir Harold looked at it for a few seconds, then smiling broadly he looked straight at Rose and said

"I think somebody here knows me almost better than I know myself, this is absolutely lovely and I shall treasure this gift. Thank you, thank you all very much.. I am going to leave the painting here for the rest of the evening so that you can all have a chance to have a good look at it. It is absolutely beautiful, a real work of art." With that he got down from the stage and walked over to Rose as Phil said

"Take your partners for the last waltz."

"Where is that scene, do you know?" Jim asked. Frank, who was standing nearby said

317

"I think it's on the Dart, a little way up from Dartmeet, probably a favourite pool that Sir Harold used to fish."

"He has certainly caught the atmosphere, and those figures in the background bring it to life, sort of tell a story don't they?"

"He is a good artist, no doubt about that" said Frank as he moved away towards Linda.

"May I have the pleasure?" asked Sir Harold.

"Thank you kind sir," replied Rose with a coquettish smile.

"That picture was your idea, wasn't it? It's very good; it certainly revived a few nearly forgotten memories from way back."

"I had never forgotten."

"Really?"

"No, a girl never forgets her first kiss."

They joined the other dancers on the floor, swaying gently in time to the music, and Rose smiled to herself. It was the first time that she had been in his arms since that summer's day all those years ago.

Linda, in Frank's arms was thinking much the same thing, as they danced around the floor. He was a good dancer leading her effortlessly, almost lifting her. She felt as though her feet weren't touching the ground, as though she was floating in his arms. At the turns and reverse turns she could feel his body pressed against hers and the strength in his arms as he held her tight. She said nothing, not wishing to break the spell of the moment, yet fearing that it couldn't last. Finally the music stopped and they all stood clapping. Few would go away that night without several wonderful memories.

"Thank you for the dance Linda, it was good, really good."

"Not at all, thank you" and with that she took him by the shoulders and kissed him on the cheek, stood back smiling at him and said

"Perhaps we could do it again some day?"

"That would be nice, very nice. Good night, and thanks once again."

He turned away, looking for his mother and cousin, while she walked over to join Beatie. The two girls headed towards the door; Linda looked back to see Frank watching her with a slightly sad expression on his face. He smiled and raised his hand; she smiled back and then was gone out of the hall into the warm summer night air.

Sir Harold thanked Rose for the dance and said "I must get my picture, it wouldn't do to forget it now would it?" then looking her straight in the eye he said "I think it would be rather nice if you were to come back for a nightcap with me, would you do that?"

Once again she gave him a coquettish smile as she said teasingly "Nightcap? Oh, to drink you mean; yes thank you, that would be lovely."

He collected his present, roughly re-wrapping it and they left the hall and walked up the drive to Edworthy Hall together.

Giles and Nancy had spent most of the evening sitting at the side of the dance-floor enjoying watching the dancing and tapping their toes in time with the music. He had noticed how well Julian and Ray had entered into the swing of things, and how well they seemed to have been accepted by everybody. It dawned on him then that he too had lost most of his feelings of unease and was at last glad to welcome them both into his home and his life. They said their goodbyes to their many friends and left the hall together; the boys on either side of Nancy with Giles walking behind with a satisfied smile on his face.

Phil and a few other stalwart helpers would stay to see everyone leave and lock up. There would be time enough tomorrow to tidy up, now it was time for home and bed after a wonderful first evening in their new village hall.

In the kitchen at Wistworthy Frank and Cathy flopped down in the chairs, worn out with their exertions and excitement.

"I'll make us all a dish of tea" said Blanche.

"Thanks Mum, I just feel the need to unwind a bit before going up."

"Was it a good evening for you Frank? You certainly seemed to be enjoying the last waltz," said Cathy.

"Yes, it was good, maybe too good; it hasn't made things any easier. I still haven't a clue as to what I can or will do next."

"You'll be alright. You know what your Mum always says, 'it'll all look better in the morning.'"

"Let's hope so," said Frank as Blanche came over to them with their mugs of tea.

FIFTY

Sunday, and a beautiful sunny morning. The sunrise had been spectacular, with shades of pink and orange lighting up the little clouds that drifted slowly across a blue sky, while high above transatlantic jumbo jets left a criss-cross pattern of vapour trails. Not many of the villagers were up to see it, their unaccustomed exertions of the previous night meant that they were having a well deserved lie in.

At Wistworthy Blanche went downstairs to make an early morning pot of tea. Having poured hers she went up with mugs for Frank and Cathy. Frank's bed was empty, obviously out early to enjoy the beauty of the summer morning, she thought. Cathy was still asleep, so leaving the tea on the bedside table she went down to drink hers in the kitchen. An hour later Cathy came down and the two women prepared and ate a light breakfast together.

"What a lovely evening that was, so nice to see every body enjoying themselves" said Blanche. "I noticed you had several dances with Ray, he seems a nice chap."

"Yes, he's very nice, so is Julian, and that painting of his was really good. I can't say that I know the location, but he has captured the atmosphere of Dartmoor wonderfully well."

"He almost seems to have fallen in love with the place, rather like Frank, to be able to paint it like that."

"Where is Frank, don't say he's still in bed?"

"No, he was out when I went in with his tea. His truck is in the yard so I reckon he's gone out over, enjoying the solitude of one of his favourite places. He does that quite often, especially when he has something on his mind."

"Like what he's going to do about Linda, you mean."

"Could be, I saw that they had the last dance together. What, if anything, has he been telling you about her?"

"Oh we had quite a long talk the other day, all about his concerns for her. He's very much in love with her, but he just doesn't know what to do. I told him he must go and have the tests."

"What tests?"

"To see if he's got Huntington's like his dad."

"Oh, I didn't know that he had told you about that, it's something he keeps very much to himself as a rule."

"Yes, I could see that he was very upset about something the other day. I told him to confide in his 'Agony Cousin' and after a bit of persuasion, well a lot of persuasion actually, he opened up and told me all about it. As far as I could make out that was the main reason for his going away to the Army. Now he's talking about going away again. He seems to think that that is the only way out for him. I wish I could help, but until he knows for sure whether or not he has the disease nobody can help him, and he seems to be convinced that he has it. Because he's so convinced he's afraid to have the test, and also he has heard that the results are not always definite. It's a vicious circle."

"D'you think he's serious about leaving?"

"You know him better than I do Auntie; I only know what he said to me. One thing I am certain of, he is madly in love with Linda, thinks the world of her. While she was married to Eric there was no problem, but now that things have changed there, the old worries have come back. More than once he said that the only way out for him was to move away, far away."

Blanche had stood up and was pacing around the kitchen obviously greatly agitated.

"It's no good" she said, "There's something I've got to do. Something that I should have done years ago, but I never did because I couldn't see that it would do any good. I was afraid of upsetting things… people."

"What things, Auntie, what people, what are you talking about?"

"I can't tell you, not now at any rate and maybe not ever. I must go out now, if Frank comes back while I'm out just tell him …. tell him….I don't know….tell him…. not to go doing anything hasty before I get back."

"OK Auntie, but I wish I knew what this was all about though, it would make it much easier to understand."

"Sorry love, I'll see you later, maybe then, OK?" and with that she grabbed a coat and was off, out into her car and down the road.

FIFTY ONE

Frank had woken early after a surprisingly good night's sleep. Seeing the lovely weather outside he was up and dressed as quietly as he could, so as not to wake the others. Then after a quick mug of tea he was off out onto the open moor. He strode easily through the dew soaked grass, making his own path up to the highest point above the farm. He paused a while to watch the sunlight as it seemed to fall into the dark shaded valleys, filling them with light and warmth. Then on again in a large circle, a walk of five or six miles, until he was at the head of the Redacre where he sat on his favourite flat rock. For a long time he just sat watching the joys of nature; a stag beetle, an almost iridescent dark blue, struggled across the rock. A tiny spider launched itself into space from the top of a blade of grass. Its life-line of silk anchored to the point that it had just left to stop it from travelling too far. As the sun got higher in the sky its warmth started to dry the dew and send tiny little wisps of steam rising from the damp ground.

Looking across the combe to the tor beyond he saw a figure on the rocks. Some one who, like himself, obviously enjoyed a walk on the moor in the early morning. The distance was too great for him to see who it was, even with his binoculars.

He lay back on the rock, closed his eyes and listened to the almost imperceptible sounds of nature all around him. Now and again the near silence was broken by some almost raucous man made sound, a plane passing overhead, a car revving on some road a mile or so away, their noise seemingly amplified by the stillness.

After a while he sat up and saw that the walking figure from the rocks was coming his way, staying on the high ground and skirting the soft wet ground that formed the Redacre Head. It was obviously some one who knew his way around on the moor or knew the area well.

To his right, looking down the valley he could see the farm with the Red Rubies grazing contentedly. They were in line abreast, almost as though some bovine sergeant major had drilled them, munching their way across the field.

The walking figure was nearer now and he didn't need to lift the binoculars to see who it was. In fact he felt that it would have been an intrusion to have done so, a sort of invasion of privacy. From her gait and general appearance he could tell that it was Linda. The mist rising from the wet ground across and away down the valley reminded him of a poem he had learned at school and liked. Though set in the evening he felt its message was appropriate to the moment and he recited it to himself under his breath:-

Another day had nearly died,
The summer sun had set
And a girl walked down across the fields
Cows in front and a dog at her heels
Trotting over the fresh-mown grass behind.

The day had been hot but the evening was cool
And the mist that came up from the brook seemed
so full
Of the heat of the day, the breath of the stream.

The breeze rose, stirred the maiden's hair
Sending silky nut-brown wisps
Tickling across her sunburned cheeks
And she smiled

For her heart like the mist in the valley
Was full, full of warmth
But the heat in her breast was the heat of her love
And the thought of her lover made her to smile.

Linda saw the figure on the rock and realizing who it was paused. Should she go on? To turn back now when he had obviously seen her would be wrong. Yet to go on might prove to be more difficult. She was glad that he was there yet she couldn't help wondering why she had come, what had drawn her to this spot. What would be the outcome? Was it all too soon; was she on the rebound and vulnerable? Was she just going to build up false hopes only to have them dashed like before?

328

'I mustn't read too much into the waltz last night and this meeting, it's just a chance encounter' she thought. But she knew full well that chance didn't come into it; she had deliberately walked over to that spot in the hope that Frank would be there.

He got to his feet as she approached a broad smile on his face.

"I thought I might find you here" she said, "It's far too nice to stay in bed indoors. When I got up on the top of the tor and looked across here I thought of how we used to sit here, so I thought I'd come over. By the time I was half way here I felt sure that I could see you, lying on this rock."

"Yes, I saw you on the tor, or a figure, I didn't know that it was you until you were much nearer. Here, come and sit, the sun has warmed up the rock."

"What a wonderful dance last night, I thought that the band were terrific. They seemed to be enjoying themselves as much if not more than we were."

"I was very pleased to see you there, I was afraid that you wouldn't come, what with …you know…"

"I know, I very nearly didn't, but Beatie came round with a bottle and we got ready together and she persuaded me. The wine might have had something to do with it." She laughed

"I liked the perfume that you were wearing, I thought it was the same one that I gave you on your seventeenth birthday, Anais Anais wasn't it?"

"Yes, I wondered if you would recognise it."

"So you wore it on purpose then?"

"Oh yes, it was all part of the clever trap that I was setting for you." She was laughing heartily now, her confidence growing. She hadn't ever thought that she could be this flirtatious but the mood, the warm sun and just being there with him in a place that used to be special to them both, seemed to have broken down her natural reserve.

"Remember how we used to sit here for hours, watching and listening to the birds?"

"Yes" she said, "And the curlews with their long curved bills and that amazing, beautiful warbling song. Are there any here now? I was hoping that I might hear one as I walked over."

"There used to be three or four pairs nesting here every year and you could be sure of hearing one calling when ever you came up here. Now there are very few, maybe just a single pair and you don't hear them that often. I don't know why it is, it's the same with the lapwings, very few of them about these days. It may be something to do with the estuaries where they go for the winter, pollution or something."

They sat talking, reminiscing about their childhood days and school, as well as catching up on more recent events. Frank hadn't heard about Marnie's baby, or that Linda had been in to help her for a couple of weeks. The old worries about children came back then and he wished the subject hadn't been brought up. Then Linda, almost as if she had read his thoughts, said

"I know that people always used to think that I was maze about kids because I was always pushing one or other of my kid brother or sisters around. It was a chore; I had to do it 'cos I was the eldest. What I really wanted to be doing was to be out playing with my friends, not baby sitting."

"So the fact that you and Eric didn't manage to have any children wasn't such a big deal then?"

"No, not really, and as things have turned out it's a blessing. Divorce without children must be a lot easier, least I hope it will be. Then I'll be free,"

They stood up to go, Frank said "I'll walk you home if you like, or to the end of the lane that leads up onto the moor."

"Thank you, you don't have to you know." But she really wanted him to.

"That's alright, I want to." They were holding hands, standing by the rock and at that moment a curlew started its warbling cry not thirty feet away from them.

"He's playing our tune" she said and turned to Frank with tears of joy in her eyes. He took her in his arms and gently kissed her on the forehead. Then she lifted her head and her lips found his. They stood there, like Cathy and Heathcliff on the wild moors, kissing and hugging each other for several minutes. It wasn't passionate, lustful, hungry kissing; it was more giving, comforting, unselfish and caring. Then without a word they broke apart and started walking hand in hand back towards Linda's cottage. Neither of them spoke,

331

though their thoughts were in turmoil. Linda excited that Frank had finally shown that he had feelings for her. Feelings that seemed to be much like those that she had for him. Frank felt strangely relieved that he had shown her just how he felt at last, yet concerned again at what he might have to do or tell her later.

They reached the head of the lane and paused. Frank took her in his arms again and kissed her gently. "I'll see you soon; I just hope that things will work out for us."

"Yes, so do I….. Bye…. love you."

She turned and went off down the lane; she felt that she wanted to skip like an excited school girl but still a slight feeling of doubt niggled at the back of her mind. 'Give it time Girl, don't rush it, you may not be ready for this even if you think you are. He may not be ready either and you don't want to drive him away. But it was lovely back there by the rock, absolutely, wonderfully lovely.'

So with these conflicting thoughts cascading in her mind she went home on her own to her cottage and her friend Beatie. What would she tell her if anything? She was far too exited to keep it to herself, but was it too soon to say anything?

Frank turned for home in sombre mood. What had he done, giving in to his emotions, was he going to regret this morning? He set off over the hill towards the clapper bridge at the end of their lane, hardly noticing the world around him, totally lost in his thoughts and his worries about the future

FIFTY TWO

Blanche drove to the end of their lane and stopped by the damson tree. She sat thinking for a minute or two, trying to work out exactly what to do next. Then taking out her mobile phone she called Phil. At first she thought that he was not at home, the phone seemed to ring for a long time but then he answered.

"Sorry to bother you Phil, but I need to see you, are you on your own?"

"I will be in a minute or two; Elaine's just off to church as we speak."

"What about Beatie, is she there, I know this probably sounds odd but I must see you on your own, it's urgent and private."

"And mysterious, by the sound of things. Yes, Beatie stayed over at Linda's last night and she's on duty from noon today so I reckon she's going to work from there. In fact I expect she's already gone, so you don't have to worry, there's nobody here but me."

"Right, I'll see you in a few minutes," said Blanche.

Then for quite a while she sat in her car looking at the damson tree and the initials carved on it. Phil had carved them there when they were seventeen, just before they left school. He had used the initials of their primary school nick-names, their own secret code, as it were. Red Barron loves

333

Snow White. Few youngsters ever expected classroom romances to last, and theirs was no exception. Phil had gone off to Bicton Agricultural College, and they had drifted apart. In any case the feud between the Leamans and the Germans, though dead and buried in the minds of the younger generation, was still very much alive as far as their elders were concerned. So any lasting relationship between them was doomed. A few years later she had met and married Stan and a kinder more loving partner she could not have found anywhere.

She drove off slowly, thinking all the while of a day thirty three years before. She and Stan had been married for two years, and then Stan's uncle in North Devon had died. Stan was his only living relative and thus his heir and executor. The estate was small; a cottage with a few acres, but Stan had felt that it would be best if he went in person to see to its disposal. It was early September; the harvest was over so it was a relatively slack time on the farm. Blanche was extremely competent and they were both confident that she could manage for the few days that he would be away.

"If you have any problems or are in need of help call on Phil. I've already warned him. That old cow, Jupiter, may calve, but she shouldn't be a problem, she's already had five calves and never any trouble."

However, four days later Blanche could see that Jupiter did have a problem. She had been messing about all day, obviously uneasy, so Blanche got her in to the shippon. It was still fitted with the old cow chains and riddle sticks so she tied her up and then rang Phil. She didn't think that she wanted to examine the old girl herself, better to leave it to Phil; it would be less upseting for the cow. She put plenty of straw around the cow and then went indoors to get hot water, soap and a towel.

Phil arrived almost before she was ready with the water and straight away took off his coat, rolled up his sleeve, soaped well and had his arm inside to see if he could feel what was causing the problem.

"Well the calf is coming the right way, that's one good thing, I can feel his nose. Yes, and I've got one front leg, I can't find 'tother though….oh yes I can, silly thing, he's got it across the birth canal so he can't possibly get out. I'll see if I can turn it. I'll have to push it back and then bring it forward the right way."

Blanche was standing by feeling rather useless as Phil gave a running commentary on his progress or lack of it.

"The trouble is that every time I try to turn the calf's leg the cow pushes and every thing goes tight and I can't move either the calf or myself."

"Should I ring for the vet?"

"No I don't think so, he wouldn't be here for best part of an hour, might be too late then. He would give her an injection in the spine to relax her; we've got to do something to stop her from pushing for just a second, that's all I would need."

He pulled out his arm and stood looking at the cow for a moment as he soaped his arm again.

"She's getting a bit weak, I don't want her to lie down if possible; we've got to do something …. I know what might work. You catch hold of her nose, finger and thumb in each nostril, and squeeze and shake as hard as you can. Don't be afraid of hurting her, that's what we want, then she may just relax for a second. Ready?"

Blanche did as she was told; the cow didn't like it much and gave a plaintive bellow. Phil, sweating profusely was busy working a way inside. Suddenly he said "Yes that's it, you've done it Maid, I've got both legs now. We'll have to rope them and pull the calf off to help her, she's tired out, reckon she's been trying to push the little devil out all day."

So they pulled off the calf, a job that Blanche had helped Stan to do on many an occasion. She wiped a bit of mucus membrane off the calf's nose but it didn't seem to want to take its first breath. Frantically she worked its front leg forward and back in a pumping motion in an attempt to stimulate the calf. Then Phil took a straw, put it into the calf's nose and wriggled it around. This made the calf sneeze and start to breathe.

"I've never seen that done before," said Blanche. She undid the chain so the cow could turn around. Then, with a little help the new-born calf, its dark brown coat wet and almost black, staggered on its wobbly legs over to suckle. No matter how many times she had witnessed it, the miracle of birth, the bringing of new life into the world was amazing. This time, in view of the trauma involved, it was particularly emotional. She turned to Phil, with tears of joy pouring down her cheeks, overcome with relief.

"Thank you so much, I don't know what I would have done without you, you were wonderful."

He put his arm around her shoulders saying, "That's alright, no need to cry" as he kissed the top of her head. She put her arms around him, feeling his naked back as she ran her hands up under his shirt.

She tilted her head back; he looked down at her and their lips met. All the pent up emotion and anxiety of the past hour seemed to flood through them in that kiss; relief and passion blended as one.

It was some time later that they were brought back to reality by the sound of Jupiter's gentle mooing.

"Oh Phil, what ever came over us, how did we get so carried away?"

"I'm sorry Dear, so very sorry, I should never......to have made love to the wife of my best friend, what could be worse than that?"

"I know, I know, but I'm just as much to blame, it takes two you know. We must just try to forget that it ever happened, we must never speak of it again."

"D'you think we can do that? It won't be easy."

"We'll just have to, that's all I know. Promise, you must promise?"

"Yes of course I promise."

"I love Stan too much to ever hurt him."

True to their word they never again spoke of that night's passionate event.

FIFTY THREE

She had nearly reached Home Farm. She was dreading meeting and talking to Phil, yet she knew that it was the only thing that she could do if she was going to have any hope of stopping Frank going away again. How would he take it, would he be angry or sympathetic, indifferent or concerned? Then there were Elaine and the girls to consider, how would they react, or did they need to be told? After all it had been a secret that no one had suspected for over thirty years, perhaps it would be best if it were to stay that way?

He was standing in the arched porch, looking out onto the yard as she arrived.

"Come in Blanche, what ever is so important that you've got to rush over here on a Sunday morning? And why all the secrecy, surely nothing can be that serious can it?"

"I'm afraid it can and it is. Can we go inside?"

"Of course" Phil saw the urgency and worry in her expression "Any thing you want."

They went into the sitting room and Blanche flopped down into an armchair facing Phil

"Do you know exactly what Stan died of?" she asked.

"No, all I know is that he once told me that he had something wrong with him and that it would probably get worse before it got better. But that was Stan, never one to ask for sympathy."

"Well what he had was Huntington's Disease and it eventually killed him. The trouble is that it's hereditary."

"Hereditary, oh my god, poor Frank, does he know?"

"Yes, he knew when we first found out about it, that was part of the reason for him going in the Army."

"I don't follow you; I thought he went in to train to be a mechanic, and because Stan really wanted him to stay on the farm."

"That was only part of it; he wanted to marry Linda but he felt that he couldn't because of the disease that he would end up getting later in life. Not to mention, of course, that he might pass it on to their children if they had any."

"I see, but why the sudden rush over here?"

"Eric has left Linda, as you know, so now she is free again. She and Frank never really got over each other; in fact they are in love, desperately in love where Frank is concerned. So now he seems to think that the only way out for him is to go away again and for good."

"I see, big problem for the lad, but where do I come in to all this, why come to me?"

"This is the worst part for me, please don't be too hard on me, I know I should have told you this years ago."

"Told me what? What ever it is you know I couldn't be hard on you, we've been friends far too long for that."

340

"That night when Stan was up in North Devon and you helped with that awkward calving, remember?"

"I'm not likely to forget am I"

She was crying now, elbows on her knees and hands over her face as she sobbed. He moved over to her and sat on the arm of her chair putting his arm around her shaking shoulders.

"He's your son, our son, and he doesn't know, nobody knows except me and now you."

"My son, what d'you mean, my son? Why didn't you tell me before?"

"How could I? Stan was so happy to have a son; everyone said how much he looked like his dad."

"They always do."

"You were away at the time and as the days went by I got to believe the lie I was telling everyone. After all you both had the same colour hair and eyes."

"But didn't Stan guess? I mean the timing, the dates and all. He knew about gestation tables for cows and they are almost exactly the same for humans. Surely he must have been suspicious."

"No, leastways he never said any thing. I had told him that the baby was due in July, and when he started coming I just said that he was a bit early. In fact, fortunately he was two weeks late."

"So what am I supposed to do now, now that I have suddenly found out that I am the father of a thirty two year old man? It's one hell of a bombshell to have dropped on a man. Do I go up and tell him?"

"No, but I've got to tell him, I've got to tell him that he hasn't got this bloody awful disease that he thinks he's got. I've got to tell him so that he will know that he can marry Linda. But I can't tell him without your say so, it wouldn't be fair on you. Now do you see?" There was a pause and a heavy silence filled the room.

"Yes, I do see, I see that you've been carrying a pretty heavy burden all these years. Wow, a son, it takes a bit of thinking about. Sorry my Dear, I was just thinking about myself."

He stood up and walked over to the drinks cabinet in the corner.

"I need a drink, can I get you one? I'm not sure if I ought to be celebrating or in shock. Feels like a bit of both."

"I won't have one thank you, a cup of tea would be nice though, I'll go and make it myself, I know my way around."

She went off into the kitchen, as much to give Phil time to think without her being near as to get herself a tea. When she came back he was sitting in his armchair again though he got up as soon as she entered the room.

"I just keep on thinking 'why didn't you tell me?' but of course I know you couldn't. It's funny, you know, I've looked at him some times and seen him hold his hands together like this, just like my mother used to. Then there's that smile of his, a sort of half smile where he only lifts the left side of his mouth; Beatie does exactly the same. Odd how I never really noticed it until now. Well I noticed it but I didn't think anything of it I should

342

say. Of course you must tell him. Don't deny the lad his chance of happiness, there's too much misery in the world as it is without our adding to it unnecessarily."

"Will you tell Elaine and the girls, it did happen before you met Elaine, for what that's worth?"

"I don't know, would it do any good? I suppose to some extent it's up to Frank, perhaps we ought to ask him first. The more I think about it though, the more I like the idea of keeping it a secret. It's been that way for so long, why stir up trouble, which it might well do?"

They sat in silence for a while, then Blanche said "Well I suppose I'd better be off and tell him. What's he going to think of me, will he hate me, despise me? His mother lying to him about his parentage all his life, how will he cope with that, will he ever be able to forgive me?"

"Would you like me to come with you?"

"No thank you, this is something I've got to do on my own."

"Well don't be afraid to shout if you need any help or anything, I'm here on the end of the phone any time, you know that."

"Thanks Phil, you're a dear."

She stood up and he kissed her tenderly on the cheek and gave her a big hug.

"Even though Stan and I weren't related, I always thought of Frank as my nephew. Now I know that he's my son.....it's wonderful.....just wonderful."

"Wish me luck" she said and was gone.

FIFTY FOUR

Back in the car Blanche found that all her thoughts and worries returned. It was all very well Phil saying that he would do all he could to help; offer to come with her now and stand by her when she told Frank, but this was something that she just had to do on her own.

How would he react to the news that his mother had been lying to him all his life? That she had hidden from him the origin of his birth. That the man whom he had always thought of as his father was in fact nothing to do with him. And yet many adopted children felt that their adopted parents meant more to them. Felt more for them because they were the ones who had brought them up, nursed them and cared for them, taught them and directed them. Stan might not have been his biological father but he had been a father and a good one to Frank in all the ways that mattered.

No, she doubted that Frank would have any bad feelings towards Stan; it was what he would feel towards her that Blanche was most worried about. She had committed a sin, in a moment of relief and euphoria she had given way to passion and ever since then she had had to carry the burden of that guilt. She couldn't expect him to understand, she barely understood it all herself.

She had loved Stan with a passion and a singular devotion. He had been not only her husband but her partner, best friend and lover for over thirty years. In all that time she had never looked at or wanted another man. For his part Stan had been a devoted husband and father providing and caring for his family. She had never told him of her one failing, she had been afraid to. She had had no idea of just what his reaction would have been, but she could guess. Once the lie had been told there was no way that it could be untold, and in fact as time went on she had almost convinced herself that Stan was Frank's real father and it wasn't difficult to believe the lie that she was telling and indeed living.

She had reached the cross road where Frank had left his taxi on his way home to Stan's funeral. She stopped the car and thought of him striding up on to the tor, his church as he called it, where he seemed to get so much help and consolation. How often had she wished that she could have found similar help from the moor or the Church or some friend? There were many with whom she had a good and friendly relationship, but no-one with whom she would have confided, and certainly no-one with whom she could have shared a secret as momentous as her brief affair with Phil.

How would Frank react? Would he hate her, despise her, walk away from her and leave her to a life of loneliness? She had always felt that their love for each other, mother and son, was strong and was a bond that would be impossible to break. Well she would find out soon enough now.

Perhaps he would ask her why she hadn't told him before, but how could she? To have told him would have meant that she would have had to tell Stan. She had loved her man too much to hurt him, as she felt sure the knowledge of her affair would have done. No, there had been no way that she could have done, said or behaved in any different manner. One mistake, one silly mistake, that had left her with a huge feeling of guilt and now a colossal problem.

But it had also left her with a son, a wonderful young man who she felt ought to find the happiness that he so richly deserved with the woman he loved and who so obviously loved him. Happiness that she knew only too well could be found with a good and loving partner.

She started the car again and drove on, following the road over the side of the hill to where the side road to Wistworthy turned off. In that moment the picture that she saw was imprinted on her mind. The road running up the valley beside the stream leading to the farm, the roofs of the buildings, the tidy little fields with the herd of Red Rubies grazing contentedly and all around the Dartmoor that she knew he loved so well. It was a picture that in that instant was stamped on her mind; almost like the perfect fulfilment of a dream, every thing that she knew he loved about the area. Would what she had to tell him make it an impossible dream or a dream come true?

Then she saw him and that horrible hollow feeling of fear gripped her stomach, the sort of feeling that she remembered having when told to report to the headmaster's office in those far off days of her schooling. And then the warm overwhelming feeling of love, of desperately needing to help him regardless of the consequences to herself, flooded over her.

Frank was sitting on the clapper bridge his legs swinging over the water, feet almost in it, a dejected look on his face. He got up slowly as his mother pulled up and walked over to stand under the damson tree beside her car.

"It's no good Mum, I love her desperately, I can't live without her, but I know I shall have to. We met this morning up on the curlew rock. I went up there to think a bit after last night. It had been so wonderful dancing with her, holding her in my arms. She came over this morning because it was always our favourite place years ago, it wasn't planned, we just think the same way about so many things, it's uncanny. We sat and talked for a long time. Then we kissed and just as we did so the curlew started singing. It was wonderful, like an omen or something, like it was meant to be. But it can't be, I can't put her through what you had to go through with Dad. And what if there were children, it just doesn't bear thinking about. No, it's no good, I was thinking that I shall have to go away again, and this time it'll have to be forever. But I know that won't solve any thing, and yet how can I stay here? I just don't know what to do …."

"I may have the answer Son. Just come and sit in the car with me for a minute. This isn't going to be easy for either of us."

"What isn't Mum?"

"There's something I've got to tell you."